ROBERT CRAIS

A
DANGEROUS
MAN

G. P. PUTNAM'S SONS
New York

PUTNAM
— EST. 1838 —

G. P. PUTNAM'S SONS
Publishers Since 1838
An imprint of Penguin Random House LLC
penguinrandomhouse.com

The Library of Congress has catalogued the G. P. Putnam's Sons
hardcover edition as follows:

Names: Crais, Robert, author.
Title: A dangerous man / Robert Crais.
Description: New York : G.P. Putnam's Sons, [2019] |
Series: An Elvis Cole and Joe Pike novel ; 18
Identifiers: LCCN 2019021247 | ISBN 9780525535683 (hardback) |
ISBN 9780525535713 (epub)
Subjects: LCSH: Cole, Elvis (Fictitious character) —Fiction. | Pike, Joe
(Fictitious character) —Fiction. | Private investigators—Fiction. |
Assassins—Fiction. | BISAC: FICTION / Crime. | FICTION /
Suspense. | GSAFD: Mystery fiction. | Suspense fiction.
Classification: LCC PS3553.R264 D36 2019 | DDC 813/.54—dc23
LC record available at https://lccn.loc.gov/2019021247

p.   cm.

First G. P. Putnam's Sons hardcover edition / August 2019
First G. P. Putnam's Sons trade paperback edition / February 2020
First G. P. Putnam's Sons premium edition / August 2020
G. P. Putnam's Sons premium edition ISBN: 9780525535706

Printed in the United States of America
1   3   5   7   9   10   8   6   4   2

for my pal,
Kim Stanley Robinson,
a witness at Beggar's Banquet

Acknowledgments

My editor, Mark Tavani, helped build this novel. Thanks for the patience, insight, and support.

My copy editor, Patricia Crais, pored over the manuscript with unyielding commitment. She made the author look better than he is. Thank you.

My inordinately talented team at Putnam: Ivan Held (the boss), Meredith Dros (the miracle worker), Elena Hershey (publicity wizard), and Karen Fink (for her work on prior novels). Additionally, thanks to publicist Kim Dower of Kim-from-LA Literary & Media Services, who has moved mountains for the author on more than one occasion.

Thanks and gratitude to the brilliant team at my publisher in the United Kingdom, Simon & Schuster UK, for their commitment and faith. Ian Chapman, Anne Perry, Suzanne Baboneau, Jo Dickinson, Bethan Jones, Hayley McMullan, Richard Vlietstra, Gemma Conley-Smith, and Jess Barratt.

And my agents: Aaron Priest and Lucy Childs of the Aaron Priest Literary Agency in the U.S., and Caspian Dennis of Abner Stein Ltd. in the U.K., I wouldn't be here without you.

A man's character is his guardian divinity.

—HERACLITUS

If you're lookin' for trouble,
just look right in my face.

—ELVIS PRESLEY
"TROUBLE," *KING CREOLE*

Her Family

Debra Sue closed her eyes and listened with all her might. The TV was off, their modest living room was dark, and Ed was sprawled on the couch. Her husband was dead to the world, but his snores were soft as a whisper. When they bought the little house a block from Sunset Boulevard, Ed worried traffic sounds would be intrusive, but they weren't, not really. Debra Sue had grown used to the noise quickly, and found the sounds soothing. She touched her husband's shoulder.

"Let's go to bed, baby. Get up."

Ed lurched awake, eyes wide and blinking.

"What happened?"

"Bedtime. Everything's fine."

Ed's eyes flagged, and he was halfway back to sleep.

"Scared me. Sorry."

"It's late. I'll be right in."

Ed swung his legs off the couch and lumbered into the hall. She heard him use the bathroom and settle into bed, but Debra Sue didn't move to join him.

She whispered his name.

"Ed."

She said her own name.

"Debra Sue."

She said their daughter's name.

"Isabel."

Debra Sue smiled.

"My family."

Debra Sue finally rose from the chair and moved through their quiet home. She made sure the front and back doors were locked, carefully checked the windows, and turned off the lights in each room. She set the alarm.

The warm night air was rich with the scent of night-blooming jasmine and orange blossoms, along with a trace of fresh paint. They had painted their little home with cheery colors after escrow closed—a bright lemony peach with a pale lime and burgundy trim—and joked that they'd given the place a new-car smell. Ed planted two orange trees in the backyard, but the jasmine had been there, and Debra Sue loved it. The jasmine was a sign. Their little house would be a happy and beautiful home.

Debra Sue turned on the outside lights, and made her way down the hall. She stopped outside Isabel's room when she heard her baby girl singing. Debra Sue stifled a giggle.

Isabel cracked her up.

Isabel was three years old. She was their only child, though Debra Sue and Ed talked about having another, and an absolute sweetheart. She was sweet, good-natured, and almost always happy.

Debra Sue moved closer, and listened.

La-la-la-LA-la-la.

Debra Sue fought not to laugh. Isabel was lying in her crib, waving her arms in the air, and singing to herself.

La-LA-la-LA.

Debra Sue didn't go in. She didn't want to disturb her daughter, and have to bring Isabel into bed with her and Ed. Right now, undisturbed, Isabel was in a wonderful, beautiful dreamland, imagining whatever fanciful stories happy three-year-old girls imagined.

Debra Sue loved Isabel so much her eyes filled with tears.

"Every day, baby girl. Every day of your life will be as happy as this. Daddy and I will make sure it is."

Debra Sue eased past Isabel's door, and crept to her bedroom. Ed was out cold, and no longer snoring. She brushed her teeth, flossed, and washed her face in the dark, then sat on the edge of their bed.

Debra Sue listened, and heard only the soft, baby-girl melody.

La-la-LA-LA. La-la-LA-LA.

But now Debra Sue didn't smile. She eased open her nightstand drawer and studied the black 9mm Sig Sauer pistol. Ed's nightstand contained an identical pistol. They had bought the guns, and learned to shoot. They practiced.

Debra Sue shut the drawer, and lay down beside her

husband. She touched his hand. She sighed like a ghost in the darkness.

"Mommy and Daddy will keep you safe."

Debra Sue listened for something she prayed never to hear, and finally fell asleep.

PART ONE

"WE KNOW YOUR SECRET."

1.

Isabel Roland

Three tellers were working the morning Isabel Roland was kidnapped. Clark Davos, a sweet guy whose third baby had just been born; Dana Chin, who was funny and wore fabulous shoes; and Isabel, the youngest teller on duty. Isabel began working at the bank a little over a year ago, three months before her mother died. Five customers were in line, but more customers entered the bank every few seconds.

Mr. Ahbuti wanted bills in exchange for sixteen rolls of nickels, twelve rolls of dimes, and a bag filled with quarters. As Isabel ran coins through a counter, her cell phone buzzed with a text from her gardener. Sprinkler problems. Isabel felt sick. The little house she inherited from her mother was driving her crazy. The sprinklers, a leaky roof over the porch, roots in the pipes because of a stupid pepper tree, the ancient range that made scary popping noises every time she turned on the left front burner. Always a new problem, and problems cost money. Isabel had grown up in the house, and loved the old place, but her modest salary wasn't enough to keep it.

Isabel closed her eyes.

Why did you have to die?

Abigail George touched her arm, startling her. Abigail was the assistant branch manager.

"I need you to take an early lunch. Break at eleven, okay?"

Isabel had punched in at nine. It was now only ten forty-one, and Izzy had eaten an Egg McMuffin and hash browns on her way into work. She felt like a bloated whale.

"But it's almost eleven now. I just ate."

Abigail smiled at Mr. Ahbuti, and lowered her voice.

"Clark has to leave early. The baby again."

They both glanced at Clark. His baby had come early, and his wife wasn't doing so well.

Abigail shrugged apologetically.

"I'm sorry. Eleven, okay? *Please?*"

Abigail squeezed her arm, and hurried away.

Isabel gave Mr. Ahbuti his cash, and called for the next customer when Dana hissed from the adjoining station.

"*Iz.*"

Dana tipped her head toward the door and mouthed the words.

"*It's him.*"

Ms. Kleinman reached Izzy's window as the man joined the line. He was tall and dark, with ropey arms, a strong neck, and lean cheeks. Every time he came in, Dana went into heat.

"*Iz.*"

Dana finished with her customer, and whispered again.

"Studburger."

"Stop."

"Double meat. Extra sauce."

"Shh!"

Ms. Kleinman made a one-hundred-dollar cash withdrawal. As Izzy processed the transaction, she snuck glances at the man. Gray sweatshirt with the sleeves cut off, faded jeans tight on his thighs, and dark glasses masking his eyes. Isabel stared at the bright red arrows tattooed high on his arms. She wanted to touch them.

Dana whispered.

"Manmeat on a stick."

Isabel counted out twenties.

As Ms. Kleinman walked away, Dana whispered again.

"Finger-lickin' good."

Izzy cut her off by calling the next customer.

"Next, please."

The man was now third in line. Dana called for a customer, and the man was now second. Clark called, and the man was hers.

"*Iz.*"

Dana.

"Ask him out."

"Sh!"

"You know you want to. Do it!"

Izzy said, "Next, please."

Dana hissed, "Do it!"

When he reached her window, Izzy smiled brightly.

"Good morning. How may I help you?"

He laid out three checks and a deposit slip. Two of the checks were made payable to Joe Pike, and the third to cash. They totaled a considerable amount.

Joe Pike said, "For deposit."

"You're Mr. Pike?"

She knew his name, and he probably knew she knew. He came in every three or four weeks.

"I've helped you before."

He nodded, but offered no other response. He didn't seem friendly or unfriendly. He didn't seem interested or uninterested. She couldn't read his expression.

Isabel fed the checks through a scanner. She wanted to say something clever, but felt stupid and awkward.

"And how's your day so far?"

"Good."

"It's such a pretty day, and here I am stuck in the bank."

Pike nodded.

"You're so tan, I'll bet you're outside a lot."

"Some."

Nods and one-word answers. He clearly wasn't interested. Isabel entered the transaction into her terminal, and gave him the deposit receipt.

The man said, "Thank you."

He walked away, and Isabel felt embarrassed, as if his lack of interest proved she was worthless.

"*Iz!*"

Dana leered across the divider.

"I saw you talking!"

"He thanked me. Saying thanks isn't talking."

"He never talks. He thinks you're *hot*."

"He didn't even see me."

"Shut *up*! He *wants* you!"

If only.

Isabel wondered if she could scrape together two hundred dollars for a new garden timer.

She glanced at her watch. Ten fifty-two. Eight minutes from a lunch she didn't want, and an event that would change her life.

2.

Karbo and Bender

Karbo and Bender missed her at home by ten minutes. Materials found inside gave them her place of employment, so now they waited at a meter six blocks from a bank near the Miracle Mile.

Karbo slumped in the passenger seat, sipping a café mocha.

"Ever kidnap anyone?"

Bender glanced away. Bender was the driver. Karbo was the smile. They had worked for Hicks before, but never together. Karbo and Bender met for the first time at four that morning outside a strip mall in Burbank. They would part in approximately two hours, and never meet again.

Karbo said, "Sorry. My mistake."

No questions allowed. They knew what they were supposed to do, how they were supposed to do it, and what was expected. Hicks prepped his people.

Bender gestured behind them.

"Here he comes."

Karbo lowered his window.

Hicks was a hard, pale dude in his forties. Nice-looking, not a giant, but broader than average. Non-threatening, if you didn't look close. A nasty edge lurked in his eyes, but he hid it well. Karbo and Bender were nice-looking, nonthreatening guys, too. Especially Karbo.

Hicks had come from the bank.

"She's a teller. Figure on making the grab at lunch."

Bender arched his eyebrows.

"Why lunch?"

"People eat lunch. Employees park in back, but with all these little cafés, no way she'll drive. She'll probably exit the front, and give you a shot. You get the shot, take it."

Bender's eyebrows kissed in a frown.

"Wouldn't it make sense to wait at her house, grab her when she gets home?"

Hicks glanced left and right, relaxed, just looking around.

"Time is an issue. You want out, say so, and I'll get someone else."

Karbo changed the subject. He didn't want out. He wanted the money.

"I have a question. What if she goes out the back?"

"If she exits the rear, you're out of the play. If she isn't alone, say she comes out with a friend, you're out of the play. Maybe she won't even come out. Maybe she brought a sandwich. No way to know, right? You have one job, and only the one."

Karbo said, "The front."

People would be watching the rear, for sure, but this was how Hicks operated. Compartmentalization. Minimum information. If an element got popped, they had nothing to give. Karbo admired the tough, precise way Hicks did business.

Hicks rested his hand on the door.

"Picture."

Hicks had given them a five-by-seven photograph of a twenty-two-year-old woman. Having changed the play, he didn't want the picture in their possession. The picture was evidence.

Bender returned the picture, and Hicks offered a final look.

"Burn her face into your brains. We can't have a mistake."

A high school photo printed off the internet showed a young woman with short dark hair, glasses, and a smile with a crooked incisor.

Karbo said, "Burned."

Bender cleared his throat. Karbo sensed the man thought they were moving too fast, but the money was huge, and their involvement would end in minutes.

Bender said, "What's she wearing?"

"Pink shirt. Kinda dull, not bright. A pink shirt over a tan skirt. I couldn't see her shoes."

Hicks tucked the picture into his jacket.

"She'll be easy to spot, but if anything looks weird, drive away. Anyone with her, drive away. Am I clear?"

Karbo and Bender nodded.

"Clear."

"Go."

Hicks walked away and Bender eased from the curb.

Their ride was a dark gray Buick SUV owned by a leasing company in La Verne, California. Late model, low miles, the full option package. They had picked up the Buick at 4:22 that morning, specifically for use in the crime. After they delivered the girl, they would hand off the Buick, pick up their cars and money, and go their separate ways.

Karbo thought Bender was having second thoughts, but Bender surprised him.

"Beautiful day, isn't it? Lovely, lovely day."

Karbo studied the man for a moment.

"Yeah."

"Gorgeous. A perfect day."

Bender hadn't said ten words all morning, even when they were searching the woman's house. Karbo figured he was nervous.

"I know we're not supposed to ask, but you've worked gigs before?"

Bender tapped the blinker and changed lanes.

"Three or four."

"This will be easy. Hicks's gigs are always easy."

"Snatching a person in front of a bank in broad daylight can't make the top of the Easy list."

"You didn't have to say yes. You should've backed out."

"Right."

"I don't want to work with someone I can't trust."

"I'm concerned, is all. He's making this up on the fly."

"A lot of these gigs, this is what happens."

"You're not concerned? You don't see the risk here?"

Karbo saw the risk. He also saw the reward.

"Look at this face."

Karbo grinned and fingered his dimples.

"I'll have her in the car in ten seconds tops. No big scene, I promise. Five minutes later, she's out of our lives. What could be easier?"

"You may be a moron."

Karbo shrugged.

"True, but you get to stay in the car. I'm the guy who gets out."

Bender finally nodded.

"You're right. And if anything looks weird, we drive away."

"Damned right we do. Fast."

Bender seemed to relax, and found a spot at a meter with an eyes-forward view of the bank.

Karbo liked the location. A commercial street lined with single-story storefronts two blocks south of Olympic. A straight shot to the freeway if needed. The girl would turn toward or away from them when she left the bank, and either was fine. A lot of people were out and about, but this shouldn't matter if Karbo did his job quickly and well.

Karbo said, "You were right."

"About?"

"The day. It's a beautiful day in the neighborhood."

"You're a moron. A perfect day doesn't make this any less risky."

They watched the bank. They didn't pay attention to the people who went into the bank, or the men who came out. They watched for a twenty-two-year-old woman wearing a pink shirt over a tan skirt.

They paid no attention to the man wearing a sleeveless gray sweatshirt. They did not see the red arrows tattooed high on his arms, and barely noticed when he entered the bank. They paid even less attention when he emerged a few minutes later.

This was their mistake.

Their perfect day was about to turn bad.

3.

Isabel

Ten fifty-three.

Isabel helped her last customer, logged out of her terminal, and closed her station. She wasn't hungry, so she wondered if she had time to run home and catch the gardener.

Dana said, "Iz?"

Dana leered, and lowered her voice.

"We can look up his number. You can call, and tell him there was a problem with the transaction."

Isabel rolled her eyes, and left the bank at eleven-oh-two.

She didn't feel up to dealing with the gardener, so she decided to get a smoothie. She was debating between chocolate and chocolate-caramel when a shiny new SUV pulled to the curb ahead of her. A good-looking guy climbed out, opened the rear passenger door, and looked around as if he was confused. He saw her, and offered a tentative smile.

"Oh, hey, excuse me?"

Izzy returned his smile.

"Yes?"

He approached and touched her arm, exactly as Abigail had touched her arm moments before. His smile and manner were halfway between embarrassed and little-boy-charming.

"I'm supposed to return this gift, and I can't find the darned address. I'm totally lost."

He touched her toward the open door, his fingers a polite invitation to help with his problem.

Isabel went with him, and saw nothing inside but a clean backseat in the clean car beneath a clean blue sky. Another man sat at the wheel, and never looked at her.

Isabel didn't have time to turn, or ask which address he couldn't find. He shoved her hard, shoulder and hip, and drove her into the car. She grabbed at the edge of the roof, trying to save herself, but her grip broke free.

"Stop, what are you—stop!"

He dove in on top of her. The door slammed.

Isabel screamed, but his hand covered her mouth. She screamed as hard as she could, but her scream could not escape.

4.

Joe Pike

Upscale mid-city area: boutiques and pastry shops, a Tesla filling a loading zone, an older gentleman walking twin beagles, a homeless man splayed in the shade from a shopping cart heavy with plastic bags. Pike wasn't looking to save someone's life on the day he left the bank.

Pike's red Jeep Cherokee was parked across the street. He departed the bank at 10:54, and slid behind the wheel. He tucked the deposit receipt into the console, removed his .357 Magnum from beneath the front seat, and considered the two female tellers.

Dana and Isabel. Pike had noticed the expressive glances and whispered comments they traded. Their infatuation might have been welcome if they worked at a coffee shop or fitness center, but not at a job where they had access to his banking information. Pike's current business interests included a partnership in a detective agency, a custom gun shop in Culver City, and several rental properties. His former employers included the United States Marine Corps, the Los Angeles Police

Department, and various private military contractors. During his contract years, his fees were paid by foreign governments approved by the United States, shell companies controlled by the CIA and NSA, and multinational corporations. This employment had been legal, but the transfer of funds from his employers had left a digital trail that a curious bank employee might question. Pike had maintained accounts at this particular bank for almost two years, and wondered if it was time to move on.

Pike was pondering this when Isabel's pink shirt caught his attention. She stepped from the bank, paused to put on a pair of sunglasses, and set off along the sidewalk. A dark gray SUV eased to the curb ahead of her. The driver's head turned as the vehicle passed, and something about the way he tracked her felt off.

Pike noticed details. The Marines had trained him to maintain situational awareness. Multiple tours in hot spots from Central America to Afghanistan had baked in his skills. The driver wasn't simply looking at Isabel; he seemed to be locked on a target.

A nice-looking man got out of the passenger seat, and opened the backseat door. Pike saw the man's head and shoulders across the roof. He turned, and Isabel smiled. They appeared to know each other, but Pike read a question in her body language.

The man touched her arm, and gestured toward the vehicle. Isabel went with him as the older gentleman with the beagles passed behind them. The older gentleman paid no attention.

Isabel and the man looked in the SUV, and disappeared so quickly the SUV might have swallowed them. In the instant she vanished, Pike saw a flash of shock in her eyes. Her fingers clutched the roof, and then she was gone. The blinker came on, and the SUV eased into traffic.

Pike wasn't sure what had happened. He watched the departing vehicle, and clocked the surroundings. The gentleman urged his beagles along, but a woman in a bright floral dress stood frozen. She gaped at the SUV as if she had seen something monstrous, but didn't know what to make of it. No one else stopped, or stared, or shouted for help.

The SUV put on its blinker, and turned at the next corner.

But the skin across Pike's back tingled as it had in the deserts and jungles. He started his Jeep, and followed.

5.

Isabel

Isabel twisted and screamed, but the man's hand covered her mouth. He crushed her into the seat. His face was inches away, and no longer charming.

He said, "Shh. Shh."

Consoling.

Izzy lay still. Her glasses askew, one eye focused, the other blurred. She heard the turn signal go on—blink, blink, blink.

Another man's voice came from the front. The driver.

"Turning."

The man on top of her glanced toward the voice.

"We okay?"

The driver didn't answer.

The man on top of her asked again.

"Are we being followed?"

"I'm looking. I don't think so."

Isabel felt the car ease through a turn.

The driver said, "What about her?"

The man on top of her straightened her glasses.

"We're fine."

Outside sounds were hushed and distant. His hand smelled of mint, and Isabel knew she was going to die. Her mind spun with the jumbled crazy memories of every sex-killer movie she'd seen, the Hillside Strangler, the Night Stalker, Manson, and Hannibal Lecter, torture and rape and murder.

The man on top of her cooed.

"Everything's fine. We're not going to hurt you. Relax."

She sobbed, and tears ran through his fingers.

The driver spoke again.

"Turn coming up. No one's chasing us."

The blinker blinked. They turned, and picked up speed.

The driver sounded calm.

"Lookin' good. We're clear."

The man on top of her grinned. She felt his body relax.

"You're okay. I promise."

The pressure on her mouth eased.

The driver said, "She okay?"

"Superb."

The man's eyes crinkled when he smiled. Friendly and charming.

"Go with the flow, and I'll move my hand. Shall we try?"

She nodded.

He lifted his hand, and words tumbled out in a rush.

"Please let me go. Please, please—"

The hand clamped her mouth, but not hard. His eyes even twinkled, as if he was amused.

"We know your secret. So let's all relax and enjoy the ride."

The driver said, "Red light ahead. Gotta stop."

She felt the car slow. A horn blared somewhere behind them, but it seemed muted and far away.

The man above her bent closer. She thought he was going to kiss her, but he whispered.

"Twenty minutes, thirty, tops, and you'll be on your way. For real. This will be over before you know it."

Rape. They were going to rape her and torture her and it would *hurt*. Isabel hiccupped. She hiccupped again, and couldn't stop.

The man grinned even wider.

"You're funny."

The driver said, "Here we go. Stopping."

They eased to a stop.

The man smiled a whisper.

"You're in control. I know it doesn't seem this way, but everything that happens now is up to you."

"Please let me go."

"Soon."

"Please. Please don't do this."

The window above her was blurry white light. She could not see where they were or what they were passing. She saw nothing of the outside world, as if she and the man on top of her were belly-to-belly in their own private crypt.

Isabel sobbed.

"Please don't hurt me. I didn't do anything. I don't want to die."

The driver said, "Green light."

Izzy sobbed so hard the world shimmered. Her pleas were as soft as a butterfly's wing.

"Help me, help, somebody please help."

The man smoothed her hair.

"Shh. It's okay. Don't be afraid. No one can hear you but us."

She sobbed again, and a shadow crossed the window.

The driver said, "C'mon, c'mon, the light's green. What's wrong with people, all he has to do is—"

The driver's window exploded as if they'd been broadsided by a runaway truck. His door flew open, and the driver vanished. Something blocked the light, and the man on top of her jerked away. He convulsed, and flew over the seat and out the door as if he had been sucked into space.

Izzy lay gasping.

The car was silent.

Isabel was alone in a suddenly empty car.

Something blocked the light again, and Mr. Pike appeared. His head turned. The dark glasses found her.

"You're safe now. Let me help you."

Isabel covered her face, and sobbed.

6.

Joe Pike

Pike secured the men belly-down on the street with plasticuffs, and took their wallets and phones. The driver was Donald Bender. The man he pulled off the teller was Christopher Karbo. Bender appeared unconscious, but Karbo watched him with rolling eyes. The right side of Karbo's face was purple, and his right eye was swelling shut.

Pike said, "Do you understand me?"

The man's eye rolled again, but he nodded.

"Stay. If you try to get up, I'll put you down."

When Pike was satisfied the men were no longer a threat, he helped the teller from the vehicle. She was shaken, but Pike saw no blood or lacerations.

"OhmiGod, OhmiGod, he pushed me into their car! He was on *top* of me."

"I saw. I was across the street."

Isabel closed her eyes, trying to steady herself.

"I feel really weird. I think I'm going to throw up."

"Breathe. It'll pass."

She drew a breath, and pressed her hands to her belly.

"He asked for help. He seemed so nice, and he just *attacked* me!"

Pike wanted to say something encouraging, but didn't know what to say. The men were nicely dressed, well kept, and their vehicle was immaculate. They looked like any other two men in the area, yet they had attempted to abduct a woman in broad daylight in front of a bank.

"Customers from the bank? Donald Bender. Christopher Karbo."

Isabel snuck a glance and shook her head.

"I don't think so. I've never seen them before."

A siren wailed, but sounded far away. Isabel noticed bystanders snapping pictures and shooting video with their phones. She looked embarrassed.

"I've never even gotten a traffic ticket. What do we do, just stand here?"

"They'll be here soon."

"I'm sorry you have to wait."

"Traffic. Traffic's a bitch even for cops."

Isabel suddenly giggled.

"Would it be all right if I texted my boss? She'll be worried."

Pike retrieved her purse from the SUV, and stood with her as she texted her boss.

The first officers to arrive were Ito and Garcia. Garcia was a P-2 with four service stripes on her sleeve. They eyed Bender and Karbo first, but Garcia's gaze settled on Pike. Ito walked over to the men on the ground, and Garcia approached Isabel and Pike.

"Someone explain why these gentlemen are proned out and bleeding."

Isabel burst into tears, and pointed at Karbo.

"He attacked me. That one—him—he pushed me into their car, and held me down. They tried to *kidnap* me. Mr. Pike saw it. He *saved* me."

Garcia studied Pike.

"You the one called emergency services?"

Pike said, "Yes."

"I know you."

"We've never met."

She glanced at his arrows.

"I know you anyway."

Garcia turned to Isabel.

"Why don't we step over here, and you can tell me what happened. Mr. Pike can wait here, okay, Mr. Pike?"

Pike said, "Sure."

A second patrol car and an EMS wagon arrived. Ito briefed the officers, and put the paramedics to work on Karbo and Bender. He finally came over to Pike.

"Okay. Let's hear your version."

Pike offered his DL without being asked, and described what had happened. He spoke in short, declarative sentences, exactly as he had when he was an officer.

"I followed them until they stopped for the light, then exited my vehicle and approached from the rear. Bender was driving. Karbo was on top of Ms. Roland in the backseat. His hand was over her mouth. She was in obvious distress."

"Sexual assault?"

"Possible, but I couldn't say. She was struggling."

"Then what?"

"I neutralized the driver, pulled Karbo off the woman, and that's it. I called nine-one-one while in pursuit, and here we are."

Ito glanced at the men.

"You neutralized them."

"Yes."

"Mr. Bender has a concussion."

"She needed help."

Ito considered Pike, and eyed the SUV's shattered window.

"So you dragged two men out of their vehicle, and basically kicked their asses."

"She needed help."

"Okay. Wait here some more."

Pike phoned his gun shop to let his guys know he would be late, then settled against the SUV. Pike was patient. He knew these things took time.

Ito secured Karbo in a patrol car, and the paramedics loaded Bender into their van. An officer asked the crowd for witnesses, but most were drifting away. Pike noticed Karbo watching the crowd, and realized the man was looking at someone. Pike searched for the person looking back, but saw no one suspicious. When he glanced back at Karbo, the man's head was down.

A gray, unmarked D-ride arrived as the paramedics left. The lead was a large, big-boned male with an over-sized head. His partner was a middle-aged woman built like a stork. They huddled with Isabel and Garcia for several minutes, then spoke to Karbo. When they finished with Karbo, they returned to Isabel and Garcia, and motioned for Pike to join them. The male was Detective Braun. His partner was Detective DeLako.

Braun said, "Here's where we are. We're going to book this as an assault and false imprisonment to get the ball rolling. We'll probably up it to a kidnap as the case develops. Okay?"

Isabel glanced at Pike, and made a shrug.

"Okay."

DeLako said, "We'd like you to come in to give a more detailed statement. One of our officers can give you a ride."

Isabel squirmed.

"Now?"

"Now is best. Everything's fresh."

"Can I come later? I can't miss work."

"Now is best. We'll clear it with your boss."

Isabel glanced at Pike again, and Pike nodded.

Isabel said, "Okay. I guess."

DeLako turned to Pike.

"Four o'clock at Wilshire Station."

Pike said, "Sure."

Braun studied Pike for a moment, and held up Pike's license.

"Joe damned Pike. I'm surprised those idiots are still breathing."

He studied Pike's license once more, and handed it back.

"You might want to lawyer up. Karbo says you attacked him for personal reasons. Says you're her boy-friend."

Isabel flushed.

"He isn't my boyfriend. I work at the bank."

Braun stared at Pike.

"Are you?"

"This is the first time I've seen Ms. Roland outside the bank."

Isabel said, "That man is lying! Mr. Pike is a customer!"

Braun softened a smile for Isabel.

"I wouldn't worry about it, Ms. Roland. Criminals lie about everything. Lemme arrange for your ride."

Isabel looked queasy as they left.

"I hope they don't believe him."

"Just tell them what happened. You'll be fine."

Pike knew she didn't believe it, and was feeling over-whelmed.

"This is so crazy. All I did was leave the bank. I came out, and they *attacked* me."

A line appeared between her eyebrows, as if she was struggling to make sense of what had happened.

"He told me they know my secret. I'm like, what secret? I don't have any secrets."

"Karbo?"

"Isn't that weird? What's wrong with people?"

She suddenly looked at him.

"I wish you could come with me."

Isabel Roland was afraid. Pike guessed her age at twenty-two or so, but she could have passed for sixteen.

Now she had to deal with things she didn't understand and people who frightened her. He took out a card, and wrote his cell.

"You'll be fine. If you want to talk, call me."

Isabel glanced at the card as if she didn't know what to say, and suddenly clutched his arm.

"We've never been introduced. I'm Isabel Roland, but everyone calls me Izzy."

Pike said, "Joe."

She took out her phone, and tapped the screen.

"Now you have my number, too."

A message arrived with her contact card.

DeLako called from behind them, saying Isabel's ride was ready to go.

Isabel looked forlorn.

"All I wanted was a smoothie."

Pike tried again to think of something assuring to say, but only managed a nod. He watched the patrol car take her away. The paramedics were gone, and the black-and-whites had left the scene. Karbo and Bender were gone. Their SUV would soon be towed. The street was busy and bright as if nothing had happened.

Pike felt a tingle kiss the base of his neck, as if someone he did not see was watching.

7.

Pike was finishing dinner that night when she called. Red bean burritos, cauliflower, and beets. Pike lived alone in a gated condo complex in Culver City, not far from his business. His phone rang at eight o'clock. Not five of, or five after, but eight on the hour.

"Hi, it's Isabel. From today?"

"I remember."

The Lakers were playing Portland. Pike muted the sound.

"I hope you don't mind. You said I could call."

"How're you doing?"

"Better, *now*."

She made a nervous giggle, somewhere between awkward and cheery.

"Janice gave me a tour. She showed me cells and where the detectives work and this man being fingerprinted. He was a thief."

"Who's Janice?"

"Detective DeLako. She told me to call her Janice. They were nice. Even Detective Braun."

She giggled again, but Pike knew this was anxiety. During Pike's time as an officer, he'd seen burglary victims sell their violated homes, assault victims crippled by PTSD, and fellow officers resign after a gunfight. Victims suffered long after perps went to jail.

"I meant with what happened. You doing okay?"

"I'm still kinda freaked."

"Freaked is normal. Janice can put you in touch with victim support groups. People who'll help you deal."

"She told me."

"Seeing someone is a good idea. Think about it."

"I will."

She hesitated, and when she spoke again her voice was low, as if she was ashamed.

"I was scared to come home. I live alone, and now being here feels creepy. I didn't want to open the door."

"You understand why?"

"I guess."

"Give yourself time."

"It's just so crazy. Who goes to lunch and gets kidnapped? Here's this stranger, and I walked over and did what he wanted. I feel stupid."

"Don't. You didn't do this to yourself."

"That's what Janice said."

"She's right."

Isabel sighed like she was catching her breath.

"Anyway, I hope they didn't keep you too long."

"Not long. We went over what happened."

Pike's interview had taken forty minutes. They asked the same questions Ito had asked, and recorded his answers. The only new information Pike provided was a description of the woman in the floral-print dress, who may have seen Karbo push Isabel into Bender's car.

"Janice told me you used to be a policeman."

"Once."

"Is the other thing true?"

"What?"

"You killed your partner and became a mercenary?"

A fountain burbled in the corner. Pike liked the sound.

Isabel said, "I don't think they like you very much. She said you're dangerous."

"That's in the past."

"Not today. Not today it wasn't."

Pike said, "No."

"Anyway. I wanted to thank you again. Thank you."

"You don't have to thank me."

"No, I do. You know what's really scary?"

Pike waited.

"You not being there. I might be dead. I could've been one of those girls you hear about, they disappear, and some maniac keeps them in a secret room."

"Stop thinking about it."

"Sorry."

"None of those things happened."

"I know. I'm going to work tomorrow. I want to be around other people."

"Good."

"I'll let you go. I just wanted to thank you."

"I'm glad I could help."

He waited for her to sign off, but she didn't.

"People were all around, but you were the one who helped. Only you."

"Good night, Izzy. Call if you need me."

"I won't bother you again."

"You didn't."

She giggled.

"You're a rockstar hero, but you're a really bad liar. Good night, Joe."

Pike lowered his phone, and returned to his dinner. He was concerned for her, and hoped she sought counseling. Pike had lived with violence for most of his life, but this was the first time violence had touched her. Pike pondered this as he ate. Once a person was touched, they were never the same.

Three days later, Isabel called.

8.

The Cherry Farm
Palmdale, California

Deputy U.S. Marshal Pryor Gregg followed his GPS south out of Palmdale along a twisting, two-lane road through low foothills and stretches of shriveled land. Gregg was tall, lean, and grim. He wore an immaculate dark brown suit, gold-rimmed sunglasses, and cowhide boots. His skin was as dark as his boots and weathered deep.

His phone said, "Turn left in one hundred yards."

Gregg keyed his radio mic.

"Ten-twenty-three."

"Copy. Inbound now."

Gregg turned past a sun-faded billboard onto a gravel parking lot with a large, plywood fruit stand. The billboard read PICK YOUR OWN CHERRIES. An L.A. County Sheriff's car was parked beside the fruit stand, and a uniformed deputy waited beside the car. The stand had been closed and locked for the season.

One car. A dep from the local substation. No tape. Gregg didn't like it.

The deputy raised a hand.

Gregg squared a broad-brimmed Stetson hat on his head as he climbed from the car.

The deputy offered his hand along with an uneasy smile. Mid-to-late thirties. Friendly. Too many donuts.

"They said you'd be right out. Cal Stella. Pleased to meet you."

Gregg flipped his commission case, flashing the badge. A silver ring surrounded a silver star, set in black leather.

"Pryor Gregg. Marshals Service. How long has the scene been clear?"

"Since yesterday. Crime scene guys finished up. Body's down in L.A. with the coroner."

Gregg had already spoken with the Sheriff's detective-in-charge and the Medical Examiner on his drive up from Los Angeles.

"We're closing it. Let's see what you have."

Stella shrugged toward the trees behind him.

"Right over here. Not far."

Gregg took a moment to consider their surroundings. Cherry trees stood in neat rows behind and surrounding the stand. The leaves were dark green and pointed, but the trees hadn't yet flowered. Gregg had studied the area using a satellite view when he got the call, but the world always changed with boots on the ground. A truck sped past. An SUV filled with women. Two kids on motorcycles.

"Let's see."

Stella led him back through the trees to a mound of

dark earth and a shallow depression. Little metal stakes marked by bright yellow tape still ringed the area. Stella pointed at the hole as if Gregg wouldn't see it.

"This is where she found him."

Gregg studied the hole and the trees. He heard cars pass on the road and the hiss of a high desert breeze, but saw nothing but trees.

"What was she doing out here?"

"Who?"

"The lady who found him."

"Irrigation. Checks the hoses couple of times a week. Checks the pH. Farmer stuff. They have twelve acres."

Heavy black irrigation hoses ran along the ground from tree to tree. Drip system.

"Same time every week?"

"We can ask."

"I'll want to speak with her."

"Sure. Whenever you want."

Gregg circled the hole. He had seen photographs of the body and crime scene, and spoken with the detective in charge. Shoe impressions taken by the criminalists suggested three people—likely male—had buried the body.

"Shallow grave."

"They didn't take a lot of time, that's for sure."

"She was just walking along and saw him?"

"Her dog. Has this German shepherd comes with her. Started whining and digging, and wouldn't come when she called. Katie."

"Katie?"

"The dog. His hand was exposed. The criminalist says he wasn't in the ground more'n a day."

"This was three days ago?"

"Found him three days ago, yes, sir. Coroner says he'd been dead a day or so when she found him."

"In the ground a day or so, or dead a day or so?"

The deputy frowned, thinking it through.

"Dead. He said dead."

Gregg squatted beside the grave, and peered toward the road. He couldn't see the fruit stand or the road, but he heard a truck. He'd passed several small houses on the drive out from Palmdale. Not close, but near.

"No one heard shots."

The deputy made a shrug.

"The wind blows pretty good out here. The wind gets to rippin', it'll snatch a sound right out of the air."

Gregg considered the hole. He wondered if they'd had this place in mind for the body dump, or if the choice was mere convenience.

"Were you one of the responding officers?"

"Yes, sir."

"Here when they recovered his body?"

"Yes, sir. All day."

"They left his badge."

"Yes, sir. Wallet, ID, credit cards. Hundred sixty-eight dollars. Keys. Cell phone. They weren't looking to rob him."

"No. I guess they were not."

Gregg thought for a moment, then stood, and brushed

at his slacks. The creases fell straight and razor-sharp true. He adjusted his hat, and started back to his car. The deputy quickly caught up.

"Got any suspects?"

"Not yet."

The local wet his lips.

"Mighta been someone he arrested."

"Might."

"Payback for something."

"Maybe."

"He was one of yours?"

"He was a marshal."

Gregg heard a helicopter, far in the distance.

"Why you figure they killed him the way they did?"

The deputy wouldn't let it go.

"Left hand, left knee, right hand. The M.E. said that's how they did it. Shot him in the left hand first, then the left knee, then the right hand before they killed him. Why you think they shot him that way?"

Gregg ignored him and pushed through the trees.

The first helicopter arrived as they reached the fruit stand. The second appeared a few seconds later, drowning the wail of sirens. Dust and sand raged in a whirling maelstrom around them, and cherry trees whipped.

The deputy squinted at Gregg. He knew Gregg was keeping secrets, and shouted to make himself heard.

"Why do you think they shot him like that?"

Gregg glanced at the dep, and decided to answer.

"They wanted it to hurt."

Pryor Gregg held tight to his hat, and watched the big chopper land. He didn't yet know what had happened here, but he had a good idea. He knew it was bad, and more people might die.

PART TWO

PERSON OF
INTEREST

9.

Joe Pike

Pike found her message after he showered at Ray De-
pente's dojo in South Central Los Angeles. It was late
afternoon. Ray, a retired Marine and lifelong martial artist, had spent the bulk of his career teaching combatives to
young Marines. These days, by choice, he taught chil-
dren, but twice a month, Ray closed his doors to regular
business, and practiced what he called "advanced techni-
cals" with a few of his friends. The guest list typically included former Delta and SEAL operators, law-enforcement
tactical cadre, and the occasional bodyguard. Pike was a
regular, and often served as an instructor.

Pike played her message as he sat on a bench in the
locker room.

"Um, hi. It's Isabel Roland. Could you call me, please?
I really, really need to talk to you."

She sounded upset, the way she sounded when he
helped her from Bender's car.

Pike checked the time. She had left the message forty-
two minutes earlier.

Pike dressed, and returned her call from his Jeep. Her voice mail answered, so he left a message.

"It's Joe."

He thought what to say.

"I'm here if you need me."

Pike didn't like the way she sounded, and wondered why she really really needed to talk.

He drove to his shop, helped the guys close up, and stopped at a market for food. An hour later, he was making dinner when he phoned her again and got her voice mail. He left a second message.

Pike liked the silence in his condominium. The furnishings were spare, and in order. The space was immaculate. Sofa, chair, coffee table, lamps. The walls were bare. No art or photos disturbed their surface. Pike kept his Jeep, his gear, his home, and himself shipshape and squared away. These lessons had been impressed upon him when he was a young Marine. Pike's childhood had been uncertain and violent. The Marines taught him the beauty of order.

Pike watched the news as he ate, then turned off the television, and changed into shorts. He spread a yoga mat on the living room floor. Pike had never been married. He had come close, once, and loved another he couldn't have. He had girlfriends, but, outside of a barracks, he had not lived with anyone more than a few days. Private military contractors with Pike's particular skill set lived demanding lives. He would leave on a moment's notice, be gone for long periods, and often could not disclose where he was going or where he had been. Pike had decided not to ask anyone to share such an unpredictable life. This was a decision he sometimes regretted. He kept no plants or pets.

Pike closed his eyes, and breathed. Slow breaths in, slow breaths out. He emptied his mind, and thought about nothing. His heart rate slowed. Forty-two, forty-one, forty beats per minute. Pike sat like this for half an hour, then stretched on the couch, and read for the remains of the evening. He wondered if Isabel would call, then put her out of his thoughts. She would, or she wouldn't.

At ten minutes after eleven, he armed the security system, shut the lights, and went to bed.

His world was silent.

Pike held his breath, and listened.

There was nothing, and no one, to hear.

10.

Pike's phone rang at six-oh-five the following morning. He had been up for hours. He'd gone for a run, finished PT, and now he was dressing. His first thought was Isabel, but the caller ID read CTY LAPD.

Pike answered slowly.

"Pike."

"This is Braun. We have a couple of follow-up questions."

A cool frost bloomed in his chest. Braun wouldn't call this early for questions.

"Is it Isabel?"

"Look out the window. We're having a party."

Pike pulled on a pair of jeans, and went to the window. Pike's condominium complex was comprised of several four-unit quads, with each quad having its own parking area. Entry to the grounds required a key card, but Braun's unmarked sedan and a black-and-white sat in his parking lot. Braun and DeLako stood by his Jeep, bathed in a milky pre-dawn glow. Two uniformed officers stood by a patrol car. The uniforms meant Braun expected trouble.

Pike said, "Coming out."

Pike grabbed a sweatshirt, then tossed it aside. He wanted them to see he was unarmed. He walked barefoot and shirtless out to the parking lot.

Braun looked tired, but wary with tension.

"Here he is now, the damsel's hero."

DeLako's eyes were cool.

"You always up this early?"

Their skin had the greasy sheen of too little sleep, and their jackets hung like wrinkled drapes. They looked like a couple of cops who'd spent the night at a crime scene.

Pike said, "Did something happen to Isabel?"

DeLako laid her hand on the Jeep's hood.

"Your engine's warm. Been out and about?"

"Sullivan Canyon. Running."

"In the dark?"

Pike stepped closer. Braun stepped back, and the uniforms shifted.

"Did something happen to Isabel?"

"Have you seen or spoken with her since the incident?"

Now Pike was curious. They were asking about Isabel, but Pike sensed their interest lay elsewhere.

"The day she was attacked, after she left you. She called. She called again yesterday. We're playing phone tag."

"Why'd she call?"

"I don't know."

DeLako patted the Jeep's hood. Pike didn't like people touching his Jeep.

"Where were you last night, say between seven and ten?"

Pike didn't like the way they were watching him any better.

"Why does it matter?"

Braun repeated the question.

"Where were you?"

"Here. Ate, read for a while, went to bed. That's it."

"Can anyone vouch for your whereabouts?"

"Got home about six. A neighbor saw me. Put out garbage around nine. The kids in the next quad were here in the parking lot, flying a drone. Now talk to me, Braun. What's going on?"

"Karbo and Bender made bail. They were released yesterday afternoon."

Pike waited. His body was still, and his face gave them nothing. They weren't finished.

Pike said, "And?"

Braun's voice turned flat as a plate.

"They were murdered last night."

DeLako touched her temple.

"Single tap here, each one. Straight-up executions. You're not playing the Punisher, are you? It's not inconceivable when we're talking about you."

"If I were, you wouldn't find the bodies."

A wispy smile touched her lips.

"Yeah, you're a killer, for sure."

"I didn't do it."

"Maybe. But now Karbo can't sue you, which makes you a person of interest."

"Does Isabel know?"

"We'll let her know at a reasonable hour."

Braun said, "She knew they were being released. Maybe she gave you a call, and you dealt some payback."

"I didn't kill them."

"No? Maybe our little Miss Isabel killed them. Sound good?"

Pike didn't like him calling her "our little Miss Isabel."

"Sounds like you don't have a suspect."

DeLako sighed, showing her irritation.

"Why were you outside the bank?"

"The story hasn't changed."

"Karbo and Bender told a different story. She got into the car willingly, but changed her mind when Karbo got grabby. They were letting her out when you popped out of nowhere."

"I saw what I saw, Detective. Isabel told the truth."

DeLako glanced at Braun, but Braun was watching Pike. After a few seconds, he made a nod.

"Maybe so, but neither of these guys had a record. Both had good jobs, owned homes, checked all the right solid-citizen boxes. Not your typical predators."

"I'm not your typical bystander."

DeLako laughed. Even Braun managed a smile.

"True. Then again, maybe what you said and what she said isn't what happened."

Pike said, "Are we finished?"

DeLako took out her pad.

"We need the names of the people who saw you last night."

They climbed into their car after DeLako copied the information. The black-and-white left first. Braun and DeLako followed. Pike watched them drive through the gate, then went to his Jeep. DeLako's handprint marred the Jeep's shining hood. He took out a handkerchief, and buffed it away.

Pike thought about Isabel as he finished dressing. She had probably called after learning that Karbo and Bender were being released. She would have been scared, which explained the urgency in her voice. When she didn't reach him, she had probably spent the rest of the evening telling her friends about it. This made sense to Pike, but she had wanted to speak with him really, really badly, and never called back. This bothered him. The nervous urgency in her voice didn't fit with her silence.

At seven A.M., Pike got her voice mail again. He wondered if he should mention Karbo and Bender, but decided against it. Braun and DeLako had been right to question him, and they would be right in questioning Isabel. Both men being killed screamed of a connection to Isabel, but the connection was so obvious it felt false.

At nine-oh-one, Pike phoned the bank.

"Sorry, Isabel isn't in today. May I help you?"

Isabel had told him she was returning to work.

"Manager, please."

His call was connected.

"AbigailGeorgehowmayIhelpyou?"

Pike identified himself, and asked for Isabel.

"Oh, Mr. Pike! I'm so sorry. She's taking a few days off. Did you hear what happened? They let those men out of jail."

"Yes, ma'am. I'm returning her call."

"She was so upset I sent her home. I couldn't blame her. How could they let them out?"

"What time was it, when she went home?"

"This was yesterday."

"I understand."

"A little after three, I guess. I told her to take as much time as she needs."

Pike thanked her and lowered his phone.

Little Miss Isabel.

He replayed her message.

"Um, hi. It's Isabel Roland. Could you call me back, please? I really, really need to talk to you."

Pike clipped his .357 to his waist, and went to his Jeep. Sometimes Pike enjoyed silence. Sometimes the silence scared him.

11.

Isabel's address led to a modest green-and-yellow Craftsman on a street lined with elms and parked cars, its sidewalks mottled with shade. A covered porch spanned the front between a pepper tree and driveway. A one-car garage in the rear looked as if it hadn't been opened in years. Pike saw nothing amiss, but nothing felt right.

Pike parked his Jeep and climbed concrete steps to the door.

He saw a small white card wedged in the jamb, and knew Isabel wasn't home. We-were-here cards had been around when Pike was an officer, and LAPD still used them. Braun and DeLako had been by to see her.

Pike knocked anyway, and rang the bell. No one answered, so he knocked again.

"Isabel. Joe Pike."

He touched the knob.

Locked.

Pike stepped away and pondered how far to take this.

The front door was clean, intact, and showed no sign of forced entry. The porch windows were closed and undamaged, and the drapes were drawn. Any other day, Isabel would be at work. On a different day, she would be having coffee with a friend or shopping on Melrose, but this was the day after the men who attacked her were murdered. He stepped off the porch and walked down the drive.

The garage shared the tiny backyard with two orange trees, an overgrown rose bed, and a dying lawn drizzled with oranges. The garage was empty and the back door was locked.

"Isabel?"

Entry was easy. A dead bolt and a knob lock. If an alarm sounded, he would have walked away, but the alarm was not armed.

Pike passed through the kitchen and dining room into the living room. A short hall led to two bedrooms with a bath between. He cleared each space quickly. Pike had cleared hundreds of structures as a police officer and professional soldier, but he felt uneasy invading her space. He finished back in the kitchen.

No signs of violence or jimmied windows. No open drawers or emptied closets to suggest she'd fled. No murdered Isabel. Pike took a breath, and let himself out. He whispered to no one.

"Call."

Pike was walking back to the street when a snow-white Volkswagen Beetle wheeled into the drive. A young woman with short mahogany hair and sunglasses clambered out. She stopped short when she saw him, and opened her mouth.

"OhmiGod. You're the man who saved her."

She took a step closer, and went on.

"I'm Carly Knox, Izzy's friend. She told me about you."

Pike dropped a hand to cover the bulge of his pistol.

"Pike."

"I know!"

Carly Knox glanced at the house.

"Would you tell the girl to answer me, please? I've texted her a million times. She's ignoring me."

The frost he'd felt earlier prickled his skin. Her calls unreturned, like his.

"I don't know where she is. I haven't been able to reach her."

Carly's smile fell.

"She isn't with you?"

Pike shook his head.

"But you're here, so I thought—"

Carly suddenly ran up the steps, and fumbled with keys.

"Izzy!"

She threw the door open. Pike heard her calling as she ran through the house.

"Izzy?? Iz! *Isabel!!!*"

Pike followed her in, and waited by the door. Before, he had moved quickly; now, he studied the room. Framed photos of a man and woman and a younger Isabel lined credenza shelves. The room was clean, but depressions on a sofa showed the weight of time. Fading prints clung to walls with a twenty-year grip. A photograph caught his attention. A younger Isabel and a younger Carly, ten or eleven, both with gigantic smiles, hugging a sloppy yellow dog.

Carly was breathless when she returned.

"They took her. I'm really scared they hurt her."

Pike knew who she meant, but asked anyway.

"Karbo and Bender?"

She blinked, and the blinking grew faster.

"They were let out. Did you know? We texted about it all afternoon. Then this car showed up, and she freaked."

Pike said, "Is she married?"

Carly looked surprised.

"What does that have to do with anything?"

"Boyfriend or brother?"

"She's *missing*, and you're asking if she has a boyfriend?"

"Karbo and Bender were murdered last night. Someone killed them."

Carly looked angry, but not because they were dead.

"They were *here*. Look!"

She scrolled through texts, and held out her phone.

"This is them."

The text window showed their exchange, Izzy's texts on one side, Carly's the other. Izzy had sent a photograph of a passing SUV, her comment beneath.

THEY'RE BACK! THEY KEEP COMING BACK!

The picture had been taken through a porch window on the down side of twilight. Pike recognized Izzy's front yard, the tree by the sidewalk, and the house across the street. The SUV was similar to Bender's vehicle, but this SUV looked like a 4Runner. Two figures were visible, but dim light and poor resolution rendered them shadows. Pike returned Carly's phone.

"Driver's side. Bender's vehicle has a broken window. This vehicle doesn't."

Carly was adamant.

"It's them! She saw them!"

She scrolled, and offered more texts.

OMG OMG IT'S THEM! THEY FOUND ME

"You see? They were *watching* her."

Pike was dubious.

"She saw their faces?"

"She thought it was them. I don't know if she actually saw them, but what does it matter? She's missing!"

Pike read their texts again.

"When did she see them?"

"Maybe five thirty? I was at work."

Izzy had called Pike earlier.

Carly went on.

"I'm like, call the police! But she wanted to leave. I told her I'd come get her, but she said they'd gone, and she was going to my place. My mom and I live right over here, like five blocks. I said, text me you're safe."

Carly caught her breath.

"Only she didn't."

She scrolled through more texts.

"This was the last text I got."

LEAVING NOW

When Pike looked up, tears etched curves on her cheeks.

"I looked for her. I came here *twice*. Her car was gone. She was gone."

Carly closed her eyes, as if she were about to say the most difficult thing in the world.

"I've been calling and texting all night. She *always* texts back. We've been best friends forever."

Pike moved to the open door, and gazed at the street.

"You still are."

He turned.

"Let's find her."

12.

The smart play was to call the police, so Pike called Braun.

"Isabel Roland is missing."

Pike waited for Braun to say something, but Braun didn't respond.

"Braun?"

"You're a person of interest. Anything you say can and will be used against you."

"I'm at Isabel Roland's home with a woman named Carly Knox. You should speak with her."

Carly nodded along, anxious to tell what she knew.

Braun said, "I thought you had no connection with this woman, and now you're at her home?"

"Sometime between five thirty and six last night, Isabel told Ms. Knox an SUV was watching her house. She believed it was Karbo and Bender."

Braun hung up.

Pike dialed again.

Carly said, "What happened?"

Pike shook his head. Braun finally answered, and started in right away.

"Stop it, Pike. Karbo and Bender weren't there. No way."

"Ms. Knox is credible. I've seen their texts."

Carly spoke loudly.

"I'm credible!"

Braun said, "Is that her?"

"Yes."

Braun made a raspy sigh.

"I can appreciate her distress, but the time line is simple. Bender lived in Northridge. Karbo lived way the hell out in Eagle Rock. Between the time they were released and the time they got popped, they didn't have time to hassle Ms. Roland."

Carly shouted.

"They were here! She saw them!"

Braun groaned.

"Jesus, Pike. You should know better."

"She took a picture of the vehicle."

"Fantastic, but Karbo and/or Bender weren't there. They were too busy getting killed."

Pike hesitated, and considered Braun's time line. He didn't like what it meant, and continued more slowly.

"Isabel left to meet Ms. Knox, but she didn't show up. No one's heard from her. She isn't returning calls or answering texts."

Carly shouted again.

"She's missing!"

Braun mumbled something to DeLako, then continued to Pike.

"I know she's not home. We were there two hours ago."

"She's been missing since last night."

"She isn't missing. You know how I know? She told me."

Pike glanced at Carly.

"You spoke with her?"

Carly shouted.

"Where is she?"

Braun ignored her.

"Yeah, when we told her they were being released. She asked if she could leave town. I told her sure, wherever you want, go. Looks like she went."

Braun hesitated before going on.

"As for her not responding and such, tell you what, you got a plate on the vehicle she saw?"

"No."

"I'll check the hospitals, see if she had an accident."

Carly tugged Pike's arm.

"I want to talk to him."

Braun heard. He made another raspy sigh.

"Give her my number. One of us will talk to her later."

Meaning him or DeLako.

Pike said, "She's here. Talk to her now."

Carly shouted.

"I'm here!"

Braun's voice came back cold.

"*Now*, we're in Culver City to question your neighbors. Best you hope these people back up your story."

"Braun?"

"Give her my number."

"You sure it wasn't Karbo or Bender?"

"One hundred percent. I'm positive."

Pike hung up, and Carly tugged his arm again.

"Are they going to look for her?"

"Izzy asked if she could leave town. Did she mention going away?"

Carly rolled her eyes.

"That was just talk. She's been threatening to leave since they attacked her. You saw her text. She was going to *my* house."

Pike nodded and studied the street. If Karbo or Bender weren't behind the wheel, then someone had taken their places.

Carly mistook his stare.

"What?"

"When Karbo and Bender took her, did Isabel tell you about it?"

"Of course she told me. We tell each other everything."

Pike waited. Carly flushed, and finally continued.

"The one man, Karbo, he told the police you were her boyfriend."

"Before. What did they say in the car, when she was alone with them?"

Carly frowned for a moment, thinking.

"Karbo did the talking. The driver didn't speak to her."

Pike prompted her.

"Karbo pushed her into the vehicle. He held her down."

"Yeah. Asshole."

"Did he kiss her?"

Carly glanced away. Uncomfortable.

Pike said, "He held her down. He was on top of her in the backseat when I pulled him off. Did he kiss her?"

"I don't think so. She didn't say."

"Did he grope her, or touch her in a sexual way?"

Carly shook her head.

"Uh-uh. I kinda asked. It was about control. She was his captive."

"He did the talking. What did he say?"

Carly frowned some more.

"Stupid stuff. Everything was up to her, they wouldn't hurt her, which she totally didn't believe."

Carly fell silent, trying to remember.

"He said it wouldn't take long."

Pike's head moved, but only a bit.

"What wouldn't take long?"

"Whatever. She thought they were going to kill her."

"We know your secret?"

Carly's eyes widened like matching balloons.

"Yes! *We know your secret*! And she's like, *what* secret? She didn't know what he was talking about."

Pike waited for more, but Carly finally shrugged.

"Then you showed up. And saved her."

Pike thought about Karbo and Bender, and their motive for taking Isabel. Her first abduction could have been written off as a crime of opportunity. A second abduction suggested Isabel was a target.

Carly said, "Why are you staring at me? I'm not making this up. They stole her *again*!"

Pike stepped outside and took out his phone. He went to the edge of the porch.

Carly said, "Who are you calling?"

She followed after him, but Pike stopped her with a finger. He would say things he didn't want her to hear.

The phone rang three times.

A familiar voice answered.

"Elvis Cole Detective Agency, two clues for the price of one. Discounts available."

"I need your help."

Cole's voice turned serious.

"Anything."

13.

Hicks

Hicks's eyes burned from a lack of sleep, and his shoulders felt tight as rocks. The night had passed like a dying freight train straining to climb a hill, and the day wasn't picking up speed. Hicks told Ronson and Stanley to keep down the noise, and pushed past the carpet they'd hung to muffle the sound. He carried his phone to a quiet part of the house. Stegner had called.

Hicks lit a cigarette.

"This is better. Tell me something good."

Hicks had sent Stegner and Wallick to search the girl's house.

Stegner said, "You said she lives alone."

Hicks knew by the tone something was off. Stegner was good, but he was one of those guys who needed his hand held.

"That's right. And?"

"We can't get in. People are here."

Multiple eyes had confirmed the girl's living arrangements. Karbo and Bender had been in her home. Hicks had seen it himself. Isabel Roland lived alone.

"What people? A gardener? A housekeeper?"

"No, man. People. A man and a woman are on the porch. A young chick, about the girl's age. A car is in the drive. A Volkswagen."

Wallick mumbled in the background. Stegner paused to listen, then passed it along.

"The front door was open, so, obviously, they have a key."

"Where are you?"

"A couple of blocks over. Not far. What do you want to do?"

Hicks wanted them to search the house.

"They're probably friends, come by to check on her. They'll leave."

"With a key?"

"Close friends, sure. You think they're police? Plainclothes?"

"Driving a Bug? I'm thinking one or both of these people live here. I'm thinking someone gave you bad intel, and she has a roommate."

The tension in Hicks's shoulders spread to his neck. He sucked the cigarette, and fired a stream of smoke out the side of his mouth.

"She lives alone. By herself."

"If Wallick and I were in her house, someone with a key could walk in. Like these two."

Wallick mumbled again.

Hicks said, "What's he saying?"

"The dude, maybe. He's got the look."

Hicks was confused. Too little sleep, not enough coffee.

"What are you talking about?"

"The dude on the porch could be an off-duty cop. A big dude. Kinda rough. He has the look."

Hicks had a weird premonition he knew the answer to the question he was about to ask.

"Dressed how?"

"Jeans, a sweatshirt like gym rats wear. You know, with the sleeves cut off?"

"You see his arms?"

"Buff. Like a jock."

"Did he have tattoos?"

"I didn't see—hang on."

Wallick again.

"Wallick says yes. Something red."

"Arrows."

"Dude. We did not linger."

A man with red arrows tattooed on his delts put Karbo and Bender down. The police report described him as a customer from Roland's bank who witnessed the abduction by chance. A bystander who had no other connection to the victim, so Hicks had let it go. Yet here he was, bystanding the kid's home.

Hicks remembered his name. Pike. Hicks decided to find out more about Mr. Pike.

Stegner interrupted his thoughts.

"What do you want us to do?"

"Kill a few minutes, and swing back around. Get the Beetle's plate."

"'Kay."

"Don't let them see you."

"I know what I'm doing."

"Stay close, and check back later. They'll leave."

"Whatever you say."

"I say we need to search her house. Do it."

Hicks ended the call, and dropped the cigarette. He watched it bounce on the golden oak floor in the gorgeous old Spanish revival, a home built in the twenties, a small mansion, big rooms, not a stick of furniture. The floors had been polished to a high luster, and truly were beautiful. Hicks crushed the butt, grinding it into the wood. The damn place was an echo chamber. This was why Hicks lined the room's windows and doors with carpet. The girl screamed. Sounds carried.

14.

Joe Pike

Pike and Carly were on the porch when Cole pulled up in his pastel yellow Corvette convertible. Pike thought the understated yellow was beautiful when the old Stingray was clean, but Cole rarely washed his car. A mottled layer of dust made the yellow look like dried egg yolk.

Carly watched Cole climb from the car.

"Is he the detective?"

"Yes. He'll look around and ask questions. He knows what to look for."

Carly seemed dubious.

"I thought he'd be wearing a suit."

Cole was wearing khaki cargo pants, a bright green Hawaiian shirt, and slip-on canvas Vans.

Pike said, "Don't let the camouflage fool you. Wait here."

Pike stepped off the porch and joined Cole at the curb.

Joe Pike had worn an LAPD uniform when he first

met Elvis Cole. Cole, who didn't yet have his license, had still worked as an apprentice for an old-line private investigator named George Feider. When Feider retired a few years later, Pike had already left the police. They pooled their money and bought Feider's business. Pike was doing contract work by then, gone for weeks or months at a time, fighting other people's wars. Pike had no interest in being an investigator, but he liked Cole, and admired him. They were friends.

Cole glanced at Carly as they shook.

"She the friend?"

Carly heard, and made an exaggerated wave from the porch.

"Hi, this is me, Carly. Izzy's friend."

Cole waved back.

"I'm Elvis. Give us a minute, okay?"

Carly didn't like it, but stayed on the porch.

Pike had sketched out the basic situation on the phone, but now he filled in the blanks with what he'd learned from Carly and Braun.

"They were texting when Isabel disappeared. She'll show you the texts."

Cole glanced at Carly, and lowered his voice.

"Maybe Braun's right. Isabel was scared. Maybe she got in her car and kept going."

"Can't see it. They're tight."

Carly shouted from the porch.

"We're tight! She wouldn't leave without telling me."

Cole and Pike both glanced at her, and Cole studied the house.

"Security cameras?"

"Zero. Not here, and none at the neighboring homes. I haven't checked farther up the street."

Cole gazed up the street.

"Might find a wit, but I wouldn't waste time now. This time of day, anyone who was home when she disappeared is probably at work or school."

Cole turned back to Carly, and raised his voice.

"Where does she park?"

Carly pointed at her Volkswagen.

"Here. Where I'm parked."

Cole turned to Pike and lowered his voice even more.

"So you think what, Karbo and Bender were waiting? They grabbed her when she came out, and fled in her car?"

"Wasn't Karbo or Bender. Someone else."

Carly shouted again.

"Izzy *saw* them! She took their picture!"

Cole stared at Carly.

"That girl has ears."

Pike said, "Her picture shows a 4Runner. Bender's SUV was a Buick. Even if the vehicles were the same, Karbo and Bender couldn't have been here."

Pike explained Braun's time line, and capped it with the murders. Cole looked surprised.

"So Karbo and Bender got popped, and two replacements showed up?"

"Yes. I figured you could track forward from here, and I'll backtrack through Karbo and Bender."

"You think we can find the new guys through a couple of dead men?"

"If the new guys are replacements, they play for the same team. They'll be connected."

"The new guys might even know who killed them."

"Either way, the trail starts where Karbo and Bender died. You good here?"

"I'm good. Go."

Pike led Cole to the porch, and briefed Carly on the plan.

Carly looked nervous.

"But your friend is here. Shouldn't you stay? Help us look for clues?"

Pike glanced at Cole.

"He's a detective. I'm something else."

Pike left them on Isabel's porch and jogged to his Jeep. He checked his watch, a plain steel Rolex he bought on his first combat tour. Isabel had been missing for sixteen hours. Time had weight. The weight was growing.

PART THREE

SIX-SIX-ONE

15.

John Chen

John Chen fired off his fourth blood request of the morning, and immediately began an evidence inventory from a drive-by shooting. Sixteen shots fired, three wounded, one dead. Two hundred fourteen pieces of evidence, all of which had to be listed by number on the appropriate form. His fingers pounded the keyboard.

John, who was a criminalist with LAPD's Forensic Science Division, needed money. Chen, who hadn't had a date in, oh, like forever, had figured out the solution to his absentee love life. John, who currently drove a molten silver Porsche Boxster, needed a Tesla.

At six three, one twenty-seven, and built like a question mark, John understood he wasn't exactly studly (the oversized glasses and pocket caddy didn't help). So, being a man of action, John had acquired the Boxster (dubbed the 'tangmobile), a reputed chick magnet that turned out to be a total fail. Case in point: The Hertzberg-Davis Forensic Science Center was located on the Cal State L.A. campus, and crawling with smokin' hot criminal science coeds. But did one of those chicks, even *one*, ask for a ride in his Black Forest love rocket? No. The science was clear: Gas-guzzling, carbon-belching Porsches were out; whisper-silent, zero-emission, hyper-fast Teslas were in. (Not that John gave two tugs and a rat weenie about his carbon footprint. Yawn.)

Only problem was, a shiny new Tesla carried a larger monthly payment. Overtime would cover some of the cost, but—despite a tsunami of crime in the City of Angels—overtime for city employees was capped. And to limit his options even more, John already worked so many overtime hours a second job was out of the question.

A lesser man would have plummeted into despair.

Not John.

John Chen threw himself into his work, determined to earn a promotion. He arrived early and stayed late, slamming out case reports and test conclusions like a wood chipper. Not that any of this was new. John had always been a hard worker, but he'd been mired in grade as a Criminalist-2 forever. A promotion to Criminalist-3 was overdue, but each time he brought it up to his boss, Harriet (a heartless, imperious bean counter), she brushed him off. In point of fact, these past few months, Harriet had grown distant, and cooler than usual. So John doubled down, bent over backward to curry favor, and set about blowing her socks off with his zeal.

"How's it going, John?"

Chen jumped to cover his screen. Habit. John didn't trust his coworkers. They resented his ambition, and looked for ways to discredit him.

Sybil Lawrence, a third-rate chemist, tried to look innocent, but John wasn't fooled. He fed her a caramel smile.

"Great, Syl. Couldn't be better."

Bitch.

Sybil took a seat next to Joel Ganowski, a management spy from the Quality Assurance Unit. Ganowski murmured to Sybil and Sybil laughed.

Spies.

John Chen was a paranoid. He knew this about himself, just as he knew he had low self-esteem, a poor self-image, and a cornucopia of insecurities. But he also knew an enemy when he saw one. Even paranoids had enemies.

Chen was finishing the inventory when Kari Logan touched his shoulder. Kari was a criminal science graduate student. Kinda ugly, but her calves were okay.

"Harriet wants you."

John startled, and covered his screen.

"Why?"

Kari laughed, and tried to peek.

"What are you hiding?"

"Nothing."

"Lemme see."

Kari angled the screen.

John said, "It's an evidence list. What's the big deal?"

"You dork. I thought you were looking at porn."

John's eyes narrowed. Their FSD computers couldn't access the internet, which Kari knew. He wondered if she was setting him up for a #metoo complaint.

"You know we can't get the internet."

"I know. I just wanted to say it. Dork."

John flushed. Dork was a word for penis, and this was the second time she'd dorked him. His #metoo fear gave way to lustful hope.

"You like porn?"

"You're such a dork."

Kari turned to leave.

"Would you like to have dinner?"

"I have a boyfriend. But thanks."

"We can ride in my Porsche."

"I have a boyfriend, John. But thanks."

"Would you go if I had a Tesla?"

"I'd go for a ride, maybe. I've never been in a Tesla."

Case closed. Porsches were out. Teslas were in.

John was watching her walk away when Harriet found him.

"John!"

Chen jumped off his stool and flashed an unctuous smile, accelerating from zero to full-on asskiss faster than a screaming Tesla.

"Going great here, Harriet. I'll clear three more cases by the end of the day. I'll have the smallest backlog in the division."

John made his unctuous smile even wider.

Behind them, Ganowski made a kissing sound, and Sybil snickered.

Cretins.

Harriet handed him an assignment slip.

"Robbery-Homicide call. I need you in Hancock Park."

Inwardly, John cringed, but his smile didn't falter.

"No problem. I'll get right on it."

Harriet seemed unmoved by his feigned enthusiasm.

"It's rich people, so give this your undivided attention."

Rich people was code. Regular people could drop like flies, and nobody gave a shit. When someone with money or connections got offed, the powers-that-be jumped.

Chen tucked the slip in his pocket.

"Always. Every case I tackle gets my undivided attention."

Harriet looked as if she wanted to say something, but walked away. Sour. John called after her.

"Thanks, Harriet. Happy to help!"

Sybil and Ganowski snickered.

John turned back to his computer and saved his work. Go ahead and laugh. They wouldn't laugh when he rolled up in a Tesla.

Chen was logging off the network when his cell phone buzzed. He felt a flash of surprise, but also excitement. The caller was Pike. Pike called only once or twice a year, but his calls usually led to breakthrough leads and face time on local TV. Hot chicks dug famous people. John Chen was all about headlines.

Chen turned his back to Ganowski and Sybil, and whispered.

"Can't talk. Surrounded."

"Can you write?"

"Not really. I'm being watched."

"Christopher Karbo. Donald Bender. They were murdered last night. Bender got it in Northridge. Karbo in Eagle Rock. I need the addresses."

Chen snuck a look at Ganowski. Ganowski glanced away. Spy.

Chen cupped his mouth, and lowered his voice even more.

"Dude. Last night? The crime scenes are still hot."

"I need the addresses, John. It's important."

John wet his lips.

"Headline important?"

"Important to me."

Chen hesitated. If Pike was onto something, which he usually was, Chen could find himself back on the nightly news. This could be the extra nudge that Harriet needed. The sour-faced bitch might finally grant his promotion.

Chen whispered.

"I'll find out. Call you in five."

Chen gathered his gear. He smiled at Ganowski as he left. Ganowski smiled back. Ganowski had never, not once, broken a headline case.

16.

Elvis Cole

Carly let him read their texts, and airdropped Isabel's snapshot of a murky SUV. Cole was impressed. Between their texting and talking, Carly and Isabel had been in almost continuous real-time contact from the moment Isabel learned Karbo and Bender were being released until the last text Carly received. The near-constant communication made Cole wonder if Isabel had been texting or talking with other friends.

Carly thought for a moment.

"Lauren and Gina, maybe. We're all friends. We go out."

"Siblings?"

Carly shook her head.

"She's an only, like me."

Cole took in the tired room and the aging family photos.

"Does Isabel live here alone?"

"Uh-huh. She lost her dad ten or eleven years ago.

Her mom died last year, which was awful. She was like my second mom."

"I'm sorry. What were their names?"

"Debbie and Ed. Debbie was really Debra Sue, but everyone called her Debbie. That's her mom and dad in the pictures."

Cole's thoughts returned to the friends.

"Lauren and Gina. If Izzy told one of them something she didn't mention to you, it might be important. Can you find out?"

Carly lifted her phone.

"Sure. Right away."

Cole stood. He wanted to walk through the house.

"One thing first. I need the basics. Her full name, her cell, date of birth, things like that. You can text it to me later."

"All right. Sure."

"And give me the make and model of her car."

Carly looked vague.

"Her car?"

"She left in her car. I need to know what she drives."

"She drives her mom's car. A green Ford. It's old."

"A couple of million old, green Fords are on the road. We need to narrow it down."

Carly frowned for a moment, then brightened.

"Wait. Her mom kept that kind of stuff in her bedroom—the house stuff and bills and things. I'll find it."

Cole motioned her down.

"I'll look. Talk to your friends."

Cole followed a short hall off the living room past Isabel's room to the master. The drapes were closed, the room was dim, and the floral spread covering a queen-sized bed sagged from a lack of use. Cole snapped on the lights, and opened the drapes. A two-drawer file cabinet sat in the corner. Cole opened the top drawer, and found it packed tight with hanging folders. The folders were alphabetically organized, and identified by neat, hand-written labels. AUTOMOBILE, AUTO INSURANCE, and AUTO SERVICE were the first three folders.

Cole smiled.

"Good job, Debbie."

Debra Sue Roland had purchased a green four-door Ford sedan twelve years earlier. Cole copied the VIN and registration numbers, but found no mention of a LoJack having been purchased or installed. So much for finding her the easy way.

Cole closed the cabinet, and studied several framed pictures on the dresser and chest. Izzy with her high school prom date. A very young Debbie and Ed at the Hollywood Bowl. Little girl Izzy on her dad's shoulders at Angel Stadium, Ed wearing a Houston Astros baseball cap. A second picture taken at the stadium showed an older Izzy and her parents with the scoreboard behind them. Angels 4, Astros 3. Cole found nothing helpful in the dresser or chest, and moved to the nightstands.

A black 9-millimeter Sig Sauer pistol was in the first nightstand he opened. The pistol was partially covered by skin cream and moisturizer, but the pistol's black shape filled the drawer like a waiting snake. Cole didn't touch it. He bent close and sniffed, but smelled no gun oil, solvent, or powder. The weapon probably hadn't been touched or handled in years. Cole closed the drawer and moved around the bed.

The opposite nightstand must have been Ed's. It was empty except for a handwritten note on lined paper torn from a small, spiral pad.

Dearest Eddie, I love you. I miss you with all my heart. You are my dearest and only love, my precious man. You will be forever. I hate living without you.

The handwriting was shaky, as if Debra Sue Roland was weak when she wrote to her husband.

Cole shut the drawer, and went to Isabel's room.

Izzy's bedroom was small, but bright and cheery. A blue frame bed with a matching nightstand, a dresser thick with earring trees, and a mirror that was too large for the room. A bookcase under the window was cluttered with yearbooks, paperback novels, and a little girl's ragged army of dolls. A floor-to-ceiling memory board was pinned with birthday and holiday cards, ticket stubs, and photos. One of the cards caught Cole's eye. A picture of Isabel in a royal blue graduation gown standing with an older man wearing a broad-brimmed Stetson cowboy hat. The photo was push-pinned to the board with a card and an envelope. Cole pulled the pin, and read a handwritten note inside the card.

Princess,

I am so proud of you and everything you accomplished. Your Dad may be up in Heaven, but I know he's proud, too. You're a special young lady, Izzy, just like your Mom.

Congratulations, and have fun with this money!

Love you,
Uncle Ted

The return address showed the sender was a Ted Kemp from Palmdale, California.

Cole took the card and envelope, and found Carly on the couch. She covered the phone when he entered.

"I'm on with Gina. I already talked to Lauren. Izzy called when she learned they were getting out, but neither of them knew about the car, or anything new."

Cole showed her the picture.

"Who's Uncle Ted?"

Carly smiled at the picture.

"He isn't really her uncle. He was friends with her mom and dad, so that's what she calls him."

"A family friend?"

"He came to her mom's funeral. He used to come to her birthday parties when we were little. We thought he was a cowboy. He was funny."

Cole thought about Isabel calling her friends. Izzy had phoned Carly, Lauren, and Gina, and now Cole wondered aloud if Izzy had phoned anyone else.

Carly blinked, her eyes wide and curious.

"We can find out. Easy."

Cole didn't understand.

She pointed her phone toward the hall.

"Izzy writes down her passwords. Check her cell account. Go look."

Cole returned to the cabinet, and found a file marked CELL PHONE. Debbie had kept meticulous, well-organized files, and Isabel had continued her mother's practice. The file contained her service provider contract along with a sheet containing her account number, user ID, and password. Cole brought the sheet back to the living room as Carly finished her call.

"Find it?"

"I did. Thanks to you."

Carly took the sheet. Two minutes later, they huddled over a billing list showing Isabel's charges for the past seven days. The column of charges showed the outgoing and incoming call numbers in chronological order, along with the date, time, and duration of each call. The most recent call was at the top of the list.

Carly pointed.

"These are all me. This is Lauren. This one's Gina. I don't know this one."

Cole recognized Pike's number near the top of the list.

Pike had phoned Isabel earlier that morning and twice the evening before. Each call showed a usage time of only one minute, suggesting Pike had left a message, or hung up when her voice mail answered.

Isabel's final outgoing call had been placed at 5:40 the previous evening.

Carly said, "See? This is when I told her to call the police."

Isabel had phoned Carly two earlier times, and Lauren and Gina an hour after her first call to Carly. She had phoned a 661 number twice, and called Pike eight minutes before she made the first 661 call.

Cole pointed at the 661 number.

"Recognize this one?"

"Uh-uh. Where's 661?"

The two 661 calls had been placed three minutes apart, and—like the call to Pike—were one-minute calls. Calling Pike had been important, but she only called Pike once. Cole wondered why Isabel called the 661 number twice.

Carly said, "What are you doing?"

"Thinking. Impressive, isn't it?"

"Is this what detective work looks like?"

"Only when I'm showing off."

"You're funny."

"A national treasure."

Cole scrolled through the entries until he found Isabel's call to Pike on the day Karbo and Bender were arrested. Isabel had phoned Pike at exactly eight P.M. Twelve minutes after speaking with Pike, Isabel phoned the 661 number. Another one-minute call.

Cole said, "I think we found a clue."

"We did?"

The 661 number never appeared as an incoming call, which meant her calls had not been returned.

Cole took out his phone, dialed, and put the call on speaker.

Carly said, "What are you doing?"

Cole said, "Being a detective. Shh."

A man's voice mail answered.

"Ya got me. Leave a message."

At the sound of the beep, Cole hung up.

"Sound familiar?"

"I don't think so."

Cole googled the 661 area code, and saw it was the area code for Palmdale.

"Uncle Ted. Ted lives in Palmdale. It has to be him."

Friend of the family. Ted hadn't returned her calls, but this didn't mean he ignored her. They could have been texting. Text messages didn't show as a call charge.

Carly said, "I didn't think they were close anymore. Why would she call him?"

"Want to see me be a detective again?"

"Yeah. It's kinda exciting."

Cole dialed the 661 number again.

"Mr. Kemp, my name is Elvis Cole. I'm calling about Isabel Roland. Please call as soon as you can. It's important."

Cole left his number, hung up, and arched his eyebrows.

"Impressed?"

"Maybe awed. I think I am awed."

Cole smiled, and gathered his notes and the pictures.

"I'd better go see."

Carly looked surprised.

"You're going to Palmdale?"

Like it was on the far side of the world.

"Yeah. Isabel called the guy three times, and he didn't call back. He might know something."

Palmdale was a desert community sixty miles north of Los Angeles, up in the Antelope Valley. The drive would take about fifty-five minutes.

Cole stood, and Carly stood with him.

"But what if he can't help? You'll go all the way up there for nothing, and it'll take forever. We could be looking for her."

Fear.

Cole saw it in her eyes and heard it in her voice. Carly was afraid for her friend.

Cole made his voice gentle.

"This is what looking for someone looks like. Not so impressive, huh?"

"I'm scared."

"I know. But I want you to remember something."

Cole tried to look encouraging.

"You helped. We have this lead because of you. We're going to find her."

They walked out together. Carly locked the door, and Cole watched her drive away. Carly didn't look particularly encouraged, and Cole didn't feel as encouraged as he tried to sound. Uncle Ted wasn't much of a clue.

Cole drove north for the desert.

17.

Traffic was light up through the Cahuenga Pass into the San Fernando Valley. Cole avoided the Ventura split, and rode the freeway north through Studio City and Valley Village and onto the Golden State Freeway. Clouds in the west promised cooler temperatures, but the heat increased as he followed the 5 into Newhall Pass, and climbed even higher as he spilled out of the San Gabriel Mountains into the great, flat expanse of the Antelope Valley. His moving map led to an exit just south of Lancaster. He pulled into a gas station, bought gas, and raised the Corvette's top. An older couple in a battered Land Cruiser at the next pump watched him. The woman's skin was dark as old leather, and wrinkled like parchment. Cole grinned at the woman. Friendly.

"This sun is something."

The woman said, "Fry your eyes right out of your head. Best you drink water."

"Good tip. Thanks."

Cole finished filling his tank, bought two bottles of water, and pulled away from the station.

Ted Kemp lived in a residential development six blocks west of the highway. The homes were small, set close, and identical, as if the developer's plan had been to cap the land with beige stucco, clay tile, and anonymity. The sun was so bright Cole squinted behind his sunglasses, but he didn't need house numbers to find Ted Kemp's home. Yellow crime scene tape stretched across the door. A Sheriff's placard identified the premises as an active crime scene.

Cole eased to a stop across the drive. The house appeared deserted, and no police vehicles were present.

Cole climbed from his car. The middle-class, midday neighborhood wasn't bustling with activity. Nobody was walking a dog, or gardening, or jogging. Everyone was probably indoors, trying to survive the triple-digit heat.

Cole walked up the drive, rang the doorbell, and knocked. He knocked again, then moved to a window, but the drapes were drawn and shades were down. He walked next door, and rang the neighbor's bell. A small dog snarled and snapped in the window, but didn't open the door. Cole walked back across Kemp's yard to the opposite neighbor, and tried again. One ring, and the door jerked open.

A withered old man with arms thin as sticks glowered.

"Are you another damned cop?"

Cole held out a card.

"Nope. Another damned private eye. I'm here on a personal matter."

The old man inspected the card.

"No shit? Like Magnum?"

"More like Rockford."

The old man looked impressed, and stuck out his hand.

"Lloyd Trent. That James Garner could act. I liked him."

A woman called faintly from inside the house.

"Who are you talking to?"

Trent flushed bright red, and he snapped over his shoulder.

"SHUT UP, GODDAMNIT!"

Cole ignored the outburst, and plowed forward. He gestured next door.

"I drove up to see Mr. Kemp. Do you know how I can reach him?"

"Get yourself a swami. He's dead."

Cole glanced over at the yellow tape.

"Dead. Dead how?"

"Found his body in an orchard over in the Leona Valley. Some bastard killed him. Been raining cops around here ever since."

The woman called again.

"What did he say?"

"I'M NOT TALKING TO YOU!"

Cole had a bad feeling about Isabel. He hoped she hadn't come up to Palmdale. He hoped she wasn't involved.

"When did this happen?"

"Couple of weeks ago, maybe? He was feeding worms before they found him."

Long before Isabel, so Cole began to feel hopeful.

"Have the police made an arrest?"

"Ain't told me if they have. You ask me, some turd he locked up evened the score."

Cole studied Lloyd Trent.

"He was a police officer?"

Mr. Trent snorted.

"A fed. With the hat, y'know?"

Trent raised his hands to his head, as if Cole might not know what a hat was.

"A marshal?"

"That's right. A marshal. Hear him tell it, he was Wyatt Fucking Earp."

Trent snorted again, as if he never thought much of Ted Kemp.

Cole showed him the picture of Kemp with Isabel at her graduation.

"Maybe you've seen her next door."

"Nope. She the one killed him?"

Cole put away the picture.

"He was a friend of her family."

The old man leered.

"Puttin' the old love stick to her?"

Cole ignored him again, and asked another question.

"Did Mr. Kemp leave behind a wife, or someone else I could speak to?"

"He was divorced. If he had kids, I couldn't tell you."

"What about a girlfriend?"

"He had women next door every so often, but I don't know as any were what you'd call girlfriends. Looked like whores to me."

The woman's faint voice came again, weaker this time, and delicate. Cole wondered if she was bedridden.

"Who are you with out there?"

"SHUT. YOUR. DAMN. TRAP!"

A tiny pain throbbed behind Cole's right eye. He decided Trent had reached the end of the information train, but showed him the picture Isabel took of the 4Runner.

"One more thing. Have you seen a 4Runner like this next door? Black or gray. Maybe dark blue."

The old man looked down his nose at the picture.

"A 4Runner?"

"Cruising past. Parked outside. Maybe in Kemp's driveway."

Trent squinted, and looked suspicious.

"Why in hell would I notice another damn car? You sure you ain't a reporter?"

The woman called softly again, her voice as light as smoke on a breeze.

"I hear angels."

Trent's face boiled with crimson fury.

"I'M NOT GONNA TELL YOU AGAIN! YOU SHUT THE FUCK UP!"

The pain behind Cole's eye grew sharp as a lance. He stepped close, and made his voice soft.

"Lower your voice."

The old man's head whipped around. His eyes crinkled to nasty, thin slits.

"What the hell did you say?"

Cole inched closer, so close they touched.

"Lower."

Closer.

"Your voice."

Trent scrambled backward, and slammed the door.

Cole listened, but heard nothing.

Cole stood outside Lloyd Trent's door until he felt foolish, then returned to his car. He opened the door, and started the engine. The interior raged with terrible heat. The air conditioner seared his face with a nuclear wind.

Cole watched Ted Kemp's house for almost a minute. The yellow tape X-ed across the windows and door made Kemp's home look like a giant cartoon. Cole didn't find the face funny.

Murder changed everything. Karbo and Bender attacked Isabel, and now they were dead. Ted Kemp, a man Isabel called Uncle, had also been murdered. Isabel Roland connected the murders, and now she was missing.

Cole was thinking about Isabel when the drapes on Lloyd Trent's window moved. Trent peered out through the break, and held up his middle finger.

Cole returned the gesture, and pulled away.

Turd.

18.

Joe Pike

Christopher Karbo was murdered in a faux-brick triplex on a winding hillside street overlooking the Glendale Freeway. Karbo had occupied the center unit of a side-by-side triplex built above a three-stall carport. A steep set of stairs beside the carport led from the street to a landing.

Two black-and-whites blocked the carport when Pike arrived. An SID wagon and an unmarked D-ride sat across the street. A uniformed officer and a detective stood talking outside an open door on the landing. An open door always marked the crime scene. Pike drove past, and did not look.

Pike continued until he was hidden from the police, then pulled over and stripped off his sweatshirt. His tattoos stood out, so Pike put on a long-sleeved blue dress shirt. He rolled the sleeves to his forearms, and walked back to a construction site two houses up and across from Karbo's town house. An empty dumpster sat out front of a home waiting to be razed, and a temporary chain-link fence surrounded the property.

Pike cut alongside the neighboring house, stepped onto a low stone wall, and vaulted the fence. A spot between the dumpster and a dying rosemary bush gave him a pretty good view.

The morning rush was over. People had left for work or school, and the neighborhood dozed in a lazy, late-morning lull. Cars passed. An older woman walked a tiny white dog. The officers had the look of men and women who'd been at the scene all night. Pike had spent enough nights at crime scenes to know how they felt. They would be tired, they would be bored, and they wanted to go home. The crime scene was winding down. Pretty soon, not long, they would leave.

A few minutes later, two uniforms came down the steps from the landing, and left in a black-and-white. One down. Three to go.

Pike's phone vibrated softly. He answered with a whisper.

"Pike."

Chen whispered back.

"It's me. Can you talk?"

"Yes."

A maroon Volvo with a rusty rear fender crept past. The lone female driver craned her head to see the police.

"Why are you whispering?"

"Talk to me, John."

"I found out a little more. Bender was shot with a

10-millimeter. Don't see many 10s. Karbo got it with a .40, so we're talking two different guns."

Pike hadn't encountered many 10-millimeter pistols, and knew Chen was right. Ten-mils packed as much punch at close range as a .45, but weren't nearly as common. A 10-mil was a signature gun, and should be easy to track.

Chen was still talking.

"Best guess on time of death is one guy couldn't make both kills. We're looking at two. One shot each in the head, and they grabbed their casings."

All of which jibed with what Braun and DeLako told him.

"Executions."

"No doubt about it. And get this—no signs of struggle, no bruising or binding. The vics either knew the shooters, or the shooters were waiting inside when Karbo and Bender got home. The one dude, Bender, he walked in with a bucket of Extra Crispy. The Colonel was all over the floor."

Chen made a gasping laugh, yonk, yonk, yonk.

Pike thought about Karbo and Bender arriving home. Something about them entering their homes didn't feel right, but the question finally occurred to him.

"How'd they get home?"

"I don't understand. What?"

"From court. Bender's vehicle was impounded. When they were released, how'd they get home?"

"Uber? I don't know. Friends? A dick over in Eagle Rock thinks Karbo's car might lead to the killer."

Pike changed his sight angle enough to see the parking stalls. A dusty Mustang filled the stall on the left, and an aging, fern-colored Pontiac Aztek filled the stall on the right. The middle stall was empty.

"What kind of car does he drive?"

"A Challenger, but get this—"

Chen let it hang, so Pike waited for the rest.

"The DMV shows no current vehicle registration for a Christopher Karbo. No record of him owning a vehicle. He's carless."

"Then how do they know what he drives?"

"Neighbors. They say the guy has a Challenger."

"Mm."

"Only it's missing, so the dicks want to find it. They're thinking the shooter took it."

"Sounds good, John. Thanks."

"You at Karbo's now?"

"Uh-huh."

"Hang tough. They're wrapping up."

Pike put away his phone and watched the police.

A woman with an FSD equipment bag over her shoulder stepped out of Karbo's town house, and spoke with the detective. The detective closed the door, and locked it. The criminalist came down the steps, stowed her bag in the wagon, and departed the scene.

Two down.

One of the uniforms went to the black-and-white, and carried a roll of crime scene tape back up the steps to the detective.

The maroon Volvo reappeared from the opposite direction, and passed as the detective stretched yellow tape across the door. A uniform glanced at the driver, and she looked quickly away.

The remaining uniforms came down and left in their black-and-white.

Three down. One to go.

The detective went to the unit next to Karbo's. He rapped at the door, and the door opened almost immediately, which meant the person inside had been listening. He was a thin guy, balding, and looked to be in his forties. They spoke for several minutes, then the thin man went back into his town house, and the detective left.

Four gone.

Pike waited to see what would happen. People always appeared after police vacated a scene, and this time was no exception.

The thin man's door cracked open, then opened wider. He stepped outside, and crossed the landing to Karbo's door. He touched the knob, then thought better of it, and moved to the window. He cupped his eyes to the glass, but shades blocked his view. He looked around at the neighborhood as if expecting a crowd to be watching, then went back into his unit and closed the door.

Pike gave it another two minutes.

The maroon Volvo returned, and this time it stopped.

The driver looked at the surrounding houses, then climbed out, and slung a large leather bag on her shoulder. Pike saw a tanned, mid-thirties blonde wearing jeans and a loose cotton top. She had frizzy hair, and wore too many bracelets. Pike thought she looked nervous.

The woman checked again to see if anyone was watching, then hurried up the steps to the landing. Pike knew by her careful gait she was trying to move quietly.

The woman went to the thin man's door, but did not knock. She listened for a moment, then hurried to Karbo's door, and pulled off the tape. She let herself in with a key.

Pike left his position behind the rosemary bush, and climbed the steps to the landing.

19.

The woman was in a dining area off the kitchen when Pike opened the door. A china cabinet behind her was open, and her purse was on the table. She put something into the purse, and was turning to the cabinet when she saw him. She gasped and threw her hands above her head.

"He owed me thirty-two hundred dollars, all right? I need that money. I got bills."

She thought he was a policeman.

Pike kept a hand on his pistol, and ordered her out from behind the table. A bloodstain shaped like a lopsided pear muddied the carpet in the center of the living room near a coffee table. The blood had soaked deep. Droplets and tissue flecked the coffee table, and fingerprint smudges dappled the door and the knob. The scent of ammonia was sharp. The door had been sprayed with ninhydrin to raise the prints.

Pike locked the door, and approached her.

"Are you armed?"

"Of course I'm not armed. Are you kidding?"

He checked her waist beneath the shirt, and her ankles beneath the pants.

"Name."

"Didi Lewis. C'mon, he owes me for the car. What am I supposed to do, eat it? This is bullshit."

Pike moved to the table and opened her purse. Two small ceramic figurines shone up at him, and three more remained in the cabinet. Little girls with pigtails. Little boys who looked like Robin Hood.

The woman looked resentful.

"He owed me, okay? Can I put my hands down please?"

"No."

Her wallet contained a California DL matching her name, but the address on the license didn't match Karbo's address.

"Do you live here, Didi?"

"For a while. Until I got tired of wasting my time with a loser. Ask Gary."

Pike tucked her wallet back in the bag.

"Gary."

She shrugged toward the wall.

"Next door. Gary knows me. Ask him."

The thin man.

"Hands down."

She lowered her hands.

Pike moved very close until he stood over her. Stealing her space. Increasing the pressure.

"Did you kill him?"

"Are you crazy? He owes me money."

"Who killed him?"

"How would I know?"

"Guess."

"Like, make up a name? I don't know. Maybe he owed money to someone who isn't as nice as me."

Pike decided she was telling the truth. He stepped away, returning her space.

"You lived with him. He was a criminal. Who were his criminal friends?"

She closed her eyes, and hesitated.

"I moved out eight, almost nine months ago. He was a loser, but the Chris I knew wasn't a criminal. He was nice."

"Isabel Roland."

"Who?"

"Know her?"

"No!"

"Did Karbo know her?"

"I don't know."

"He mention her?"

"No! I don't know! I haven't spoken to him in a couple of weeks. He stopped returning my calls."

Pike watched her for a moment, and believed her.

"What about Donald Bender?"

"I don't know these people. I'm sorry!"

Pike believed her again.

"Karbo and Bender kidnapped Isabel Roland a week ago. Yesterday, they made bail. Last night, a person or persons came here, and shot him. See how it fits?"

She closed her eyes again.

"I was shocked."

"You seem more upset about the money."

Her eyes were sad when they opened.

"I've been gone a long time."

She took a breath, and glanced at the cabinet.

"Are you a cop? I don't think you're a cop."

Pike shook his head.

"He owed me thirty-two hundred dollars. He promised I'd get it."

"For what?"

"My car. I should've made him pay for it up front, but I was stupid. I let him make payments. Big. Effin'. Mistake."

"The DMV says he doesn't own a vehicle."

"I didn't sign over the title. That was our deal. He got to use it, but he wouldn't get the pink slip until he finished paying. Which he didn't."

"What kind of car?"

"A Challenger. Midnight blue, and pretty as hell, but, man, that ride could drink. I couldn't afford to keep it, not with a kid."

The missing muscle car. Parked cars lined the street outside, but Pike didn't recall a Challenger.

"Is it down below?"

She snorted and rolled her eyes.

"Of course not. The idiot left it up in Burbank. It was towed. Now I gotta pay the citation *and* the impound fee, and if I don't pay the stupid citation, it goes on *my* record, not his."

Pike was silent for several seconds.

"The tow company contacted you because you're the registered owner."

"Yeah. I damn near died when I saw how much they want. I don't have that kind of money. Chris didn't return my calls, so I called Gary, and Gary told me he'd been arrested."

"He was in jail when the car was towed?"

"I guess so. He got arrested, so there it sat. Boom."

Pike wondered why Karbo left his car in Burbank. Maybe Bender had picked him up, and someone had seen them. Maybe this person or persons knew them, and knew why they wanted Isabel.

"Where in Burbank?"

"I don't know. In Burbank. It's in my purse."

Pike motioned to her purse, and she took out the citation and paperwork she'd gotten from the tow company. Like all parking tickets, the citation showed the date, time, and location of the infraction. The midnight blue Challenger had been cited for overnight parking without a permit and towed the day after Karbo's arrest. Pike copied the Challenger's citation number and the Burbank address.

When Pike finished, Didi Lewis was staring at the figurines in the cabinet.

"They were his mom's. He told me they're worth a couple of thousand dollars."

The blood in the carpet had darkened, and the closed air in the town house smelled medicinal. Pike checked the time. Isabel had been missing for eighteen hours.

"How'd you expect him to pay for it?"

"What?"

"The car. You sold it to him on time. How'd you expect him to pay for it?"

She looked surprised by his question.

"Christopher worked. He drove trucks. Short-haul delivery. He was with them for years."

"So why didn't he pay?"

She stared a long moment before she answered.

"He liked cards. Some months were leaner than others."

Pike glanced at the figurines in the cabinet, and went to the door.

"Take what you want."

Pike hurried down to his Jeep.

20.

Pike hit Burbank, dropped off the freeway, and followed his map to a tired neighborhood strip mall shaped like an L. A taqueria advertising flautas and tortas bordered the main entrance, and a liquor mart anchored a side-street entrance at the rear. Typical East Valley corner location. Nothing out of the ordinary, no resident bruisers; a long way from Eagle Rock, and farther from Isabel.

The parking lot was crowded, so Pike left his Jeep on the side street. Signs warning VIOLATORS WILL BE TOWED AT OWNER'S EXPENSE in English and Spanish dotted the mall. Karbo should have paid attention, but maybe he'd felt it hadn't been necessary.

Strip malls in high-crime areas often hired security guards or installed surveillance cameras. Pike saw neither, and decided to go door-to-door. He googled a photo of a dark blue Challenger, and started with the taqueria, asking if anyone remembered the car and the driver.

A few people lied, but most tried to help.

Two cooks in the taqueria and a cashier with ink on his face claimed they knew nothing. A slender dude with slick hair in a weight-loss clinic also feigned ignorance, but two women at a hair salon, one older, one young, both recalled the car being towed. Neither saw it arrive, or the driver. Pike struck out again at an appliance shop, but a young woman at a thrift shop told him to check at the liquor mart.

"Ask Ekizian. It was parked outside his place, and nothing makes him angrier."

"Next door?"

Ekizian's Liquor and Jr. Market.

"Yeah. Ekizian doesn't take shit. He probably called."

Pike headed next door, and immediately spotted a camera hanging from the ceiling inside Ekizian's store. Hand-painted signs advertising an ATM machine and lottery tickets had hidden it earlier. The camera hung above the door, peering out at the parking lot through the O in Lottery.

Pike pushed through the entrance, and found himself in a fortress. A heavy, middle-aged clerk sat behind a counter protected by a Lexan shield. More cameras hung above her and above each aisle, feeding multiple CCT views to a monitor beside her.

Pike went to the counter, and showed her the picture.

"A dark blue Dodge like this was towed a few days ago. Know anything?"

Small eyes in a fleshy face scowled.

"Mr. E! Get out here."

A short, furry man stepped from a storeroom behind the glass. His black eyes were fierce. Bushy black eyebrows bristled like porcupines. The clerk nodded at Pike, and Ekizian drew himself taller.

"I am Ekizian. What it is you want?"

The woman interrupted.

"He's here about the car."

Ekizian angrily slapped the counter.

"Is this car yours?"

"The man who left it and an accomplice kidnapped a friend of mine. Later that day, they were arrested. Someone here at the mall might know them."

The fierce eyes grew wary.

"And you?"

"I want to speak with whoever knows them."

Ekizian hesitated.

"You are a police?"

"No. Not police."

"If you make trouble, the police will come."

Pike put away his phone.

"No trouble. Tell me about the car."

"There is nothing to tell. The car was here. It stay all day, and the night. It was here the next day, stealing the parking from my customers. To steal from my customers is to steal from Ekizian."

He slapped the counter again.

"Did you see the driver?"

"I come to work, the car was here. I see no one."

"Early?"

"With the sun. Every day, I come at six."

Pike glanced at the camera above the door.

"How about the camera? Did the camera see?"

"The camera sees everything. We look. Maybe the camera remembers."

Ekizian pressed a button beneath the counter. A lock buzzed, and he stepped out from behind the Lexan with an iPad.

Pike said, "This would have been last week."

"Ekizian knows. Look here with me. I show you."

Ekizian opened an app, dialed in a date, and a frozen image of the empty parking lot appeared. The high-def image was sharp, well lit, and as still as an Edward Hopper painting. The camera above Ekizian's door gave a fish-eye view down the length of the parking lot. The main entrance was in the background with the taqueria to its right. The side entrance was out of frame to the left.

"You see? This is one second after the midnight before. The car is not here. Nothing is here, but we will see."

Ekizian scrolled the time line forward. Red and white lights jerked past the entrance like firefly streaks.

Pike glimpsed a shadow dart past.

"Stop. Let's back it up."

Ekizian rolled back the recording.

At two twenty-five, a homeless person pushed a shopping cart past the entrance.

Ekizian grunted. Approving.

"You have the fast eyes. I did not see."

They rolled forward again.

The parking lot remained empty until sixteen minutes after four, when headlights swept the storefronts. Ekizian froze the image, backed up, and advanced the video in real time.

Ekizian said, "Maybe this him."

At four sixteen, headlights flashed again as Christopher Karbo's Challenger entered from the left of the frame. The Challenger swung toward the camera, and stopped directly outside Ekizian's door. Karbo was behind the wheel. He was alone.

Ekizian scowled.

"This is him?"

"Yes."

Ekizian shook his fist.

"You see? An empty lot, but he takes the place for my customers!"

Pike wondered why Karbo had come so far from Eagle Rock at such an early hour. He and Bender wouldn't encounter Isabel for another seven hours.

Pike learned the answer eighteen seconds later.

Donald Bender walked into the frame from the left, passed behind the Challenger, and rapped on the trunk. Karbo climbed out, and the two men shook. Bender must have left his Buick on the side street.

Ekizian tapped the image.

"And this one? He, too, is a kidnapper?"

"Was. He's dead. They're both dead."

Ekizian studied Pike. A scimitar smile slashed his face.

"I see."

Pike shook his head.

"Not me."

"No?"

Pike shook his head again.

Ekizian looked disappointed.

Karbo and Bender continued talking, but Pike sensed something off in how they related to each other. Karbo flashed a perfunctory smile and Bender seemed uncomfortable. Their handshake had been businesslike, and they stood a step too far apart. They seemed more like strangers who were meeting for the first time than friends who would commit a spur-of-the-moment abduction.

Ekizian said, "You see enough?"

"Let's watch a little more."

Karbo turned to the Challenger and raised his key. The car's lights flashed, indicating he had locked the vehicle. Then Karbo took a small black box from his pocket, placed the fob in the box, and got down on all fours by the driver's-side rear wheel. He reached under the Challenger with the box.

Ekizian frowned.

"What is it he's doing?"

"Leaving his key. Maybe someone was supposed to pick up his car."

The scimitar flashed again.

"Someone did, yes? The police."

Pike expected them to walk out of the frame, but they remained by the Challenger. Bender crossed his arms. Karbo leaned against the car. Their conversation died, and both men looked bored.

Ekizian scowled.

"Now they just stand? They come this early for why?"

"Let's see."

Ekizian waved his hand at the image.

"They just standing."

"They're waiting."

Two minutes later, headlights flashed again as a new vehicle swung through the entrance. Bender had not arrived in the Buick. The Buick had just arrived.

The Buick pulled forward, and parked beside the Challenger. A man wearing a sport coat climbed out, and handed the key to Bender.

Ekizian said, "Another? All these men, did all of them kidnap your friend?"

"Looks like."

"This new one, is he also dead?"

"Not yet."

The scimitar smile returned.

The new man looked to be in his early forties. He was taller than Karbo and Bender and solidly built. His face was so pale, the lights in the parking lot made him seem ghostly.

The pale man did most of the talking. Karbo and Bender listened, facing him like employees. They spoke for exactly four minutes and twenty-two seconds before headlights flashed again. A 4Runner entered the parking lot, and stopped broadside to the camera. It looked identical to the 4Runner outside Isabel's home. The pale man climbed into the shotgun seat, and the 4Runner pulled away. Karbo and Bender went to the

Buick, and left a few seconds later. An eerie, nighthawk stillness settled over the parking lot.

Pike said, "Once more. Do you mind? I'd like to see the Buick arrive."

"I no mind. You want pictures? I can take grabs from the screen and make pictures."

"Pictures would be nice. Thank you."

Ekizian rolled back the video.

The Buick pulled forward, and parked beside the Challenger. The driver's door opened, and the pale man climbed out. When he stepped from the Buick, he gripped the top of the door and faced the camera.

The corner of Pike's mouth ticked. A tiny twitch, too small to see.

Karbo, Bender, the pale man, and the 4Runner's driver.

Four.

Four people had taken Isabel. Pike wondered if others were involved, and why so many conspired to steal her.

We know your secret.

Pike had a secret, too.

The pale man was in his sights, and none of them knew.

21.

Elvis Cole

Cole stopped at a minimart not far from Ted Kemp's home. He grabbed a Diet Coke from an upright cooler, and scoured a rack of newspapers. The *Los Angeles Times* and *USA Today* were available, but he saw nothing local. Cole glanced up, and found the clerk watching.

Cole said, "What's the local paper up here?"

The clerk was a thin guy in his early twenties with limp hair and a spray of zits on his chin. His eyes were lifeless and dull, like a daydreaming cow.

"We have three or four, but we don't carry them."

The death of journalism.

"Name one."

"The *Desert Breeze*. It's a weekly."

Cole paid for the Coke, and settled against the cooler. He googled the *Desert Breeze*, and found a story dated four days earlier.

LOCAL MAN MURDERED

by William F. Wu
for *The Desert Breeze*

A body discovered in a Leona Valley cherry orchard has been identified as Theodore Kemp, 64, an area resident.

Ms. Janice Webb, 47, was inspecting the irrigation system early Tuesday morning when her German shepherd discovered the body.

The cause of death was a gunshot wound to the head.

Sgt. Ray Pierce of the L.A. County Sheriffs Palmdale substation is in charge of the investigation.

"Mr. Kemp was murdered at a separate location, and transported to the orchard postmortem. His body was found partially interred. If anyone has information regarding the crime, please contact Detective Donna Baez or myself at the Palmdale substation."

Mr. Kemp has been an Antelope Valley resident for twenty-six years, and was well liked in the community. An Air Force veteran, Mr. Kemp was a retired United States Marshal, an avid golfer, and a member of the West Desert Country Club. He was divorced, and has no survivors.

> Funeral arrangements have not been an-
> nounced, pending the investigation.

The lack of details was disappointing.

Cole glanced up. The clerk still watched him, but didn't react.

Cole said, "Hey."

The clerk said, "Hey."

"Mind if I stand here?"

"Uh-uh."

Blank.

Cole found the *Desert Breeze* phone number, and put in a call. A woman answered with a rough smoker's voice.

"*Desert Breeze.*"

"William Wu, please."

"He's out. Want his voice mail?"

"I'm calling in regard to a story he wrote about the Kemp murder."

"He still isn't here. Whatcha need?"

"The story's dated four days ago. I was hoping for information about Mr. Kemp."

"Sorry. I cover local politics."

"Can you tell me if an arrest has been made?"

"Bill covers crime. Let me give you his voice mail."

"One more thing. The story says Mr. Kemp was divorced. Would you know his ex-wife's name, and how I can reach her?"

"Even if I knew, I wouldn't tell you. Here's his voice mail."

"How about I give you my number, and you see she

gets it? This regards an old friend of Ted's. It has nothing to do with the murder."

"Leave it with Bill."

Cole heard a click, and Wu's prerecorded voice.

Cole left his name and number, and lowered the phone. He shrugged at the clerk.

"Voice mail. They stick you with voice mail, they never call back."

The clerk's vague expression didn't change.

"Hope they catch his killers. Mr. Kemp was nice."

"You knew him?"

"He was a regular. Bought gas, a six-pack, whatever. Stopped in all the time."

Cole realized this should have been obvious. Kemp lived only seven blocks away.

"You said killers, as in more than one?"

Wu's story hadn't mentioned the killer or killers.

The clerk shifted on his stool.

"Two for sure, and might be three. Shoe prints around the grave, and they got some DNA. One's an Anglo male, for sure. They don't know about the others."

The lifeless clerk was a gold mine.

"'They' being the police?"

"I'm here by the highway. Deps stop in all the time."

Cole smiled. A mother lode.

"Regulars."

"Uh-huh."

"They have any suspects?"

"Not yet, but they'll break it. The feds came in. We got feds everywhere."

"Makes sense, him being a retired marshal."

"That, and the way he was killed. Gruesome."

"The story said gunshot."

"That's how he died, but they messed him up first. Shot him in the hands. Shot his right knee. Beat him and cut him something awful."

The clerk's voice faded, and his expression finally changed. The lifeless eyes turned sad.

Cole said, "I'm sorry."

"Yeah. Messed up."

The clerk managed a shrug.

"He was nice. Always took time to talk. Liked to tell stories."

"Sounds like a good guy."

"Yeah."

Cole told himself this couldn't be connected to Isabel Roland, but he knew he was lying. He wondered if the DNA matched Karbo or Bender.

"Did the deps say why he was killed?"

"Don't know for sure. Probably somebody he busted, is what they're saying."

Lloyd Trent's theory was the consensus opinion.

Cole finished the Coke, and dropped the empty into a recycling bin. He turned to leave when the clerk spoke again.

"I heard what you told the newspaper, you wanting to ask Mr. Kemp's ex about a friend of his."

"That's right. Know her?"

"Nope. Didn't know he'd been married. You might

try up at the country club. Mr. Rose, maybe, or Mr. Baum. Mr. Hollis for sure."

Cole returned to the counter.

"The country club?"

"Golf. Mr. Kemp was big on golf. Half the times he stopped in, he was on his way to play golf. Loved it."

"The people you mentioned, a foursome?"

"Uh-huh. Wait a minute—"

The lifeless eyes stared into space.

"The Baums are off on a cruise. Try Mr. Hollis. They were close. Mr. Hollis might know."

"First name?"

"Rich. Richard, I guess."

"At the country club?"

The lifeless eyes lost focus. Cole was thinking the clerk had lapsed into a fugue when he lifted a phone and tapped at the screen.

"Try the jewelry shop first. I got it here somewhere."

"He's a jeweler?"

"Kinda retired, but yeah. Mr. Kemp liked him the best. They had a lot in common."

"They did?"

"Drinkers."

The clerk held out his phone, and Cole copied an address and number.

"What about Rose?"

"Him, I don't know. Mr. Hollis can put you in touch."

Cole tucked the address into a pocket, and went to the door.

"Thanks. You saved me a lot of time."

The faraway eyes suddenly focused.

"He loved golf. He really loved it."

Cole hesitated.

"I'm sure he did."

"The best part about being retired was the golf. Said he'd show me how if I wanted. Said I could go along."

"Did you?"

The lifeless eyes lost their focus.

"Uh-uh. Wish I had."

Cole wished he had, too.

"You're going to miss him."

"Yeah."

Cole pushed through the door, and stepped into shimmering heat.

22.

Hollis and Hollis Fine Family Jewelers referred to Rich and his daughter, Rachel. Richard Hollis was a thin man in his early seventies with steel gray hair and a nose laced with capillaries. His daughter was almost fifty, and thin like her father. She speared Cole with a hateful glare when he interrupted their work.

Mr. Hollis stepped from behind a display case, and led Cole to the side.

"Did they catch the bastards?"

Cole caught a whiff of gin, but ignored it.

Drinkers.

"Sir, I don't know. I'm not with the police."

"He was a marshal, you know?"

"Yes, sir. I came up to see him about this young lady."

Cole flashed the photo of Kemp and Isabel at her graduation.

"That's Ted, all right. Poor Ted. Jesus, I'm still in shock."

His daughter speared Cole with another glare.

"Dad? You don't have to stick around. Go play golf."

Hollis ignored her, and studied the picture.

"Who's the young lady?"

"Isabel Roland. Her parents were Debra Sue Roland and Ed Roland. Did you know them?"

Hollis shook his head.

"I'm sorry, no. I didn't."

"Isabel knew him as Uncle Ted."

Hollis smiled sadly.

"Nice to hear."

"Ted was a family friend."

Hollis returned the picture.

"Why are you asking?"

"Isabel is missing. She tried to contact Ted last night, so I had hoped he'd know something helpful. I didn't learn of his death until I got up here."

"Ted's been gone for almost two weeks."

"I'm told you and he were close."

"We were. We'd be on the links right now if this hadn't happened."

His daughter muttered.

"Drinking."

Mr. Hollis closed his eyes.

"Don't start."

Cole said, "I understand Mr. Kemp was divorced."

"Mm-hm. That'd be Delores."

"Maybe she knows the Rolands. Could you put me in touch?"

"Hardly. Ted pulled the plug on that one thirty-odd

years ago. Back east somewhere, before Teddy came west. Marshals move around, you know."

So much for the ex.

"How about a girlfriend? Was he close to anyone here in the area?"

His daughter snorted.

"Besides my father?"

Hollis gave a sly wink.

"Plenty of someones, if you know what I mean. Teddy was quite the swordsman."

His daughter groaned.

"It's called bullshit, and you ate it up. Please."

Hollis stared at his daughter.

"The man is dead. We were friends."

"He was a bullshitter, and you ate it up with a spoon."

Hollis glared at his daughter.

"Ted was a United States Marshal, for God's sake. He had stories. He was interesting."

The daughter glanced at Cole, and arched her eyebrows.

"And after a few drinks, which was always, Ted was the most interesting man in the world."

"You're embarrassing yourself."

She returned to her work, but didn't stop talking.

"My father hates his life. Since the day they met, he's wanted to be Ted."

"You're absurd. You sound like your mother."

"She's right. Ask her."

"We were friends. I enjoyed the man's company, and why wouldn't I?"

Hollis turned to Cole, and tugged him away.

"The day we met, the day *this one*—"

He jabbed a thumb at his daughter.

"—likes to complain about, Ted came in to have his watch repaired, older, but a very nice Hamilton."

His fifty-year-old daughter rolled her eyes.

"Here we go. A story I've heard a thousand times."

"You brought it up."

Hollis continued the story.

"Anyway, this man comes in, he's browsing, and he starts asking questions. Do we buy direct from the manufacturers? Do we file written transfer tracks? Are our gems cut with markers? I thought he must be a sales rep, so I asked which company he was with."

His daughter answered in a deep, manly voice.

"The United States government, retired."

She sighed, and went on with her work.

"This is my father's favorite part of the story."

"Even your mother laughed. She was here."

"She didn't laugh when you started coming home drunk."

Hollis stared at his daughter, and finally shrugged.

"Ted was funny. He'd just retired, and we both liked golf. We hit it off."

His daughter rolled her eyes again.

"Golf and gin was what you two liked, in no particular order."

Cole was curious.

"Why was he asking questions?"

"Insurance fraud case. One of his wits was a jewelry fence from Chicago. A mob guy. The Mafia."

Hollis gave Cole a look when he said the word Mafia.

"Fourteen jewelers and six insurance executives went to prison."

Cole stared at Hollis, and glanced at his daughter. Her head was down as she fixed the clasp on a bracelet.

"One of his wits. A witness?"

"Teddy helped government witnesses set up new lives. This is how he knew so much. The wit told him how fake gems were being swapped and resold."

"A witness in the witness protection program."

Hollis smiled, and blew more juniper.

"That's right. Ted was a security marshal. They call it wit-sec."

Hollis didn't seem to realize what he was saying. The identities of people in the witness protection program were among the most closely held secrets in law enforcement.

Cole said, "Mr. Hollis—"

Cole decided to be tactful.

"I'm not sure he should have told you about someone in the program. These things are supposed to be secret."

His daughter mumbled.

"Except when they drank. Which was always."

Hollis waved a hand.

"No, no, don't get me wrong. Teddy never used names. He was discreet."

Hardly.

"You should tell the authorities. This could have a bearing on their investigation."

Hollis answered proudly, and fogged Cole with juniper.

"I did. I was one of the first people the marshals interviewed. Everyone loved Ted's stories."

His daughter chirped up again.

"Not everyone."

Cole shook his head.

"Wait. How many witnesses did he tell you about?"

Hollis ticked off a list, citing a hit man from Seattle, a drug-smuggling airline pilot from Miami, a kleptomaniac pimp from Biloxi, a getaway driver from Detroit who ran over two little girls, a bank robber from Detroit who killed his mother over a parakeet, a coke-addled hedge fund executive from San Francisco, a syndicate lawyer from Boston who wouldn't stop seeing transgender prostitutes, and a one-eyed rapist from New Orleans who flipped on a drug-dealing African prince.

Hollis would have kept going, but his daughter had heard enough.

"Please. Stop."

Hollis shrugged.

"Awful people make for good stories."

His daughter interrupted again.

"They weren't all awful, and they weren't all criminals."

Her father made an agreeable nod.

"This is true. Some were good people trying to do the right thing, like the lady from Houston."

Cole felt a jolt, as if a passing temblor rolled the floor.

"Houston?"

Cole recalled the photo of Ed and his family at Angel Stadium, Angels 4, Astros 3, Ed wearing a Houston Astros cap.

Cole's mouth felt dry.

"Ted relocated a witness from Houston?"

"Mm-hm. Now in this particular case, bad medicines were killing people, and his witness helped stop it. Here's a lady, she knew it would be a hardship, testifying and all, but she stepped up when it counted. Folks like this, Ted admired."

Cole said, "A federal case in Houston?"

Hollis glanced at his daughter.

"Yeah. What'd he call it?"

"Counterfeit pharmaceuticals."

"That's it. Fake pills, bad medicine, drugs with all this contamination. Teddy heard so many awful stories, he wouldn't take an aspirin unless he knew where it came from."

"Stories he heard from his witness."

"Mm-hm."

"He say anything else about his witness?"

"I doubt it. Ted was careful. These people changed their lives for a reason."

His daughter said, "Go play golf, Dad. Have a drink."

Cole thanked the Hollises, and returned to his car. An

overhead sun baked the sky, only now the heat seemed farther away.

Cole imagined Kemp and Hollis and their buddies out on the links, everyone hitting a flask, and laughing at Ted's funny stories. Back at the clubhouse, the stories would grow, spreading with each retelling like migrating doves.

Sooner or later, the wrong person might hear.

Sooner or later, the wrong person might come to call.

Cole took a breath. He started his car, and headed for home.

He was afraid for Isabel Roland. More afraid than before.

He thought about Isabel as he drove away, and did not see a tan car follow.

23.

John Chen

The Hancock Park location should've brightened John's day. Most murders brought him to squalid neighborhoods and lice-ridden hovels. John preferred wealthier crime scenes. Wealthy people had nice things (like Teslas) and beautiful homes (a boy can dream, can't he?). Also, wealthy women (almost always work-out fanatics with smoking-hot bodies) were known to be lonely and desperate for love (John believed this to be true, despite having no evidence).

Not today.

The decaying old-money mansion smelled of urine and mothballs. And if hot, horny, lookie-loo wives lived nearby, they were nowhere to be seen.

Six black-and-whites, two D-rides, and two L.A. County emergency vehicles were out front when John arrived. A Wilshire Station Homicide dick walked him through the scene. The dick blew Cheez-Its, so John kept his distance.

The skull of a wheelchair-bound, ninety-two-year-old female had been split with a hatchet. Her sixty-seven-year-old son (a self-loathing mama's boy) had struck her three times above the right eye (twice through the frontal bone, once through the parietal), after which he wandered out to their pool with the hatchet, phoned the emergency operator, and shot himself in the head with a .32-caliber pistol. His only words to the operator were "Am I really so bad?"

Douche.

John Chen was thrilled.

Three perfect splatter lines traced the arc of his swings. Blood drips from the hatchet marked the son's path to the poolside chaise longue where he'd sat, made the call, and buttoned his play. The pistol remained in his hand, the phone rested in his lap, and the hatchet lay on the deck beside him. Barring a staged scene by malevolent actors (which, c'mon, happened only on television), the crime was a grounder.

The Cheez-It dick studied the old lady's bloody chair.

"Shouldn't take long, right? Looks like a grounder."

"No time at all. It's a grounder."

Chen opened his equipment case. A grounder was a slam-dunk, open-and-shut case.

The Cheez-It dick walked to an open French door, and stared at the pool.

"Messed up. Poor guy must've been in a lot of pain."

Chen rolled his eyes, wishing the dick would leave.

The Cheez-It dick shrugged.

"Just sayin'."

The dick walked away.

Chen pulled on his gloves and opened his equipment case. Couple of hours, tops, he'd be back at the lab, knock out the report, and present it to Harriet like a gift. One crime scene analysis for Rich People, please! Would you like fries with that?

John had just begun making his first measurement when Harriet called.

"Have they arrived?"

"Who?"

"Joel and Kimberly. They'll arrive soon. Don't worry."

Joel being the aforementioned Ganowski. Kimberly being Kimberly Silas, a photographer from the Technical Investigation Division's Photography Unit.

John was instantly suspicious. Harriet had never sent Ganowski to one of his crime scenes before.

"I'm not worried. Why are they arriving?"

"To make sure we're covered."

A flash of adrenaline made his head throb.

"It's a grounder. I don't need help."

"Not help. Coverage. In case someone has questions."

Meaning, in case someone, for some as yet unknown reason (almost certainly an heir or business associate), challenged John's findings in court.

John was pissed. Ganowski and Silas might slow him down. Worse, they might try to take credit for his work. Either might make him look bad, and wreck his chance at a promotion.

"Really, Harriet, I can—"

Harriet hung up. She actually *hung up*.

Chen lowered his phone, and wondered why Harriet was acting so weird.

Ganowski strode in two minutes later, looking smug.

"How're you doing, John? Everything going well?"

"I've been here ten minutes. How well could it be going?"

"Don't mind us. Pretend we're not here."

"Are you a C-2 or a C-3?"

"A C-3. Why?"

Silas began taking pictures without saying a word.

Spies.

John cleared the interior crime scene quickly. He graphed and charted the scene on the appropriate forms, measured and logged the splatter angles and radii, then numbered, photographed, and collected bits of bone, hair, and blood from the wall and surrounding floor. Fast, thorough, professional, suspicious. Every time he looked at Ganowski, Ganowski was watching him.

One hour and fourteen minutes later, Chen was by the pool, bagging and tagging the hatchet, the pistol, and the phone, when Joe Pike called for the second time that day.

Chen snuck a glance at the house. Ganowski and the Cheez-It dick were yakking it up in the family room.

John casually stepped behind a banana tree, and whipped out his phone.

"I'm at a scene. Rich people."

"Bender's vehicle. LAPD towed it when he was arrested."

Chen knew nothing about Bender's vehicle.

"I don't know. You want me to find out?"

"They have it. A Buick SUV. Gray."

"This was the vehicle used to grab the girl?"

"Yes. Bender was driving, so it'll be filed under his name and the case number. Can you find out if prints were pulled?"

Chen glanced at the house again. Ganowski and the Cheez-It dick were laughing.

"I can find out, but I can already tell you the answer. They wouldn't need to pull prints. Karbo and Bender were found in the vehicle."

"Karbo and Bender weren't working alone."

"They weren't?"

"A third male delivered the Buick to Bender the morning they kidnapped Isabel."

Chen felt a flash of excitement.

"No shit?"

"Print the top of the driver's door. He touched the frame above the window. Try for a hit."

John glanced at the house again, and his stomach clenched. Ganowski was at the window. Frowning.

"I can't just print an impounded vehicle. This isn't my case."

"The vehicle isn't anyone's case, John. They're dead."

John wet his lips, thinking. This could be his break. This could be the door to his promotion.

"Do the police know about this guy?"

"No. Not yet. No one knows but us."

Chen took another peek. Silas stepped up beside Ganowski, and took John's picture.

Spies.

Chen checked the time. He might be able to do it. Sneak into the impound yard, grab the prints, and still clear his cases. Maybe.

Pike spoke again, interrupting his thoughts.

"Isabel is missing, John. They took her again. This man has her or knows where she is."

John peeked out from behind the banana tree. Ganowski was making a call.

"Harriet's waiting. She's expecting me."

"I know what I'm asking."

"She sent spies. They're watching."

"Has to be now, John. Isabel needs us."

Ganowski raised the phone to his ear, staring at John as he spoke.

Chen smelled a breakthrough.

"Karbo and Bender. He might be behind their murders."

"He might be, John. He probably is."

Chen took a breath. The upside potential was enormous. The Tesla was already in his garage.

"I'm on it. Call you ASAP."

Chen put his phone away, bagged the remains of his gear, and steamed into the house.

Ganowski flashed his smarmy, superior smile.

"Personal call?"

"My oncologist."

Turd.

Chen glanced at the Cheez-It dick without slowing.

"Your scene. I'm clear. Reports in the morning."

Ganowski frowned. Silas took his picture as he left.

24.

Joe Pike

Pike left Ekizian's, and thought about Bender as he returned to his Jeep. Bender had entered the parking lot on foot. So unless someone had dropped him off, he would have left his personal car on the same residential street as Pike.

Pike stopped at his Jeep, and studied the street. Parking by the mall was metered, but parking along the side street was free. With the lunch hour approaching, vehicles lined both sides of the street, but at four in the morning, parking would have been easy. Bender would have parked close.

Pike walked up the street, considering each car, but nothing stood out.

On the way back, he passed two teenaged boys jumping a skateboard in a driveway. Both were skinny, with dark hair and baggy shorts. One was taller, and older. Pike made them for brothers.

"Hey."

They stopped with the skateboard, and bunched together. Worried.

The taller kid shifted.

"Hey what?"

"You live here?"

"We didn't do anything."

Pike glanced at the cars lining the street.

"These cars."

"What?"

"The cars along here, they belong to your neighbors?"

The taller kid shrugged.

"I don't know. Why?"

"If you lived here, you'd know."

Pike pointed at a white Toyota.

"This car. Does it belong to you?"

The older boy looked about fourteen. He snickered, showing off for his younger brother.

"You wanna buy it? How much you gimme?"

Pike stared.

After a few seconds, the boy stopped smirking, and shrugged toward the house next door.

"She owns it. Ms. Renfro."

Pike tipped his head at a black Chevrolet.

"How about the Chevy?"

"Belongs to the guy across the street. He's a dick."

"Any of these vehicles show up last week? A vehicle you didn't know. Just showed up, and hasn't moved?"

The younger one glanced at his older brother. The

big one toed his skateboard, and shrugged. The younger one cut in fast, anxious to take part in the drama.

"Are you a police?"

The older one sneered, and shouldered his brother.

"Of course he's a cop, stupid. Can't you tell?"

The younger one elbowed his brother.

"The red car."

His brother shoved back.

"No way. You don't know anything."

The younger one came down the drive, and pointed at a burgundy Subaru across the street.

"The red one. Ms. Gonzales asked about it. Her husband's pissed. He parks here when he gets home, and now he can't."

Pike crossed to the Subaru and peered through the windows. The brothers followed him into the street, and watched.

The Subaru was dusty, but no more than the surrounding vehicles, and cleaner than some. A pad for jotting notes was clipped to the console, but Pike couldn't tell if anything was written on it. A cell phone bracket was mounted to the dash. The bracket was empty. Pike circled the vehicle, and lowered himself into a push-up position by the driver's-side rear wheel. He checked the wheel well, but found nothing. Pike moved to the front wheel, and lowered himself again.

The younger brother said, "What're you looking for? Drugs?"

A black magnetic key box was stuck to the chassis. Pike pulled it free, and removed the fob.

The older brother hooted.

"Damn! If I knew the key was here, we coulda gone riding!"

The younger brother crept closer to Pike.

"Who does it belong to, a criminal?"

Pike pulled on a pair of black nitrile gloves.

"A dead man."

The older brother grinned.

"Awesome! That why you put on the gloves?"

His younger brother said, "Of course, stupid. Everyone knows that."

Pike unlocked the Subaru, and slipped in behind the wheel. A Proof of Insurance slip in the glove box identified the vehicle's owner as Donald Thomas Bender.

Pike searched under and around the driver's seat, and found a Ruger .380 semi-automatic pistol in a soft case. The pistol was loaded, but the scents of burnt powder and cleaning solvent were close to nonexistent. Pike decided the pistol hadn't been fired in years. He returned the pistol to its place under the seat, and examined the notepad. The strip mall's address was written on the top sheet along with a time and name. 4:30. Karbow. Bender had misspelled Karbo's name. This confirmed Pike's read from the video. The two men knew little or nothing about each other. The next page contained Isabel's home address, along with the make, model, and license number of her car.

Pike found a cell phone and a company ID badge in the console. The cell phone was a high-end Android model, and fit the dashboard bracket. Pike had taken inexpensive throwaway phones from Karbo and Bender the day they attacked Isabel, so the Android was probably Bender's actual phone. The phone powered up, but required an entry code. The company ID was a plastic card on a lanyard identifying Donald Bender as an employee of Stolder Direct Trucking Company, San Dimas, California. A driver, like Karbo. Pike slipped the phone and ID into his pocket.

Pike found two fresh burners and a deck of prepaid calling cards behind the passenger seat. The burners were unopened in their packaging. Spares.

Pike photographed the relevant pages, and let himself out. He photographed Bender's vehicle and license plate, then opened the trunk. Both brothers moved closer.

The older brother said, "Maybe he'll find a body. Wouldn't that be cool?"

His younger brother tried to see.

"Maybe he'll find a head. A head would be cooler."

The trunk contained a tan windbreaker, a set of jumper cables, and a dog's red rubber tug toy.

Pike closed the trunk, and locked the vehicle. The Subaru beeped. Pike slipped the fob into his pocket, and turned to the brothers.

"The police will come in the next day or two. Tell Mr. Gonzales he'll have his parking place soon."

Pike started away, then turned back.

"Stay groovy."

The brothers grinned, but the younger kid looked confused.

"What's groovy mean?"

Pike walked back to his Jeep, thinking about the things in Bender's Subaru. Bender had Isabel's home address, but they grabbed her outside the bank. They had probably gone to her home, missed her, and pivoted to her place of employment. Pike wondered if this had been their decision, or if the pale man had made the call. Waiting until Isabel returned home would have been the safer play, but they had assumed a higher level of risk to take her outside the bank. The willingness to ignore the risk implied a pressure to grab her quickly. Pike wondered why, but the why didn't matter. People made bad decisions if they couldn't handle pressure, and the man in the parking lot had made a bad mistake. He failed to anticipate Pike.

Pike emailed the screen grabs to Cole, and called. Cole answered on the second ring.

"Did you just send something?"

"Pictures. Karbo and Bender with a third man on the morning they grabbed Isabel. The 4Runner is in one of the shots. Can't see the driver, but at least four people were involved with Isabel's kidnap."

Pike explained about the Challenger and Subaru, and the burners and addresses in Bender's car.

"They were told when and where to pick up the Buick. The man you'll see with them delivered it."

"A dummy car. If someone saw them make the grab, the plate wouldn't lead back to them."

"That's how I see it. After he dropped the Buick, the 4Runner picked him up."

"Hang on. I'm on my way back. Let me pull over."

Pike listened to traffic sounds until Cole returned.

"Okay. I'm looking at him. Got an ID?"

"No. I spoke to Chen. He'll pull prints, and try for a hit."

Cole was silent for several seconds.

"So we have a boss, a crew, and multiple vehicles attempting to kidnap a twenty-two-year-old bank teller. I think I know what we're dealing with."

Cole was leading up to something.

Pike said, "What?"

"The Rolands had a close friend named Ted Kemp. So close, Isabel called him Uncle Ted. After Karbo and Bender grabbed her, she reached out to him. Yesterday, after she learned they were being released, she reached out again. Ted didn't return her calls. His body was found eleven days ago."

"How does this fit?"

"Uncle Ted worked Witness Security for the Marshals. He was tortured before he was murdered. Could've been payback for something else, him being a marshal, but Ted liked to talk about his wit-sec days. And the witnesses he helped relocate here in Southern California."

Pike felt pieces of the puzzle shift, one piece nudging the next as they tried to fit together.

"The Rolands were in the witness protection program?"

"I don't know, but I'll try to find out. I'm heading back to my office now."

Pike said, "Witness protection."

"Crazy, huh?"

"Her parents are dead."

"I know. But here we are."

We know your secret.

"If this is true, would Isabel know?"

Cole hesitated, as if he had to work his way to an answer.

"Kemp was part of their lives, especially when Izzy was a child. But this doesn't mean she knew they were in the program. If they were, and if her parents were smart, they would have kept it from her."

Pike thought about Carly. Carly's vibe hadn't suggested any big family secrets in the Roland household, but Pike still didn't like it.

"Let me know what you find."

"Will do."

Pike hung up, and sorted the screen grabs again. Karbo and Bender made two. The pale man and the 4Runner's driver made four. The snapshot Izzy sent to Carly showed two murky figures in the 4Runner. Might be the pale man and the same driver, or two additional players, which would make a total of six. Crews cost money. Pike wondered who mounted a six-man crew to kidnap Isabel, and why they had made such a hefty investment.

Karbo's Challenger had been towed to a lot on the eastern edge of the Valley. Pike started the Jeep, and headed for the freeway.

PART FOUR

THE TALL MAN

25.

Elvis Cole

Cole grabbed a pastrami on rye from the little deli on the ground floor, and climbed four flights to his office. The building had an elevator, but Cole took the stairs. Stairs made you tough.

Cole let himself in, closed the door, and settled behind his desk with the sandwich. He took a bite. Nothing to write home about. He found two packets of Chinese hot mustard in his desk, and applied the mustard. Better. Cole glanced at the Pinocchio clock.

"What do you think? Witness protection?"

Pinocchio's plastic eyes slid from side to side. Pinocchio wasn't impressed.

"Yeah. Me, neither."

The odds were too crazy small. Like most experienced investigators, Cole did not believe in coincidence, so the notion that Hollis—Hollis being the first and only friend of Uncle Ted Kemp he had met—happened to mention a witness from Houston felt way too coincidental.

On the other hand, Kemp was a drunk who talked too much, and likely told the same stories to everyone. If Kemp's buddies knew the same stories, then any of them could have told him about the Lone Star witness, or the kleptomaniac pimp from Biloxi or the mom-killing bank bandit from Detroit.

Cole ate the sandwich, and thought through the facts.

Kemp had been with the Marshals Service. Check. Uncle Ted Kemp had been a longtime friend of the Rolands. Check. The Rolands rooted for the Houston Astros baseball team. Check. All of which added up to nothing. Check.

One man's coincidence was another man's probability.

Cole felt he was making progress. If the Marshals suspected Kemp had been tortured to reveal a witness's identity, they likely didn't know which witness, if any, Kemp gave up. If they suspected the Rolands of being the compromised witnesses, they would have been all over Isabel. They weren't, which suggested the Rolands were simply civilians or the Marshals were clueless.

Cole finished the sandwich, and opened the French doors to his balcony. A low haze hid the sea. The heavy clouds he'd seen earlier had grown into towering giants.

Cole opened his laptop and went to work.

Identifying federal trials related to counterfeit pharmaceuticals proved to be easy. Cole ran an Internet search, limiting results to stories in Texas appearing more than twenty years ago.

A list of links appeared, most referencing a case tried in the U.S. District Court in Houston. The People of the United States v. Jonathan Dennis Darnel and Samwell Lockhart Fundt, M.D. Darnel and Fundt were described as the owners of New Way Healthful Choices, Inc., a distributor of nutritional supplements. Together, the defendants had been charged with one hundred sixty-eight federal counts including fraud, conspiracy, sale and distribution of fake or illicit medicines, smuggling of same, trafficking of same, money laundering, and nine counts of manslaughter, the manslaughter counts derived from deaths caused by contaminants found in the counterfeit medicines. At the end of a three-week trial, the jury returned guilty verdicts on all one hundred sixty-eight counts.

Cole read the first three stories, and skimmed the rest. Twenty-three witnesses appeared for the prosecution. Identifying information was minimal, but names and ages were given. Cole ran individual searches, and found her.

DeeAnn Ryan had been Darnel's twenty-four-year-old office manager and bookkeeper. Cole found Dee-Ann's high school graduation portrait. She looked so much like Isabel they could have been clones.

Cole tipped his chair back, and grinned at Pinocchio.

"The World's Greatest Detective strikes again."

As with five other New Way employee witnesses, DeeAnn had not known the pharmaceuticals distributed by the company were fraudulent until the FBI approached her. She cooperated willingly, and agreed to provide ongoing information regarding Darnel and Fundt, as well as information regarding the quantities and sources of pharmaceuticals and weekly accountings of monies received and disbursed by the company. The monies received had been large. The prosecution alleged New Way collected as much as three-point-four million dollars each week. In cash.

Cole felt uneasy, and wondered if he had missed something obvious. The Marshals had been investigating Kemp's murder for two weeks. Maybe they knew exactly who Kemp gave up, and had taken steps to protect them. The men in the dark SUV Isabel mistook for Karbo and Bender could have been marshals. The marshals would insist on radio silence, which would explain Isabel's disappearance, and the silence that followed.

Cole was feeling proud of this deduction when the door opened, and three people entered. The first was a midsized woman with sandy hair and grim eyes in a navy pant suit. A bald man the size of an NFL lineman lumbered in next, and a tall, lean man entered last. Six five, maybe six six, but some of his height came from boots and a custom-made Stetson. The tall man closed the door. He locked it.

Cole cleared the computer's screen, and closed his laptop. He held up the remains of his sandwich.

"Sorry. We're closed for lunch."

The NFL lineman said, "Is he closed?"

The woman said, "He's open."

The tall man came closer, and gazed down at Cole from so high above he was part of the ceiling.

26.

The tall man reached under his jacket. A pistol peeked out, but the man didn't touch it. He flashed a badge case and showed his credentials.

"Pryor Gregg, Mr. Cole. I'm an Inspector with the Marshals Service. These are Deputy Marshals Steinaway and Urman."

Steinaway was the woman. Urman was the lineman. Neither changed expression nor acknowledged the introduction.

Cole nodded at Urman.

"Didn't you play in the Rose Bowl?"

Pryor Gregg was putting away his credentials when Cole's cell phone buzzed with an incoming call. Pike. Cole picked up the phone and sent the call to voice mail.

Gregg said, "Don't you want to get it?"

Cole slipped the phone into a pocket.

"Robocall. They're trying to sell something."

"Why were you asking about Ted Kemp?"

Cole glanced at Urman and Steinaway. News traveled fast in Palmdale.

"I'm trying to find a woman he used to date named Frances Pomeroy. I made the drive thinking he could help. I didn't know he was dead."

"Why not just call?"

"I did. He didn't call back, so I made the drive. Guys like me, people don't call back. I'm used to it."

"Did you kill him?"

"Why would I go to his house and talk to his friends if I killed him?"

Steinaway said, "Maybe you're stupid."

Urman nodded.

"That, or you wanted to find out what the police were doing. Maybe both."

Cole made a brushing wave at the lineman.

"Could you move? You're blocking the light."

Gregg said, "Who's the woman you're trying to find?"

Cole had spoken to three people, and asked all three about Isabel. Gregg probably knew he had asked about a woman, but he might not know which woman.

"A client's ex. Family stuff. Nothing dramatic."

"We'd like to speak with your client."

Cole tipped back.

"The word confidential on my door means something, Inspector. Sorry."

Steinaway said, "A word on a door."

Urman said, "Impressive."

Gregg took a seat opposite the desk. The director's chair squeaked.

"It means what we allow it to mean, Mr. Cole. You know why we're here."

"Someone killed him."

"Then you showed up. Coincidence?"

The C word again.

"He was a marshal, like you. Retired. Liked women and golf, one of those women being my client's ex. I drove up to see if he was still in touch with her, or knew how to find her. Call it whatever you like."

Gregg peered out from under the hat, testing the weight of the lie. Thinking was good. Thinking meant he might go for it.

"And you knew nothing about it before today?"

"No, sir. I did not."

"No idea who murdered him?"

"No, sir."

Gregg shifted as if the chair wasn't comfortable.

"Or why?"

"Him being a marshal, I could guess. A kid at a minimart said it was ugly."

The brim of Gregg's Stetson dipped, down just a bit, and up.

"Kemp was a lush."

Urman cleared his throat, and Steinaway murmured.

"Boss."

Gregg stared at Cole as if they were the only two people in the room.

"Average marshal, pretty good record, but he forgot himself. Spoke about matters we don't mention. You reading me, Mr. Cole?"

"Secrets. Sounds like witness security secrets."

"The nature of Kemp's murder suggests the killers wanted information. Whether he identified a particular witness, we don't know, so I'm forced to assume he did."

"Maybe this wasn't about a witness. Could've been a vengeance killing."

"I hope you're right. But until I know otherwise, we have to see after the people in our program. We protect people, Mr. Cole. That's the deal. We've never lost a witness who plays by our rules. We do not intend to start."

"I hope Mr. Kemp didn't blow it for you."

The hat dipped again.

"I can't undo what he did. If he gave up one of our people, we can offer a fresh start. Set them up with a new life, do what we do, and try to make it right."

Cole thought it sounded like a sales pitch.

"Sounds good, but I can't help you."

"You sure?"

"Positive."

Gregg stared for a while, and finally stood.

"Well, maybe that's true, and maybe it's not."

Gregg adjusted his hat.

"But I think you know something. Maybe not about the murder, but you're nibbling at the edge of this. I can smell it."

"What's it smell like?"

"Fear."

Gregg slipped a card from his jacket, and placed it on the desk.

"Us coming here like we have, knocking, talking, this is because we heard good things about you. Know why an SOG team didn't haul you away?"

The Special Operations Group was the Marshals Service's version of SWAT.

Cole said, "Because you heard good things?"

Urman said, "Genius."

Steinaway nodded.

"Above average, for sure."

Gregg went on as if they hadn't spoken.

"Smells like fear because you're torn. You know something, and you want to help. You might even know who these bastards killed my marshal to find."

"I don't know anything, Inspector. I usually don't."

Gregg shrugged.

"This may be, but I think not, and now here we are, and it's taking everything you have not to tell me, because I'm making sense. The not telling, you don't like it. You're thinking, if you don't tell me, someone else might die, maybe even the person you're trying to help."

Cole said nothing, hoping his silence didn't look like a confession.

Gregg tapped the card one time.

"Think on it, Mr. Cole. If you need to discuss this with someone, discuss it, and tell'm we're here to help. Either way, we'll be in touch."

Gregg turned to leave, but seemed to think better of it and slowly turned back. The Stetson's wide brim split his face with a shadow.

"By the way, I understand you're associated with a gentleman named Pike."

Cole felt the floor tilt, just a bit, and tried not to show it.

"That's right. He's my partner."

"Have you seen him recently?"

"He travels a lot."

Gregg was a thousand feet tall. He peered down from the heights, and showed no reaction.

Cole said, "Why?"

Gregg left, and Urman followed. Steinaway headed out last, and stopped at the door.

Cole gave a little wave.

"Pleasure to meet you. Stop by anytime."

Steinaway said, "Wake up."

She closed the door when she left.

Cole closed his eyes and wondered how much they knew. The marshals had not accused him or tried to muscle him. Gregg had taken a different approach, making an appeal for Cole's cooperation. Cole wondered what this meant, and decided it probably meant something bad. And Gregg had saved Pike for last. Cole was certain this meant something even worse, but he couldn't see what.

Cole grabbed a fresh bottle of water, and stepped out onto the balcony. The offshore clouds were darker and swollen like coiling, knotted muscles. Overhead, a helicopter carved a lazy arc against the gray sky.

Gregg was good.

He was good because he was right.

Cole returned to his desk, opened his laptop, and reread the clippings. He studied the picture of DeeAnn Ryan and held the photo of Isabel beside it. Clones.

Cole spent another forty-five minutes researching the trial and its aftermath. Then he called Pike.

27.

Joe Pike

The Challenger gave him nothing. Where Bender had left scrawled notes, addresses, and burners, Karbo left his Challenger immaculate. Pike was walking to his Jeep when Cole called.

"Can you talk?"

"Go."

"Three marshals left my office forty-five minutes ago. Two grunts and an inspector named Gregg. They believe Kemp gave up witness information."

"About the Rolands?"

"I don't think they know, but it's definitely the Rolands. I'm sending you something—"

Pike's phone vibrated with the incoming email. He climbed into his Jeep and pulled the door shut as Cole continued.

"Isabel's parents were in the program. Specifically, her mother. Debra Sue Roland's original name was Dee-Ann Ryan. Her husband, Ed, was Nick Ryan, both from Sugar Land, Texas. Under the name Ryan, she helped put the whack on a large-scale counterfeit pharmaceuticals ring almost twenty-five years ago. The links I sent tell about the trial."

"This was in Texas?"

"Federal court in Houston."

Twenty-five years was forever ago. Yet here were the pale man, Karbo and Bender, and other men mounting a major effort.

"Her mother is dead. Her father's been dead for years. This doesn't track. Nobody's left to punish."

"Yeah. Twenty-five years after the fact, and they're taking it out on a dead woman's daughter?"

"So something else is at play."

"Could be. DeeAnn wasn't the only State's witness. I clocked fourteen names. Of those I've checked, six went on with their regular lives under their original names. Only DeeAnn and her husband vanished. So only DeeAnn and her husband entered the program."

"Was there a mob or cartel connection?"

"Not from what I saw in the coverage. Two principals were named in the indictment, a cat named Darnel and a doctor named Fundt. They were amateurs— slimeballs who thought they were smart."

"Both convicted?"

"Convicted, sentenced, and put away, but get this— both were murdered during their incarceration."

Pike's phone suddenly buzzed with an incoming call.

"Hang on. It's Carly."

Pike put Cole on hold, and took Carly's call.

"Pike."

"They're back! It's the 4Runner! They're back!"

The words came in a rush, her voice excited and tight.

Pike immediately started the Jeep, but kept his voice calm. Panic bred panic. Calm inspired calm. These were lessons he learned in the battle space.

"Are you safe?"

With no change in his tone, Pike swung the Jeep through a hard turn, and jammed on the gas.

"I think so. They left."

"I'm coming now. Hang on—"

He left her on hold and toggled to Cole.

"She's at Izzy's. The SUV's back."

"You still up in the Valley?"

"Yes."

"I'm close. Leaving now."

Pike flipped back to Carly.

"Elvis is coming, too. I want you to leave. Walk or drive, doesn't matter. Go."

Carly hesitated, and Pike knew she was peeking out the window.

"The mailman is across the street. A lady is walking her dog. I'm okay. They're gone."

Pike slowed for a red, but did not stop. A gap opened between cars. He powered through, and veered around a truck.

"They might come back. I want you to leave."

"They must be looking for Izzy. If they had her, they wouldn't be *here*, right? She must have escaped."

"We don't know, Carly. We don't know why they came. Leave. Don't stay."

"I'm okay. Really."

Pike said, "Carly."

"It wasn't gray like in the picture. It was blue, like a midnight blue. I got some of the license number—"

Pike weaved through traffic, flashing past cars as if they were parked.

"Six, U, J, B. I couldn't see the rest."

Six-U-J-B matched the first four digits of the 4Runner in Ekizian's video.

"You should leave."

"If they come back, I'll get the rest of their license number."

Pike was getting a headache.

"Call the police. Tell them the men in the car are stalking you, and you fear for your life. Do it, Carly. Do it now."

"I don't want to scare them away. If they come back, we can catch them."

A stabbing pain punched through his eye. Staying calm was a test.

A freeway entrance was coming fast, but a line of cars clogged the ramp. Pike swung onto the shoulder, and powered around them.

"Say your location."

"Inside. I'm in the living room."

"If you're not going to leave or call the police, go outside. Stand on the porch. Stay in plain view where people can see you."

"I'm starting to feel silly."

"The porch. Please."

"Okay. I'm on the porch. I waved at the mailman."

She giggled, but it sounded brittle.

Pike careened between cars and blasted ahead.

"Okay. Stay outside. Wave at everyone. I'm coming."

"You're funny."

Pike checked the time. He was twenty-two, twenty-three minutes away, but Elvis was closer. Eight minutes, ten minutes, tops, and Elvis would reach her.

"Carly? You still waving?"

She giggled again.

"No, silly. I'd feel stupid."

Pike flashed past cars as if they were parked. He didn't feel funny or stupid. He felt helpless.

28.

Elvis Cole

Cole pulled out of the parking garage and turned toward Sunset. He hadn't taken the time to put on his shoulder holster. It sat wrapped in the light cotton jacket he wore to cover it on the passenger seat.

Traffic was lousy, but bad traffic in Los Angeles had become the new normal. He drove aggressively, ducked up side streets to avoid the worst of it, and made good time.

Cole was less than half a mile from Carly when he changed lanes and noticed the tan sedan. He had seen the sedan twice before, and thought nothing of it. The first time, the sedan had been ahead of him, waiting to turn from a cross street. The sedan had turned when he passed, and joined the flow of traffic two cars behind him. The second time, Cole ducked down a side street to avoid a construction site, and the sedan made the same turn. Other cars were taking the same side street, so Cole wrote it off.

But here they were again, two cars back.

Cole was in the right-hand lane. He put on his left blinker, and moved into the left lane as if he planned to make a left turn. The sedan drifted into the left lane. Two blocks later, Cole put on his right blinker, and eased into the right lane. He slowed as he neared the next cross street as if he intended to turn.

The sedan followed him into the right lane.

Cole thought about Carly and the men in the SUV and didn't like where the thoughts led.

He changed lanes again, and glimpsed two shapes when the sedan changed lanes with him. Cole didn't make out their faces, but the shape filling the shotgun seat was huge. Urman.

Carly was three minutes away.

Cole slowed and let the traffic stack up behind him.

He slowed even more, and straddled the divider line so both lanes behind him backed up. Horns blew, and the woman behind him gave him the finger.

Cars stacked up until a rolling parking lot trailed in his rearview mirror. The marshal's sedan was surrounded by irate drivers and cars, and trapped three rows back.

Cole kept them locked in the herd of cars behind him until he reached the next cross street. Then he turned hard, punched the gas, and his old Corvette roared.

Cole didn't get far.

Halfway up the block, a blue sedan and a gray sedan screamed around the corner. The blue sedan blocked the street, and the gray sedan came toward him. Pryor Gregg was driving.

Cole thumb-dialed Pike, who answered with his ETA.

"Twelve minutes out. Maybe less."

"The marshals jumped me. I'm done."

The tan sedan raced up behind and screeched to a stop sideways. Urman, all right. And Steinaway.

Cole turned off his phone and shut off the engine. In the silence, he heard the whup-whup-whup of a helicopter. The bird flew past overhead, and banked into an orbit. It was the same helicopter he'd seen from his balcony.

Cole made no sudden moves. He grabbed the top of the steering wheel with both hands, and hoped Carly was safe.

29.

John Chen

John Chen rode a wave of adrenaline-fueled, double-Y-chromosome, male-conquest *power* when he returned to the lab. Success!! He had slipped in and out of the impound yard with no one the wiser (heart revving so hard he thought he would stroke), pulled eight quality prints (using the screenshot Pike sent, showing the man touching the top of the SUV's door), and *still* made it back to the lab before six. Chen bumped into Harriet on his way in, and she didn't even scowl. John, feeling all badass and rippling with confidence, gave her a cheery wave.

"You'll have my report in the morning. First thing."

Harriet walked away looking sad.

The prints were things of beauty. The ridges and bifurcations were sharp, the crossovers were clean, and most showed minimal obscuration.

Chen transferred the prints to plastic slides, and scanned their images into the Forensic Science Division's computer. Software analyzed and compared the digital images with those contained in the California DOJ Criminal Information Services database, and kicked back the results. Two hits appeared on the screen.

Chen glanced around to make sure no one was approaching.

Three of the eight prints were left by Bender.

Five of the eight belonged to a Nathan Daniel Hicks.

Chen brought up the information on Hicks. The dude was a beast. An ex-con and convicted felon with a lengthy record.

Chen glanced around again, then photographed the information with his phone. Printing the document would have been easier, but if someone walked up, he might have to explain.

The rap sheet was long. Chen had to photograph the screen three times, and grew worried Harriet or one of her spies would catch him. He checked to be sure each image was readable, took a last look around, and cleared the screen. *Gone!* He was safe. He had done it! John Chen, superhero criminalist, was doing his part to save Isabel Roland!

Chen smiled to himself, and his smile became a giggle. Arli Scruggs, a DNA specialist at the gas spectrometer, glanced over. Bitch. Chen smirked, and swaggered away. Screw you, Arli.

Chen filed the slides, and went to his workstation. He needed to call Pike, but he would log the Hancock Park evidence first. Harriet might check on his progress, so he needed something to show her. John logged on to his terminal, and got down to business.

"John."

Harriet's voice startled him. Chen lurched sideways and almost tipped over. He caught the desk just in time.

"Oh. Hi, Harriet. It's coming along great."

Harriet stared at him like a mortician who hadn't been paid.

"Come to the conference room, please."

Harriet didn't wait for a response. She left.

"Harriet? But I'm writing the report."

Harriet walked away faster.

Chen glanced at Arli Scruggs. Scruggs gave him the finger.

Chen logged out of his terminal, and hurried to the conference room. It was a large room with a long oval table. Harriet sat at the head. Her hands were folded on papers. She was alone.

John entered and stopped by the door. His stomach did a little flip-flop.

"You'll have it first thing. I promise."

Harriet picked up the papers and dealt them across the table. They were photographs printed on regular printer paper.

"How do you explain these?"

John stepped closer to see. The photographs showed John at the impound yard. They showed him entering, handing his creds to the gate guard, and standing by the SUV. The pictures showed John inside the SUV, squatting beside the SUV as he reached into his equipment case, lasering the door as he looked for prints, and dusting the prints he found.

John, feeling as if he would vomit and totally panicked, stammered.

"This looks like me."

Harriet sat back and stared.

John hiccupped and tasted acid. He flushed, and stammered again.

"What is this?"

"This is you. The vehicle was associated with a kidnap filing approximately eight days ago. A case to which you were not assigned. Care to explain?"

"Who took these? Was it Ganowski? It was!"

"The driver of this vehicle has since been murdered. Another case to which you have not been assigned, yet here you are, collecting evidence. I ask again, for the last time, do you care to explain?"

John's mind reeled with a panic-driven cacophony of thoughts. He couldn't tell her the truth. The truth would be an admission of guilt, and, even worse, implicate Joe. He grasped for an excuse.

"Instinct."

"Excuse me."

"Just a, um, feeling I had. Yes, you're right, not my cases, but I had this weird feeling—"

John was flying blind and making it up as he went.

"—that, you know, Bender knew his murderer, so I thought maybe I could—"

Harriet raised her palms.

"Stop it, John. Don't lie. Saying nothing is better than lying."

"I'm not lying!"

"Are you working for a private entity or individual?"

"No!"

LAPD criminalists were forbidden to work for any other entity. The potential for conflicts of interest and claims of tainted evidence were too great.

"I'm not, Harriet! C'mon. I know the rules!"

Harriet closed her eyes. She sat with her eyes closed for several seconds, then gathered the pictures together.

"You do, John. I know you do. I've heard rumors for years."

"Lies! They suck up to you by shitting on me! It's envy! They get ahead if they bring me down!"

"You've done the job for them."

Harriet stood, and the mortician's mask was gone. She looked sad.

"Despite your eccentricities, I've always respected your work. You're so good at this, John. You're excellent."

John made a last desperate grab at saving himself.

"Hancock Park. I'll have it on your desk in the morning. First thing, Harriet. The very first thing!"

She stepped out from behind the table and went to the door.

"No, John. You're done. You'll receive a disciplinary notice tomorrow. As of now, you're suspended until such time a hearing is scheduled."

John Chen grew smaller and smaller. He felt himself shrinking.

Harriet stopped in the door, and gave him a final glance.

"You won't have trouble finding another job. But please, don't ask me to recommend you."

Harriet walked away. Each footstep sounded like the boom of heavy artillery. Each thundering shell headed his way.

John didn't move.

He felt empty, so empty he faded away.

30.

Joe Pike

Pike flipped back to Carly. He was concerned about Cole, but he didn't want to alarm her even more, or leave her alone.

"Eight minutes now."

"They haven't come back."

Carly had gone home to ask if her mother knew Ted Kemp, or anything about him. She'd changed clothes, and stopped for a coffee on the way back to Isabel's. When she had reached Isabel's house, a dark 4Runner was at the curb.

Pike said, "Did you get a picture?"

"I didn't realize it was them until I was in the driveway. OhmiGod, I almost hit the porch. The one man, he was on the sidewalk. They were looking at me. I was *so* scared, but he got in and they left."

Their leaving when Carly arrived was good. This meant they didn't want to involve anyone else, or draw attention to themselves.

"You saw their faces?"

"Yes! They were *right here*, looking at me."

"Tell me what they looked like."

Carly described two men, one behind the wheel, and the man on the sidewalk. Longish dark hair on the driver, a broad face, looked mean. A big man. She thought he had a mustache, but wasn't sure. The man on the sidewalk was wide and thick; she used the word burly. Short hair, a weathered face with lines and creases, and a zigzag scar on his forehead. Bulging eyes set wide apart, like a pug dog, but not cute.

Pike said, "I'm close. You good?"

"My butt hurts. People are out. Kids are getting home. Everything looks so normal."

The distance spiraled down, twenty blocks, fifteen, ten.

Pike said, "You can leave now, Carly. I've got it."

"Why? You're close."

Beyond stubborn.

Five blocks. Four.

"Gotta hang up. Might be six or seven minutes before I call."

"I'm fine. Millions of people are passing by."

Pike passed Isabel's street, turned on the next, and parked six houses up from Sunset. He waited as two women passed, then climbed out, and collected a lightweight ballistic vest from the rear. Returning to the driver's seat, he stripped off his sweatshirt, and strapped on the vest. Police officers usually wore Level 2 vests, which were lightweight, comfortable for long shifts in a patrol car, and offered protection from 9mm,

.40-caliber, and most common pistol rounds. Pike wore a custom Level 3A vest. Five millimeters thick, and only a pound heavier, multiple layers of a polymer matrix laminate would stop double-aught buckshot, edged blades, 9-millimeter submachine gun bullets, and all handgun ammunition up to and including the .44 magnum. Pike was a strong man, and fit. He didn't mind the extra weight.

He pulled the sweatshirt over the vest, and clipped the Python to his hip. Pike sipped from a bottle of water. Not much. Three sips. He pictured the house across from Isabel's house. Two elms in front, a similar porch, enormous green beach ball shrubs huddled at the porch like nursing puppies. The house he pictured was directly behind the house where he'd parked.

Pike stowed the bottle, checked the surrounding homes for eyes, then climbed out, and walked up the yard to the side of the house. He paused at a wooden gate, heard nothing beyond, and let himself through. He moved silently along the length of the house, and across a backyard cluttered with gnomes, bird feeders, ragged lawn furniture, and empty planting beds to a rotting wood fence at the rear. Another quick pause to check, then quietly over. Pike reached the side of the next house easily, and slipped between windows and shrubs to the front and finally into the voluminous green shrubs massed by the porch.

He crept forward on his belly until he found the right spot.

Isabel's house was across the street, and directly ahead.

He had a clear view of her house.

Carly's Beetle was in the drive. Carly sat on the porch with her feet on the steps, and a Starbucks cup beside her. She held her phone.

Pike eased his phone from his pocket, and tapped out a message.

> do not look up.
> eyes on your phone.
> i'm here.

Carly raised her phone when it chimed with the incoming text. She seemed to stiffen, and did not move for several seconds, but she did not look up. After a few seconds, she tapped a response.

Where are you?

Pike answered.

> close. do not look up.
> do not try to find me.

He sent the message, and saw her frown. She tapped at the screen.

OKAY!!! I'M NOT!! CAN'T YOU CALL??

Pike tapped again.

> no.
> is there an outside porch light?

He waited, and watched her answer.

Yes, sir.

More tapping.

> turn off the inside lights
> turn on the porch light
> lock the house
> leave
> do not return until you
> hear from me.

Pike watched as she read, holding the phone like a difficult book. She held it for a very long time before she answered.

Are they here, too?

Pike cut and pasted his answer.

> turn off the inside lights
> turn on the porch light
> lock the house
> leave

> do not return until you
> hear from me.

Then he added.

> please.

She laughed. He saw her laugh from across the street, then she stood, and went inside. The sun was still high, but beginning to dim. The day was dying to darkness. Carly was still inside when he received another text.

Are they coming back?

Pike gave the answer.

> not until you leave.

Pike thought she might fire off another text, but she did not. She locked the front door, and went to her car. She did not sneak peeks at the surrounding houses, or try to find him. She climbed into her car, backed out the drive, and left.

Pike settled into the earth beneath the branches and leaves, and felt himself fade into the soil and the shadows. After a few minutes, he lifted his phone, and called Elvis Cole.

Cole's voice mail answered.

Pike whispered, "Call."

Pike watched Isabel's house, and let his thoughts drift.

This one time, during his contractor days, Pike and his guys were hired to shut down a poaching outfit in southern Africa, a gang of battle-scarred, ex-insurgency lunatics who would roll on an elephant herd, pound them with heavy weapons, and sell off the ivory to Chinese smugglers. Dudes who lived in the bush, never slept in the same hut two nights in a row, running with warlords and maniacs. Word came down they used an old drug-smuggling route to pack out fresh ivory. A local led Pike and his team to a wet spot in the mud he claimed was on the old route. So Pike and his guys set up, dug in, and waited, night-vision goggles, commo buds in their ears, weapons locked and hot, good to go. Later, had to be two, three in the morning, a leopard strolled in, an old male, silent as a dream. The big cat walked past Pike and a gunner named Ross Stevens less than six feet away, and climbed a leafless, gnarly old tree overlooking the mud. The leopard picked a strong branch, settled in, and stayed.

A day passed.

Two days passed.

No poachers showed. No ivory. No living creature.

The old leopard, he stayed in the tree.

Pike and his guys were hard-core professionals. Combat discipline was sacrosanct. If they had to pee, they peed in their pants. Had to poop, go to it. They communicated with one another by gestures so small the leopard did not see them. By this time, none of them believed the poachers were coming, but discipline was a matter of pride.

On the third day, a sat-link whisper came through their earbuds. The poachers were spotted in another grid of the sector. Pull out, relocate, reposition.

Pike's guys looked at him. Pike looked back. He glanced at the cat. Each of his guys glanced at the cat in turn. As long as the cat stayed in the tree, they would stay, too.

They waited.

Dawn of the fourth day, a purple glow warmed the horizon when a muffled snort came from the brush. Pike and his guys instantly woke. A second snort followed. Three young warthogs stepped from the brush, and made their way toward the mud. They passed directly beneath the tree.

The leopard drew himself up, a glowing green mass in the NVE, and dropped.

Two pigs ran, squealing. The leopard took the third. Snapped its neck like a twig, and held it until the kicking stopped. He carried his kill up the tree.

Pike stood.

"Let's boogie."

His guys stood, grinning and laughing. The big cat watched them go.

Pike and his guys discussed the leopard as they hiked out, and often thereafter. They admired the cat's patience and resolve. They admired his skill, his cunning, and his deadly efficiency. Leopards did not chase prey like cheetahs, or stalk the tall grass like lions.

The leopard simply set up on a wet spot, above the mud, out of sight, hidden. The leopard didn't need a cheetah's speed, or have to search for prey like a lion. The leopard knew if he staked out something his prey wanted, his prey would come to him.

31.

Heavy clouds dimmed the evening light. The little house beside him belonged to an older couple. Nicholas and Faye spent most of their time in the rear, but when they came to the front of the house, Pike heard them clearly. He listened to note their movement, but tried not to hear. When the couple returned to the back of the house, their voices blurred to a mumble. Pike preferred the mumble.

An incoming call disturbed his peace. A slight vibration, and Pike checked the screen. He made no sudden moves, and did not disturb the branches. Chen. Pike answered as soft as a falling leaf.

"Yes."

"Joe, this is John Chen."

Chen's voice was unusually calm.

"Yes."

"The man from the SUV is Nathan Daniel Hicks. I got his prints, right where you said."

Pike's mouth twitched. The pale man had a name.

"I'm sending his sheet. I didn't get all of it. It's long. The dude's pretty bad."

Pike felt another vibration as whatever Chen sent arrived. He listened for Nicholas and Faye. They were still in the rear.

"Bad how?"

"Armed robbery, aggravated assault, grand theft. It goes on. Hijackings and warehouses, mostly. Did two stints in prison. You'll see."

Chen delivered the news in the same distant voice.

"Wants or warrants?"

Rap sheets provided a record of an individual's criminal history. This included prior arrests and prosecutions, convictions and dismissals, sentencing and parole information, and pretty much any and all contact the individual had with the criminal justice system. The California DOJ's sheet would also include outstanding criminal warrants.

Chen said, "None. Last arrest was eight years ago. Nothing since then."

Pike knew the lack of arrests didn't mean Hicks had stopped doing crime. Professional criminals did crime for a living. Hicks would have continued taking scores. He'd simply grown smarter, and figured out how to avoid arrest.

Pike listened for Faye and Nicholas again, and once again heard nothing. He wanted to get off the line and study the sheet.

"Thanks, John. This helps."

Chen hesitated, but didn't sign off.

"Isabel. Is she nice?"

Pike was surprised by the question, but, as always, he showed nothing.

"Yes. She's a nice person."

"I hope you find her."

Chen's voice held a numb quality Pike didn't like.

"John? Are you all right?"

"I'm fine."

"What's wrong?"

"I was just thinking—you know, like if someone was holding me hostage or torturing me or—"

"John—"

"If I needed help, you'd be the first person I'd call. Assuming I could call."

"Are you okay?"

Chen fell silent again.

"John?"

"I never told you this, but you were the first person who ever showed faith in me. The Sobek murders. Remember?"

"I remember."

A lunatic named Lawrence Sobek had set about murdering the people he blamed for the death of his pedophile lover in prison. Pike, as the arresting officer, had been among Sobek's targets. So had Karen Garcia, a young woman who had once been Pike's girlfriend.

Chen was still talking.

"I was up at Lake Hollywood. Alone. The sun was setting. Man, you scared the hell out of me. You just, I don't know, appeared. Poof, and there you were, looking all you. I thought you were going to kill me."

"You didn't know me."

"You helped. Pointed out evidence I'd missed. Taught me to see a crime scene through different eyes. Your eyes. Did my job for me, I guess."

"Why are you thinking about this?"

"I think about it a lot. I wouldn't have made the big breakthroughs without you. I wouldn't have gotten the press, but I did, then, and all the times since. I want you to know. It's meant a lot."

"Two-way street, John. You've helped me and Elvis. It's a partnership."

Chen's soft voice broke.

"This makes me cry. A man like you, being so kind."

"I'm not being kind. It's true."

"Here's what mattered most. All this time, you've never, not once, disrespected me. You've never treated me like a geek. Or a creep. This is a kindness I'll never be able to repay. Thank you."

"John. Please tell me what's wrong."

"You find her, Joe. I know you'll find her."

Chen hung up.

Pike stared between the leaves at the Roland house, wondering why his friend sounded so sad. The sun settled, the clouds thickened, and the light within the bush faded to shadows. The front door opened a few feet away, and the older woman came out. He followed Faye's footsteps across the porch and down the steps, but he could not see her.

Inside, Nicholas called, his voice moving.

"Goddamnit, where are you? Faye!"

The television came on. Pike heard voices, but could not understand what they said.

A few minutes later, Faye returned. Pike followed her footsteps up the steps, and across the porch.

Inside, Faye said, "Oh, shut up. You make me so tired I don't know what to do."

Isabel's home and yard and the street deepened to a purple gray as the porch light Carly left on seemed to brighten. Pike hung his sunglasses on the neck of his sweatshirt.

Behind him, Faye spoke loudly as she stomped through the house.

"Put on music, for pity's sake. Do you have to watch the news? The news makes you crazy."

Evening arrived, and gave way to night. A light rain began to fall, tapping the leaves, and dripping from the branches. His clothes grew wet. Water leaked from his hair. Pike didn't move. His thoughts were still. His heart rate hovered at forty-two beats per minute. A couple hurried past, caught by the rain. Cars passed, following headlights.

Isabel's home waited peacefully.

More headlights appeared, but this time the vehicle slowed.

The corner of Pike's mouth ticked. Once.

The 4Runner crept into his field of view, moving left to right, and Pike saw the backs of two heads. Two men looking at Isabel's home.

Pike did not move. His heart rate did not change. He watched the vehicle.

The 4Runner passed from his field of view, and was gone.

One minute.

Two.

Lights approached, this time from right to left. The 4Runner stopped at the curb directly in front of Isabel's house. Pike heard their engine stop. Their headlights went dark, the doors opened, and the driver and his passenger slipped from the vehicle. Each man quietly closed his door, and moved up the walk.

The driver was taller, with square shoulders, a wide body, and a large head. Pike decided he looked like the Frankenstein monster, so Pike dubbed him Boris. The passenger was built low and burly, with a broad face, a heavy chest, and thick legs. Pike thought he looked like a bulldog, and dubbed him Spot. Neither was Nathan Daniel Hicks.

The men climbed onto Isabel's porch into the golden light, and went to her door.

Pike checked the time. Isabel had been missing exactly twenty-five hours.

Spot slid a key into the lock.

Pike wondered if the key belonged to Isabel. He decided it did.

The front door opened.

The men stepped inside, and Boris closed the door.

Joe Pike backed from beneath the branches and leaves, and ran through the rain alongside the house to the rear. He moved quickly, and did not care if anyone heard.

Her presence was somewhere ahead and out of view, pulling him closer.

Be alive.

Be alive.

Pike slipped across a fence and ran for his Jeep.

32.

Hicks

The Adderall kept him going, but didn't do squat for exhaustion. After all night and all day with the girl, Hicks was bone-deep tired. A weird buzz in his head made him wonder if the speed was cooking his brain. Hicks was down in the kitchen scarfing stale tortilla chips and brown guacamole when Riley called. Hicks snatched up his phone, thinking Ronson or Stanley had called, but saw it was Riley. Hicks wanted to duck. The old man wouldn't like what he had to say, but he answered.

"What's up?"

"Time to talk. Come see me."

Hicks checked the time, irritated. Ronson and Stanley should be out of the house, and on their way home. As soon as they unloaded the take, the entire crew would return to the house for a final time, and rip it apart. Before then, in the next few minutes, Hicks planned to take a final shot at the girl. He was convinced she knew nothing, but you never knew. Then he would kill her.

Hicks said, "Listen, can it wait? I'm in the middle of it, up here."

Riley said, "Now."

Riley was the old man's assistant. Or his son, or enforcer. Hicks didn't know which. Riley named a Cuban restaurant on Sunset over in Silver Lake, and gave him the address. Food wasn't part of the deal. Riley met him at restaurants to avoid confusion. Signs made them easy to find, and restaurants had parking lots.

Hicks told the others he was leaving, then brushed his teeth and changed shirts. He smelled like a goat, but left without taking a shower. Hicks took a pistol.

The restaurant was twenty minutes away. Hicks spent the drive deciding whether he should lie. Lying might buy him some time, but lying to this particular old man could be a serious mistake.

Hicks was still deciding when he entered the parking lot and spotted Riley's car. He also spotted Riley's goons. The same three goons were around wherever they met. Big, raw-boned shitkickers straight out of Central Casting. Dark from long days in the saddle, gunfighter eyes, bad demeanors. Cowboy boots. They never spoke. They just watched Hicks, and looked like they wanted to kill him.

Hicks parked in front of the Cuban restaurant, and climbed into Riley's car. A rental. Riley, like the goons, had flown in from Texas.

Hicks started off light.

"This little mall here is kinda famous. A few years

ago, a lunatic set off a bomb right down here in the dumpster. Killed a guy. Blew out all these windows, the windows across the street. Made the national news."

Riley ignored him.

"She come across?"

Hicks hesitated, debating all the way down to the moment of truth, and shook his head.

"No. She's a dead end. Useless. It's all about the house now."

Riley didn't react. He simply raised his phone, and dialed the old man. This was how they did business.

Riley was a big boy, too, six two, six three, but he dressed nicer than the goons. Had the boots, but he wore slacks and a sport coat. A polite guy, well-spoken, Hicks even kinda liked him, but every time they were together, Hicks was ready to kill him. Scars slashed his forehead and nose, and ginormous knuckles bulged from catcher's-mitt hands.

Riley put the call on speaker.

Riley said, "My employer will answer."

This was how their calls began. Riley never used the old man's name. It was always "my employer."

Couple of hundred rings later, the old man finally answered. His voice was hard as a spike.

"Well? You earning your pay?"

"Searching their home as we speak. I'll get back to you as soon as I know what we've found."

Hicks regretted the dodge as soon as the old man chuckled.

"You'll get back to me?"

"We're attacking the house. The men I sent are—"

The old man talked over him.

"What you're saying is, at some point in the future, not now, but later, when it's more convenient, you'll maybe give me a call?"

"It came out wrong. What I—"

The old man's voice rose. Riley raised a finger, telling Hicks to let him finish.

"I want to know what's going on. You've had her damned kid all last night and all day today! This thing oughta be over, and you're gonna get back to me?"

Hicks simply told him.

"She doesn't know."

Hicks heard the old man breathing, and the breathing scared him. He pushed ahead.

"The marshal told us she didn't know. Correct? Well, he told the truth. She doesn't."

"You think not?"

"I know not. She's done. She has nothing to offer."

"Riley, you listening to this?"

Riley said, "Every word."

The old man snorted.

"Well, here's what I think. She's smarter than you. She is holding out, and you have been fooled. A little girl like this, maybe you haven't been hard enough. Maybe you need to try harder."

"She doesn't know. We're wasting time. Time is our enemy."

"Riley?"

"Right here."

The old man was silent for a moment.

"Never mind. You and I will talk later."

"You bet."

The old man resumed with Hicks, and now his voice seemed calmer.

"Forgetting the girl for a second, which we'll return to, what does the highly recommended, professional badass I hired out there in California plan to do now?"

Hicks glanced at Riley, and felt himself flush. His temples throbbed, and his neck hardened to ropes. Riley shook his head, telling Hicks to stay calm, let it go.

Hicks worked up some spit, and took a breath.

"Attack the house. Her house is the only path forward."

"That bitch had more than one, believe me."

"The West Hollywood house, where she lived with her husband and daughter."

"People know this girl is missing. They'll come around."

"Already have. And worse, maybe tomorrow, the police will roll in. Then it becomes a crime scene. Available hours remaining? Twelve to fifteen, max."

"I'm listening."

"My guys are inside now. First pass, they'll pull paperwork—bills, files, correspondence, et cetera. Also, phones and computers, anything with a memory. Odds are, if the Ryans left physical evidence, it's somewhere innocuous."

"Agreed. But odds go both ways."

"These people lived off the grid and undercover for twenty-five years. They knew how to hide. They were good at it. Once we secure the paper, we'll pull the house apart. Garage, attic, air ducts, floors, fixtures, closets, everything."

"Tonight."

"Right away."

"You're talking more than twelve to fifteen hours."

"One man has to stay with the girl. That gives me three men in her home, and a guy with a metal detector checking the yard. Maybe she hid a can under a rosebush."

Hicks hoped the old man would chuckle again, but he didn't, so Hicks pressed ahead with his case.

"Twelve hours is wishful thinking. One of her friends, she has a key. The friend comes back, we're done. If the cops roll in sooner, kiss the house and everything in it good-bye."

The old man grunted.

"All right, then. So do it."

"Only way to find is to look, and looking takes people and time. We're short on both. An extra guy could save us."

The old man paused.

"What're you getting at?"

"The girl's gotta go. It frees a man to help clear the house. Simple as that."

"Whatever she knows goes with her."

"She doesn't know anything."

Now the old man stayed quiet forever. Hicks looked at Riley, and made a should-I-say-something? shrug. Riley shook his head. Wait.

Finally, felt like hours, the old man cleared his throat.

"You're hot to kill this girl."

"She's gotta go sooner or later. Rule Number One. Leave no witnesses. If she goes now, we see a benefit. *You* see a benefit."

The old man cleared his throat.

"I appreciate what you're saying. I do. But you ain't killing shit. We clear?"

"You hired me to do a job. This is me doing it."

"She knows, boy. That girl knows everything. Don't blow it."

Hicks glanced at Riley, but the man's eyes were blank.

The old man said, "Riley?"

"Sir?"

"Get Mr. Hicks on his way."

"Will do."

Riley lowered the phone, and considered Hicks for a moment.

Hicks said, "What?"

"You should've just killed her."

"You know what? Fuck this. I know what I'm doing. You *know* I know what I'm doing. That's why you hired me."

"He's been after the girl's mother for twenty-five years. He has been hating that lady for one-quarter of a century. Think."

Hicks didn't get it.

"What?"

"Won't be as good as killing her mother, but he is a hateful, vengeful man. He'll kill her himself."

Riley considered him a little bit longer.

"You're working for us. You took our money. Best you remember."

Riley's eyes were empty. Hicks figured he had a gun, but this didn't mean he could use it. He glanced at the goons. Big men, big targets.

Hicks said, "Best you remember why I'm the guy you hired."

Hicks got out and returned to his car.

33.

Elvis Cole

They marched him into Hollywood Station like they owned the place, Gregg and a herd of U.S. Marshals. The watch commander led them to a conference room. It was one of the nice conference rooms with a big-screen monitor, a large shiny table, and clean chairs. The Marshals had juice.

Gregg and his herd walked past, but Urman steered Cole into the room and pulled out a chair.

"Sit."

Cole sat.

"Can I have my phone?"

"What phone?"

Marshal humor.

Urman left, and locked the door. They had taken Cole's phone, his wallet, and his watch. They locked him in the room, but they did not book him, photograph him, or handcuff him. They did not advise him of his rights. Cole told himself this was a good sign, but knew it meant nothing. Something had changed.

In the time since they left his office, the marshals had learned something new, and gone to battle stations.

They made him wait.

The door opened after about an hour, and Gregg and Steinaway walked in. An older man with a big head and a thin woman with spiteful eyes came in with them.

Cole smiled brightly.

"Thank you all for coming. Meeting's adjourned."

Zero reaction.

Gregg introduced the man and the woman as they sat.

"Detectives Braun and DeLako with LAPD. You've already met Deputy Marshal Steinaway and myself."

Cole recognized Braun's name, but ignored him.

"It's been all of two hours, Inspector. What's with the show of force?"

Gregg removed the Stetson and placed it on the table. The hat was as big as a manhole cover.

"Have you spoken with Mr. Pike since we last saw you?"

"No, sir. I have not."

Steinaway grinned, as nasty as a razor cut.

"Liar."

Gregg met Cole's eyes and did not look away. His eyes were calm.

"Who is Isabel Roland?"

"Never met the lady. I don't know."

Cole waited for Steinaway to call him a liar, but she rattled off a series of facts.

"Your partner and known associate is one Joseph Pike,

no middle initial. Several days ago, Mr. Pike prevented two gentlemen—a Christopher Karbo and a Donald Bender, both now deceased—from kidnapping Ms. Roland."

Cole said, "He's a good man, that Joe."

Gregg nodded toward Braun and DeLako.

"Detectives Braun and DeLako are the case detectives. They've interviewed both Mr. Pike and Ms. Roland."

Braun started to say something, but Steinaway cut him off.

"That same evening, Ms. Roland phoned Ted Kemp two times, and left messages on his voice mail."

Cole was watching Gregg. Gregg nodded along with Steinaway, but his eyes never left Cole.

"We have the voice mails and phone records."

Steinaway wasn't finished.

"Late yesterday afternoon, Ms. Roland phoned Kemp again. The timing and content of the three calls suggest she was unaware of his death. Further, materials found in Kemp's home indicate a longtime relationship with the Roland family, particularly her parents."

Steinaway smiled. Her smile was wide and mean, and said she had saved the best for last.

"And earlier today, Kemp received two calls from Elvis Cole. The first was a hang up. The second, Mr. Cole left a message. He mentioned the name Isabel Roland. Shall we play it?"

Cole shrugged.

"Imposter. Probably a Russian agent."

Steinaway smiled even wider, and looked at her boss.

Gregg laced his fingers and took over. His hands were so big they looked like giant tarantulas.

"Ted Kemp was tortured. He was repeatedly cut, beaten, shot multiple times with a 10-millimeter pistol, and finally killed. We believe he was tortured to extract witness information. We believe one or both of Ms. Roland's parents were that witness, and the person behind Kemp's murder sent Karbo and Bender to kidnap their child."

Cole sat back. The amount of information the marshals developed in very little time was impressive.

"Believe? Don't you know? You're the Marshals Service."

Steinaway flushed.

"Fuck you, Cole. You think we keep a big book, we can look it up? This shit is secret."

Gregg silenced her with a wave.

"We'll know by tonight. Until you showed up in Palmdale, Ms. Roland wasn't a factor. But you did, and you led to your partner, who's connected to Ms. Roland."

Steinaway finished strong.

"Who left messages on a dead marshal's voice mail. Like you. You see how this works?"

Braun cleared his throat and spoke for the first time.

"Pike phoned this morning from Ms. Roland's home. He was concerned. She'd told a friend Karbo and Bender had found her."

DeLako said, "The friend thinks they kidnapped her, but Karbo and Bender are dead. They got popped last night."

Braun made a grunt.

"So if she got took, someone else took her. Maybe the same turds who murdered Kemp."

Braun leaned forward.

"Pike isn't a target here, Cole. Nobody thinks he killed Kemp or harmed Ms. Roland. But if he knows something that can help us, we need to know."

"I don't know what to tell you."

"Where's Pike?"

"I don't know."

Steinaway said it again.

"Liar."

Cole tried to figure out how much he could give.

"After you left, I called him. He hasn't called back. I'm not his keeper, Gregg. He has a business. Other interests."

Steinaway rapped the table.

"We tried his business. They weren't cooperative."

"They're all former LEOs, Steinaway. Maybe it's you."

A LEO was a Law Enforcement Officer.

Gregg seemed to be studying him. Cole wondered what he was thinking. Gregg had brought the full weight of the U.S. Marshals Service to bear, and probably had half the marshals in California working the case. Cole found himself liking Gregg's determined loyalty, and wondered how deep it ran.

Cole said, "Are we finished?"

Steinaway smirked.

"Not even close."

Cole placed his palms on the table.

"Talking about killers makes me concerned for my partner. I think I'll go try to find him."

Cole watched Gregg, and Gregg watched him back. Cole slowly stood.

DeLako jumped to her feet and opened the door.

"Sit down, Cole. Officer, inside."

A uniformed cop the size of a mountain was waiting outside. The cop started in, but Gregg raised a hand. His eyes remained calm.

"Where will you look?"

"Dunno. Something will come to me."

Steinaway said, "It better come to you right god-damned now or you'll never leave."

Cole didn't look at Steinaway. His eyes didn't leave Gregg.

"I've answered your questions as a courtesy. Since I haven't been placed under arrest, I did so voluntarily. Am I being placed under arrest?"

Gregg was thinking. Calm.

"I understand you and Mr. Pike co-own your agency."

Gregg wasn't asking. He was making a statement.

"I'm sure you know we do. Yes."

"Together, you and he purchased the agency from a Mr. George Feider, so you've been partners since the beginning."

"We have."

"No office staff. No other employees. Only the two of you."

Cole wondered where he was going.

"That's right."

"So in many ways, you and Mr. Pike, you're a very small family."

Cole nodded, and this time said nothing.

"The Marshals Service is a small family. If someone murdered your family, what would you do?"

"I'd find them. I would do whatever it took to find them. And I would have justice."

Gregg slowly stood.

"You can go."

Braun jerked back and glared at Gregg.

"That's it?"

Steinaway gripped his arm.

"Settle down, Sparky. That's it."

Gregg wasn't finished.

"I have two priorities here, Mr. Cole. To assure the safety of Ms. Roland, and to identify the person or persons responsible for killing a member of my family."

Cole had laid out his offer. Gregg had responded.

Cole turned to the door. The big uniform still blocked the way, but he stepped aside. Cole looked back at Gregg.

"I'll see what I can do, Inspector. If I can help find whoever killed your marshal, I will."

Gregg nodded.

"All right, then."

Gregg sat, took out his phone, and didn't look up again. Cole was dismissed.

Steinaway returned Cole's phone, wallet, and watch, and the mountainous uniform showed him out. A marshal was waiting outside with his Corvette, and tossed him the keys.

"You should wash this thing. It's a mess."

"You have a good evening, too."

Cole pulled out of the parking lot, and immediately phoned Pike.

34.

Pryor Gregg

Urman joined them as Gregg finished checking his messages. The two city cops, Braun and DeLako, simmered like irate alley cats. The moment Gregg lowered his phone, Braun started.

"We should've kept him. I've sweated guys like Cole for days. Whatever Pike knows, he knows. Trust me."

Gregg leaned back, and turned to Urman.

"How we doing?"

Urman dropped into Cole's seat.

"All good. We'll have his phone records before midnight."

Steinaway said, "Pike's, too?"

"Affirm. Landlines, cell, business lines, all of it."

DeLako glowered at Braun.

"You see these guys? Takes us forever, but these guys? The government."

Urman arched his eyebrows at Gregg, asking a question.

"What about the other thing?"

"It's on."

Braun glanced from Urman to Gregg.

"What other thing?"

Steinaway went to the door.

"I'll get the car. Urman. You walking?"

Urman pushed to his feet and followed her out.

Braun asked again.

"What other thing? What's going on?"

Gregg placed his hat on his head, adjusted the fit, and stood.

"We appreciate your cooperation, Detectives. You've been invaluable. Thank you."

Braun glanced at DeLako.

"Do we look like office help?"

He turned back to Gregg, and spread his arms to encompass the room.

"This is *our* house. And this is our case. You're a guest."

Gregg regretted his choice of words. He took off the Stetson, and sat.

"You're right. I apologize. I was trying to express my gratitude, and it came out wrong. Your cooperation has been invaluable. I hope we'll continue to have it."

DeLako still scowled.

"Works both ways. Cole's full of shit. We should've kept him here, and squeezed his 'nads dry."

Steinaway appeared in the door.

"Boss?"

"Right there."

Steinaway disappeared.

Gregg looked back at DeLako, and thought care-fully before he responded. He wasn't sure how much to reveal, and didn't want to misspeak again.

"We've been looking into Mr. Cole and his partner all day. Mr. Cole doesn't seem like a man who can be squeezed."

Braun leaned back. He seemed more thoughtful than his partner.

"The kid has a good rep. He does. But I guarantee he knows where Pike is. Everything Pike knows, Cole knows."

Gregg smiled. If they only knew.

"Probably not everything."

DeLako sneered.

"Everything. Those dudes live in each other's pockets."

Gregg was careful with what he said next.

"Mr. Pike has a good reputation, as well, if you ask certain people. You're aware of his work as a military contractor?"

Another sneer. So far, DeLako had sneered, scowled, frowned, glowered, and glared. Gregg wondered why Braun put up with such a negative partner.

DeLako said, "Pike's a lunatic. This Gun for Hire bullshit."

"Particularly interesting when we learned he carries a TS/SCI DOD security clearance."

DeLako frowned at Braun, not understanding.

"A TS what?"

Gregg noted Braun. The senior detective's dark eyes were thoughtful as he answered.

"Top Secret. Issued by the Department of Defense."

Gregg nodded.

"That's right. Top Secret, sensitive compartmented information. The SCI designation means the DOD trusted Mr. Pike with tasks requiring more than a Top Secret clearance."

DeLako grinned like she didn't believe him.

"Waitaminute. Pike? Pike's a thug. He's one bullet short of prison."

Gregg spoke directly to Braun.

"He may be, but he chose interesting jobs for a thug. Most of his contracts involved hostage rescues and re- coveries, and high-value-subject security."

DeLako squinted, still trying to get her head around it.

"For the Department of Defense?"

"Among others. If you were held captive by, say, Boko Haram in Africa or narco-terrorists in Central America, Mr. Pike is the man they'd send. He's the man you'd want them to send."

Making Joe Pike exactly the right person to find and recover Ms. Roland.

DeLako scowled and squinted, but Braun's gaze was steady.

"This isn't Africa. We have laws."

Gregg rose, and put on his hat. He adjusted the fit.

"Yes, sir. We do."

Gregg went to the door.

"Anyway, thank you again. Sorry to pull you away from your homes."

DeLako said, "Hey. What do you think Cole is doing right now?"

Gregg paused at the door.

"Calling Joe Pike. Might be they'll even hook up."

DeLako made her best scowl of the evening.

"Yeah. And if we'd kept Cole just a little bit longer, we could've set up an SIS tail."

Gregg readjusted his hat. Just a smidge, until the fit was perfect.

"Wish I'd thought of it. G'night, Detectives. Thank you again."

Gregg left, and hurried out to his car. He didn't need an SIS surveillance team. The U.S. Marshals had something better.

35.

Joe Pike

Pike rounded the block and parked at the top of Isabel's street, three houses up and five cars behind the 4Runner. The rain fell harder, coating the windshield with shimmering waves. Pike shut the lights and wipers, and slipped his gun from its holster.

Sixteen minutes later, a shadow returned to their vehicle, and appeared to be holding a box or a shopping bag in his arms. A smaller shadow returned a few seconds behind, and carried a suitcase. Both shadows made one more trip into the house, and carried more bags away.

The 4Runner's lights came on. Pike watched their vehicle nose from the curb ahead of him, and cruise to the end of the street. Their brake lights flared, their turn signal came on, but he did not move until they turned. Then he hit the lights, hammered the gas, and caught sight of them two blocks later, turning again. Boris and Spot didn't seem to be in a rush. They took their time. Pike trailed them like a shark trailed a ship, unseen, unknown, there.

Pike followed them east into Hollywood, passing the Chinese Theatre and the Wax Museum. Traffic was heavy and sluggish, but Boris did nothing to draw attention. He drove with the flow.

Good boy, Boris.

They hit a drive-thru burger restaurant south of the freeway, and took forever getting their food. Pike picked them up when they left, and headed north toward the Hollywood Hills. Griffith Observatory lay dead ahead, a bright gold star beneath the overcast, calling for a future that could have been. At the base of the hills they turned east again, climbing into the Los Feliz foothills.

Traffic thinned to residents, so Pike killed his lights again. An oncoming car flashed its headlights. When Pike didn't respond, they flashed again. The driver shouted as the car passed.

"No lights, stupid!"

Pike tried to spot the 4Runner ahead, but it was gone.

Pike drove faster, hoping to catch sight of them on the other side of each curve, but one curve flowed into the next, and the 4Runner didn't appear. Then he rounded yet another curve at the top of a ridge, and stopped short. The 4Runner was disappearing into a three-car garage directly ahead. Pike reversed into shadows, and watched the garage door rumble closed.

Pike pulled to the curb, and shut the engine.

The three-car garage belonged to a large, Spanish-style home with white stucco walls, arched windows, and a heavy tile roof. A dim ochre glow leaked from a second-floor window at the far end of the house, but the home was otherwise dark. A FOR SALE sign stood near a decorative gate by the street. Pike saw no movement or life even though Boris and Spot had arrived.

Pike wondered if Isabel was in the mansion. Hicks might be inside, and more men like Boris and Spot, but Pike finally decided none of this mattered. Isabel was in the house, or she wasn't. Only Isabel mattered.

Pike googled the broker's website, and checked the listing. The home contained five bedrooms and seven baths spread over fifty-six hundred square feet. Photos revealed a third level below, a pool, and a deck and balconies with "breathtaking" views of the city. Pike also learned that terraced steps on both sides of the house led down to the pool, and a grand staircase in the entry climbed to the upper-floor bedroom suites. A second, smaller staircase on the far end of the house, dubbed a "servants' stair" by the realtor, connected all three floors. Pike knew the layout when he left the realtor's website.

Pike clipped the Python under his shirt, snugged the straps on his vest, and made his way to the side of the house. He saw no cameras or motion sensors, but knew they were easily hidden.

Pike followed the terraced steps down to the pool, and stood in the darkness at the edge of the deck. Rain dripped from his hair and ran down his face. He tucked his sunglasses into a pocket. The rear of the house was as dark as the front except for a single lit room on the main level above. Pike crossed the deck for a closer look.

The main floor above opened to a balcony overlooking the pool. Glass doors faced the balcony, allowing residents to enjoy the view, and Mexican tile steps provided easy access to the pool. Boris stood in the kitchen, holding a long-neck bottle of beer and a bag of French fries. A balcony door off the kitchen stood open for air.

Spot paced into view, talking on a cell phone. He took a fry from Boris's bag, and left the kitchen.

Pike drew his pistol, climbed to the balcony, and stepped through the door into a large, empty room. On the realtor's website, the room had been described as a family room, and was beautifully decorated. Now, the room was empty, and as dark as a closet. Pike moved to the edge of the light.

Boris stood at the kitchen's island, dealing burgers and fries from a white paper bag. His back was turned. Pike listened for Spot, but heard only the crinkle of wrappers.

Fully loaded, Pike's pistol weighed almost three pounds. He stepped into the kitchen, and hit Boris behind the right ear with the flat of his gun. Half-chewed burger and lettuce sprayed the island, and the bag of hamburgers fell. Pike hit Boris again. The big man sagged, but Pike pinned him upright against the island, and covered the door with his gun. Pike held the aim, but no one approached.

Boris made a low groan.

Pike twisted Boris's arm behind his back, locked the elbow, and swung Boris around to face the door. Pike showed Boris the Python, and snugged the muzzle under his jaw.

Pike whispered.

"Make noise, I'll kill you."

Pike stressed the arm, and whispered again.

"Don't speak. Nod. Do you understand?"

"Yes."

Pike stressed the arm harder.

"Don't speak."

Boris nodded.

Pike whispered, "Isabel."

Boris nodded.

"She's here?"

Nod.

"Where? Answer."

Boris whispered.

"Upstairs."

"The other guy, he's with her? Answer."

"He's coming back."

"Others here? Answer."

"Could be. I dunno. We just got back."

"Shoes. Right foot first. Take'm off."

Boris toed off his right shoe first, then his left.

"Fight or make noise, you die. Tell me you understand. Answer."

"I understand."

"Go."

Pike steered Boris into the dark beyond the kitchen. The absence of furnishings made navigating the space easy, but also magnified sounds. Pike kept Boris close, and moved softly. A hall off the family room led to the servants' stair, so Pike steered Boris along the hall. Bo-

ris tensed when they reached the landing, so Pike sand-
wiched his pistol between them. He pulled Boris
closer, and thumbed back the hammer until it locked in
the cocked position. Pike wanted Boris to feel the Python cock.

He whispered again.

"Clear?"

Nod.

Pike nudged him onto the stairs.

"Up."

The stairs creaked as they climbed. Halfway up, Spot's
voice echoed from far behind them.

"Hey! You gonna clean this up? Hey!"

They reached the top-floor landing, and another
long hall, the hall leading past bedrooms to the grand
staircase. A single wall sconce glowed weakly, lighting
the landing, but leaving most of the hall dark. Pike
counted four doors, all closed, two on each side of the
hall, but the nearest door, the first door on his right,
was draped with a heavy piece of carpet. The carpet
had been nailed above the door, and hung like a cur-
tain. Pike had seen carpet covering doors and windows
in high-conflict regions from El Salvador to Sierra Le-
one, and knew its true purpose. Carpet was used to
muffle screams.

Spot called again, downstairs and farther away.

"Are you sick? Damnit, where are you?"

Pike stopped Boris at the carpet.

"Isabel?"

Boris nodded.

"Anyone else?"

Boris shook his head.

Pike assumed he was lying.

Spot called, louder now. Closer.

"This isn't funny! Asshole!"

Pike touched the Python's muzzle to Boris's jaw, and whispered again.

"Push aside the carpet. Open the door. Slow."

Boris followed directions, and pushed the door open.

Isabel lay curled on her side in the far corner of the dimly lit room. Zipties held her wrists behind her back, and duct tape bound her ankles. She was naked except for a bra and panties, and a blue nylon bag pulled over her head, but Pike knew she was Isabel.

Spot called again, his voice approaching the servants' stair below.

Whisper.

"Tell him you're coming down."

Boris shouted.

"I'm coming down."

As Boris shouted, the door across the hall opened, and a shirtless man with a pistol stepped out. Boris heaved backward, slamming Pike into the wall as the shirtless man raised his gun.

The .357 boomed as loud as a bomb.

The shirtless man stumbled, and cracked off two wild shots—BAMBAM. The bullets punched into Boris as Pike fired again—BOOM. The shirtless man fell, and Boris collapsed.

Isabel called out, but Pike barely heard her. A raging

hum filled his ears, drowning her voice and creaks from the servants' stair behind him.

Pike kicked the shirtless man's gun aside when something heavy slammed his back and knocked him forward. Pike dropped to the side, and saw Spot on the landing. He stood in a two-hand combat stance, aiming a weapon. FLASHFLASH. Yellow-white flashes strobed from Spot's gun, and a second sledgehammer slammed his chest. Pike staggered and fired—BABOOM. Spot twirled across the landing like a dancer, and slid down the wall. Pike sank to a knee, and then to a hand. His eyes watered. He could not breathe. The tone roared.

Go.

Move.

Get her.

Pike forced himself up, and took a position in Isabel's door. He fed the Python a speedloader, and watched for pop-up gunmen. His arms felt leaden. Breathing hurt. He thought he might be bleeding to death, but he didn't have time to die. Pike strained to hear if others were coming, but heard only the tone.

Clear the area.

Get her to safety.

Move.

Pike shouted over his shoulder, hoping she heard.

"Stay down. *Lie flat on the floor.*"

His voice sounded hollow, as if a desert wind had stolen his voice.

Pike moved down the hall. He cleared each room in turn, finding sleeping bags and personal gear, but no gunmen. He finished in seconds, and fell back, gun up and ready. Pike quickly searched the dead men, and snapped photos of each. He took their wallets and phones, and checked their weapons. A .40 and a 10. Spot's pistol was the 10. Pike left their guns, and hurried to Isabel.

"I'm here."

Isabel twisted, trying to roll toward him.

Pike knelt beside her and pulled the nylon sack from her head. Her lips moved, but her voice was a mumble.

Pike shook his head, and touched his ear.

"Can't hear. Be my ears. Listen. Is someone coming?"

Isabel listened, and shook her head.

"I don't think so. I don't hear anyone."

Pike clipped the ties from her wrists and peeled off the tape. He dumped the phones and wallets into the nylon sack.

"We have to leave. Can you stand?"

Isabel stood without help. Her skin was pasty. Bruises and pink blotches marred her arms and shoulders. Pike stripped off his sweatshirt, and pulled the wet garment over her head.

She shouted, and pointed to her eyes.

"I need my glasses. I can't see."

"Where?"

"I don't know."

"We have to go."

"*I can't see!*"

Pike got lucky. Her shoes and clothes were missing, but her glasses and wallet and phone were in the next room. Pike gave her the glasses, and led her into the hall. Isabel stepped over the blood.

Pike went down the grand staircase first, and cleared the entry before letting her follow. Sharp rakes of pain stitched his chest with each step.

Pike wanted the boxes and bags Boris and Spot had taken from Isabel's home, but Hicks was missing, and others like Boris and Spot could arrive.

Pike opened the entry door, took Isabel's hand, and hurried into the rain.

PART FIVE

LEOPARDS

36.

Joe Pike

Pike swerved across traffic at the base of the hill and stopped on a cross street three blocks away. Saw-toothed pain stitched his chest when he jammed the brakes. Isabel didn't expect them to stop, and frantically looked around.

"Did they follow us? Is it them?"

Pike stripped off the vest, and ran his hands over his belly and sides. Isabel realized he was checking for blood, and grew even more frightened.

"OhmiGod, are you shot? Did they shoot you?"

"Not today. I'm good."

The polyethylene layers had stopped the 10-millimeter bullets cold, but each bullet carried seven hundred foot-pounds of energy. The vest had been designed to minimize blunt force trauma by dispersing the energy, but a large purple bruise was spreading across his chest. Pike figured two ribs were cracked, and maybe his sternum. He settled back, and studied her.

"How about you?"

Isabel seemed unable to answer. Her breathing was shallow and fast. Her eyes seemed unnaturally wide, and frantic thoughts played in their shadows. Rain danced like jewels on the windshield as the wipers arced back and forth. Shhchoonk, shhchoonk, shhchoonk. Pike made his voice gentle.

"We can go to a hospital. See a doctor."

She turned away. Numb. Shhchoonk-shhchoonk.

"I don't need a doctor."

"A woman doctor. For evidence."

"I wasn't raped."

She turned back, and searched his face.

"I never believed in angels. Maybe they're real."

She gazed out the window again.

Pike found the mug shots of Hicks, and held out his phone.

"Was he involved?"

Her eyes widened again.

"OhmiGod. Yes."

"Nathan Hicks. Why did he take you?"

"He's crazy. He thinks I'm some girl from Texas."

There it was. They blindsided her with her parents' past, and left her upended.

"He's a thief. Runs crews, mostly. Big jobs, like warehouses and armored cars. Cash depots."

"He said all this crazy stuff about my parents. Crazy. I tried to tell him, but I was so scared."

Isabel had been through a terrible experience. She was confused, shaken, and deserved time to make sense of what happened, but he needed to know what she learned. Pike put away his phone, and tried to be gentle.

"Crazy stuff about your mother?"

She glanced away, nervous, as if some of the crazy stuff had rung true.

"My parents weren't from Texas. I've never been to Texas. It's all a mistake."

"Hicks wasn't here. Do you know where he went?"

"No. How could I know?"

"Overheard, maybe."

"No, I—"

She shook her head. Struggling.

"Hicks is based here in L.A. He's local, so someone back east probably hired him. Maybe you heard something."

"Back east? No. Why would—?"

"This is happening for a reason."

"Yeah. They're stupid, and they made a stupid mistake. They think I'm somebody else."

Pike found the picture Cole sent of her mother, and held out his phone. Isabel went very still, and seemed even younger and more fragile.

"She's so young."

"High school. My partner found it. Elvis. He's been helping me look for you."

Isabel stared at the picture.

"I've never seen this."

"Her name wasn't Debra Sue then. It was DeeAnn Ryan."

Isabel stiffened, and her eyes flashed.

"Then she isn't my mother. Your friend doesn't know what he's talking about."

"I'm sorry we have to talk about these things. I wish we didn't."

"Then stop. Shut up. This is stupid."

"Your parents were in the government's witness protection program."

"Shut. Up."

"Your mother helped put bad people away, and now they've come for their pound of flesh."

"Do I look like I have nineteen million dollars? I can't even pay for new sprinklers."

She sat perched on the far side of the Jeep, gasping.

Pike said, "Nineteen million dollars."

"He said my mother took nineteen million dollars. They want it back."

Pike stared at Isabel in the darkness and heard the wipers.

Shhchoonk-shhchoonk-shhchoonk.

Karbo and Bender. Hicks and his crew. So many people after Isabel, and now it made sense. They didn't come for vengeance. They were taking a score.

"Hicks believes you have nineteen million dollars."

"Isn't that stupid? My *mother*?"

Pike's phone buzzed with an incoming call. He would have ignored it, but saw it was Elvis. He answered.

"She's safe. She's with me now."

Isabel said, "Who is it?"

Pike raised a finger, asking her to be silent.

Cole said, "Can you talk?"

"No."

"The marshals just cut me free. We need to talk."

"Can't go home. Your place is out. We need somewhere safe."

Cole thought for a moment.

"Peter's?"

"Works."

"I'll set it up."

Isabel was waiting when Pike lowered the phone.

"We should call the police. Those men are dead. It looks like we're guilty."

Pike held out his hand.

"Take my hand."

"Why?"

"Please."

She took his hand.

"Squeeze. Hold tight."

She squeezed.

"I shot two men. Three men are dead. If we go to the law, the police will put me in jail while they investigate."

"But those men kidnapped me. You saved me."

Pike squeezed back, not hard, but firm. An anchor.

"Hicks is still free. Whoever sent him is free. They still want their money."

"But I don't have their money."

"Here, with you, I can protect you. I can't protect you from a cell. Do you understand?"

She nodded and let go of his hand.

Pike started the engine, and headed for the freeway.

Isabel stared out the window for a while, but finally turned back to him.

"Who's Peter?"

"A friend. He has a place we can use."

"Where?"

"Malibu. You'll meet Elvis. He can fill you in about your parents."

She crossed her arms, and gazed out the window.

"No one needs to fill me in."

They rode in silence to the end of the block.

"I need clothes. I need clothes, and toiletries, and my things. Can we swing past my house?"

"Your house is the first place they'll look."

"They're dead."

"Not all of them."

Pike glanced over.

"Peter's place is set up for guests. There'll be clothes. Toiletries. Things."

Isabel suddenly faced him, her eyes bright with a frantic energy.

"We have to get my car! I know where they left it! I want to get my car."

"It's not at your home."

"I know. It's like two blocks away. I ran out to my car. I got in, and this guy must've been hiding. He just jumped in and pushed me aside, and drove me around the corner. The other man was waiting. They put me in their car, and they must've left mine. I know right where it is."

Pike wanted to get the Jeep off the street. A neighbor might have clocked his tag. He might have been captured by a security camera.

"We don't have a key."

"They probably left the key. And if they didn't, I have a spare at home. In the kitchen."

"Home isn't safe."

She leaned close again, and gripped his arm.

"This was my mom's car. She gave it to me, and I can't just leave it sitting there. I'm sure they didn't lock it. They probably left the key in the ignition. Someone might steal it."

Isabel tugged.

"C'mon. It isn't far out of the way. I know right where it is. Two blocks over and around the corner."

She gripped him with both hands.

"*Please.*"

Pike doubted her car remained. The pale man ran a tight, professional operation, and professionals would have disposed of her vehicle. Pike decided to let her see for herself.

"If the key is missing, we're not going home for the spare. Agreed?"

"Yes."

"If the key is with the vehicle, we'll secure your car, lock it, and leave it. We won't drive it home. Agreed?"

"It's only two blocks."

"No driving. Moving your car keeps us in the area too long."

"Two blocks?"

"The police might have my tag. If they do, we're vulnerable until we're off the street."

"I guess."

"We'll secure your vehicle, leave it in place, and go. Agree?"

She grudgingly nodded.

Pike turned away from the freeway, and headed toward her home. Isabel said nothing more, and neither did he. The windshield wipers were soothing. Shhchoonk, shhchoonk, shhchoonk.

Eight minutes later, she peered ahead through the rainy windshield. Shhchoonk.

"Here comes my street. Go past. Not the next street, but the one after. Slow down. I'll show you."

Pike knew where to turn, but said nothing.

"The next one. Coming up. Here. Turn here."

Pike turned, and eased up an obsidian neighborhood street exactly like Isabel's street. Small homes, trees, and residents' cars snugged at the curbs.

Isabel peered into the watery dark.

"On the right. About halfway up."

She rolled down the passenger window.

"The other man was waiting. It's right up here."

Pike touched the brake.

Shhchoonk, shhchoonk.

The Jeep crept to a stop.

Pike saw no aging Ford sedans. He sat with his hands on the wheel, and waited.

Isabel stuck her head out the window. She studied

the parked cars ahead, and turned to see the cars they had passed.

"It was here. This is where we got out."

Rain slapped her head.

"He pulled me out, and dragged me to their car. They put a bag over my head, and held me down."

Her voice grew louder, and brittle with anger.

"It was here. My mother's car. It was *right HERE*."

She shouted.

"My mother gave me that car. My mom."

She turned to Pike with wild, glaring eyes. Wet hair hung across her face like scars.

"They stole it! They stole her car, and I want it back!"

She convulsed with a terrible sob.

"Where is it? Where's her car? They stole it!"

Isabel gasped as if she were drowning. She covered her face with her hands, and sobbed, and the sobbing continued.

Pike placed his palm gently on her back. He would have said something if he knew what to say, but he didn't. He pictured Hicks, and Karbo and Bender. He pictured the men he had killed. Pike wished he had killed them sooner.

They had stolen more than her mother's car.

37.

They followed Sunset Boulevard through the Palisades on a winding downhill slide to the sea. The rain slowed to a dying drizzle. Pike turned west on the Pacific Coast Highway, and followed the black edge of the ocean. Isabel stared out the window, watching darkness roll past. A mile beyond Tuna Canyon, Pike turned through a private gate, and arrived at a featureless concrete monolith.

With no windows or glass, and side gates blocking access and views past the front, the structure presented an unknowable face, ensuring the occupants' privacy. A steel door offset to the side was the lone point of entry. Cole's Corvette sat by the door.

Isabel said, "Whose car, the detective?"

"The detective."

"This is so messed up."

Pike showed her through the door into a long slate hall. Framed one-sheet movie posters hung along one wall, opposite doors to a powder room and a very large screening room. Isabel eyed the posters as they passed, but Pike didn't slow. At the end of the hall, they turned past a floating staircase, and Isabel gasped.

A single, cavernous room spanned the width and length of the house, stretching from the hall to a twelve-foot wall of glass overlooking the beach. An ultramodern European kitchen segued to a formal dining area featuring an anthracite table with sixteen zebra-skin seats. The dining space dissolved into a lounge area designed around a twelve-foot circular fireplace and an art deco mahogany bar. Custom-made, oversized couches and chairs divided their attention between the fireplace and a 100-inch flat screen set up for video games. A championship pool table anchored the far end of the room, beyond two vintage Triumph motorcycles, three Stern pinball machines, a vintage Wurlitzer jukebox, and two foosball tables, all of which suggested a rich boy's frat house reimagined by an Oscar-winning set designer with an unlimited budget. Which was how the owner described it.

Isabel said, "Oh. My. God."

Elvis Cole said, "Not really, but we're often confused."

Pike dropped the sack of phones and his go-bag on the anthracite table, and set his pistol beside it.

"This is Elvis. Elvis, Isabel."

Cole came from the kitchen and joined them.

"I picked up takeout. Thai. If you'd rather something else, the kitchen is stocked."

Cole offered his hand.

"Hi, Isabel. I'm sorry this is happening."

Isabel turned away, and went to the bar.

"That isn't a picture of my mother."

A one-sheet from a film called *Chainsaw* and another from a film called *Hard Point* hung behind the bar. She studied the one-sheets as if nothing else mattered.

Cole glanced at Pike, and arched his eyebrows.

Pike said, "She didn't know."

Isabel tossed a response over her shoulder.

"There's nothing to know. We should call the police. Detective DeLako was nice."

Cole edged closer and lowered his voice.

"Is she wearing your sweatshirt?"

Pike upended the sack. Wallets and phones clattered onto the table.

"It was bad. Three down."

Pike flipped through the wallets, and passed them to Cole. A California driver's license issued to an Edward Francis Healey showed a photo of Boris. Spot had carried a New Mexico DL as Walter Hartwell from Albuquerque. Both wallets were fat with cash, but neither contained credit cards, membership or discount cards, or photographs.

"What about Hicks?"

"Hicks wasn't there. These two and a third, but not Hicks."

Cole lowered his voice even more.

"Can you be tied to the scene?"

"Maybe. Isabel for sure."

Isabel heard, and turned.

"Why me?"

"They took something from your home. Looked like suitcases and bags. That's how I found you. I followed them."

Isabel returned from the bar.

"What did they take?"

"I don't know. It's in their car."

Cole was staring. He touched Pike's shoulder.

"Look at me."

Pike looked.

Cole leaned closer, and touched his own cheek.

"Get your face. Blood."

Pike checked the backs of his hands and his forearms. Specks. Blood splatter from the gunfight.

Pike turned to Isabel.

"We have a lot to do. Would you like to wash up first, or eat?"

"I hope you don't think they found money. If there was money in my house, I would know, and there isn't. I've lived there since I was born. I don't know what they're talking about."

Cole glanced from Isabel to Pike.

"What money are we talking about?"

"They think she has nineteen million dollars. They didn't come for payback. They said her mother took it."

Cole smiled, like maybe they were pulling his leg.

"No way."

Isabel rolled her eyes.

"They have my mother confused with someone else. I'm telling you. This is so *stupid*."

Pike wanted to touch her, but didn't. He struggled to imagine a word of comfort, but no ready word appeared.

He said, "Gotta be tough."

Isabel rolled her eyes.

Cole walked back to the kitchen, and returned with a stapled sheaf of pages.

"I thought you might want to see this."

He offered the pages, but Isabel didn't take them.

"Your mom helped a lot of people. She didn't have to, but she did. It took a lot of guts."

Isabel stepped back.

"I know you mean well, but this person wasn't my mother."

"You don't have to read it, up to you, but I found her high school alumni association online, too. And her yearbook picture. It's all in here."

Isabel glowered at Pike, anxious and irritated.

"I've seen the picture. Yes, there's a resemblance, but what's the word? There's a word when two people look alike. Not a clone."

Cole kept going. His voice was soothing, and his eyes were kind. Pike was glad Cole was here. Cole always knew what to say.

"I found your dad's picture, too. Wasn't looking for it, but there it was."

"Doppelganger! That's it. A person who looks so much like you they could be your twin, but isn't. Yes, she kinda looks like my mom, maybe, if you reach for it, but that's all it is. Two people who look alike. A co-incidence."

Cole turned to a particular page, and held out the sheet to show her.

"And this handsome young dude is your dad. They were classmates."

Isabel stared at her father's photograph.

Cole said it again.

"They were classmates. Same school. Back in Texas. A long time ago."

Isabel stood absolutely still. She stared at her father's old photograph. Pike watched her eyes, and knew she was seeing more than the image on the page.

Cole folded the pages together, and set the pages on the table.

"This sucks. I know it sucks. I'm sorry."

Isabel swayed. She stared into space, where the pages had been.

Pike picked up the pages.

"C'mon. The shirt's wet. Let's find something dry."

"I don't have clothes."

"We'll find something. C'mon."

She looked down at herself, and saw the stains on his sweatshirt.

"Is this blood?"

Pike touched her arm.

"You can shower. Get clean. I'll show you."

He guided her toward the stairs.

38.

The upper floor held four immaculate bedrooms, each with an en suite bath. Pike showed Isabel to the master. It was the largest. The bathroom was stocked with toiletries and towels, and the closets contained new, unused robes, beach clothes, sandals, and swimsuits. Everything a drop-in guest might need.

Pike said, "Here. Robes. Shirts and shorts. Things. Use whatever you like."

Isabel stared at the closet like a zombie.

"I don't have their money."

"I know."

"My parents worked. You've seen our house."

She turned from the closet as if she were numb.

"They said they'd kill me. If I don't give them the money, they'll kill me, and I don't know what they're talking about."

Pike set the articles about her mother onto the bed. Isabel had been kidnapped twice, threatened by people she didn't know about things she didn't believe, and felt as if her fate rested with others. It was the same way with young troops in a battle space. She needed to feel as if she had some say in the outcome.

Pike said, "Do you trust me?"

"Of course I trust you. What kind of question is that?"

"I need your help."

"I don't know what they're talking about."

"You were with them. They talked. You heard. Something you know might help."

"Like what?"

"Names, locations, intentions. Like that."

"I didn't hear anything."

"How many people are we dealing with?"

"I don't know. A lot."

"Count faces. Like this—Karbo and Bender. That's two. Hicks is three. The three tonight. Six. Anyone else?"

Pike could tell she was trying, but he pressed ahead. The more answers she found, the more control she would feel.

"Is Hicks the boss?"

"I don't know. I think so."

"Did he tell the others what to do?"

"Uh-huh. Yes."

"Then he's the boss. Question is, does someone tell Hicks what to do?"

Isabel brightened, as if the teacher had asked a question she could answer.

"Yes! He definitely has a boss. I heard them."

"Hicks and his boss?"

Isabel scrunched her face, working her memory.

"No. Hicks and one of the others. I heard them through the vent when I was alone."

"Okay. What did you hear?"

"Something about not getting paid. He was mad. I thought they were talking about me, but they weren't."

"Complaining about their boss?"

"Hicks was. Something like, he shouldn't have taken the job, the guy didn't listen, he was nuts, like that. He was definitely talking about someone they work for."

She made a halfhearted shrug.

"I didn't get a name."

"Good start. This helps. Anything you remember will help."

Isabel adjusted her glasses, and glanced away.

"He asked about you."

"By name?"

Isabel glanced away again.

"He saw you save me. At the bank. He thinks you're my bodyguard."

Karbo had looked at someone in the crowd. Pike remembered a feeling of danger.

"What did you tell him?"

"The truth. You were a customer. You'd just left the bank, and happened to be outside. He didn't believe me."

"Want some good news?"

"I could use some."

"You're here. You're safe. What he believes doesn't matter."

Isabel didn't look encouraged.

"No. Not now."

"Shower. Take your time. When you're ready, come get some dinner."

Isabel made a queasy face.

"Can I call Carly? She's gotta be frantic."

"We'll call her together."

Pike left her, but didn't go down. He entered the bedroom next to the stairs, and went into the bathroom. He took off his shades and looked in the mirror. Speckles dotted the side of his face. Thin brown streaks striped his nose and forehead, matching the marks on his arms. Taking off the T-shirt hurt. A bulging hematoma had grown at the bottom of the bruise. He took out his folding knife, wadded a handful of toilet paper, and made a small cut at the base of the bulge. When the blood finished draining, he flushed the paper, rinsed the sink, and washed his arms and face and chest with soap. He needed a shower, but the shower could wait. He put on his glasses, pressed more toilet paper to the cut, and went down.

Cole was looking through the wallets at the long table. He glanced up when Pike came down, and followed him to the kitchen.

"She okay?"

"Dealing."

Pike drank a glass of tap water, then cracked a tray of ice into a Ziploc bag. He pressed the bag to the bruise. Cole found two bottles of Victoria beer in the fridge, and offered a bottle to Pike. The cold Mexican beer had a crisp, bitter taste Pike enjoyed. He took a black T-shirt from the go-bag, and paused to figure out the least painful way to put it on. Cole took the shirt without asking, pulled it over Pike's head, and held it so Pike could wiggle his arms through the holes.

Cole glanced at the stairs and lowered his voice.

"Close call, brother. What tagged you, a .45?"

"A 10. Twice, chest and back."

Cole made a soft hiss.

"Damned close. What happened?"

Pike described Boris and Spot, and the shirtless man, and the empty Los Feliz mansion. He recited the address from memory, the listing broker, and the tag number from Boris's vehicle. Cole copied the numbers into a pad, tucked the pad into a pocket, and glanced at the recovered phones.

"High-quality burners. They're locked. The DLs—"

Cole flashed the DLs, and pocketed them with the pad.

"If they're fake, they're excellent. I'll check on the house, but the owner and agent probably didn't know it was being used."

Cole took a small gray box from his pocket, and set it on the counter. Pike had seen similar boxes many times.

"A location transmitter?"

"A gift from the marshals. Found it on my car when they cut me loose."

Cole dropped the box in the trash.

"I killed it."

"Gregg thought you'd lead them to me?"

"Yeah. Braun and DeLako were with him. They know you're hunting for Isabel."

Cole told him how the marshals tried to follow him, and what happened at Hollywood Station.

"Braun was clear. They don't believe you killed Kemp, or had anything to do with it, or anything to do with Isabel's disappearance. They want the people who murdered Kemp. They're thinking you know."

"Hicks is running the crew, but he's hired help."

Cole raised his eyebrows.

"Does Isabel know who sent him?"

"No. But Hicks said her mother stole the money from someone she worked for, and he wants it back."

"The person she stole from wants it back?"

"Yes."

Cole shook his head.

"They're dead. Two guys owned the company her mother worked for. Both were indicted, and both were convicted. And both of them died in prison. Murdered."

Pike made a grunt.

"Looks like they had a silent partner."

"I didn't see anything about missing money in the coverage. No accusations, no complaints, nothing."

Cole shot another glance at the stairs, and lowered his voice even more.

"Think her mother really stole nineteen million dollars?"

Pike shrugged, and a flash of pain spiked his ribs. He adjusted the ice.

"Doesn't matter, did or didn't."

"The dudes in Los Feliz believe she took it."

"Not anymore. Dead men have no beliefs."

"True. But Hicks isn't dead. What do you think he'll do?"

"Only two options. Cut and run, or take a Hail Mary shot at finding her."

Pike checked the time. Seventy-four minutes had passed since they left Los Feliz.

"The police will be all over his house. The streets will be blocked. Hicks will know he's lost her again, but he won't know what happened, or where she is, or even if she's alive or dead."

"Or whether she's picking his face from an LAPD six-pack. Personally, I'd cut and run."

Pike had pondered how Hicks would react.

"Not this guy. He answers to someone. He takes risks, and he'll go for the long shot. He'll try to find her."

Cole said, "Her home."

"Yeah."

The only possible place Hicks could hope to find Isabel was at her home.

Cole glanced at the stairs again, and turned to leave.

"I'll go watch her house."

"I'll make sure she's okay, and I'll be along."

A fist bump, and Cole left.

Pike took a fresh Victoria from the fridge, and added ice to the Ziploc bag. The Thai food smelled good. Red curry vegetables with crispy tofu. Pineapple fried rice. Pike ate standing at the sink, holding the ice to his chest.

When he finished, he put the leftovers in the fridge, and took the beer out onto the deck. The heavy glass doors opened easily.

Outside, the rolling crash of the surf was loud. The low overcast, a deep charcoal gray, gravid with moisture, hid the stars and moon, and their light. The beach and the ocean were invisible. Pike took off his shades, but the dark gave no ground.

The owner had installed spotlights to illuminate the beach, but Pike did not turn them on. He held the ice to his chest, sipped the beer, and stared at an ocean he could not see.

39.

Pike left the deck and heard water running upstairs. He decided Izzy was taking a shower, so he went out to his Jeep for the vest. He brought the vest inside to the big table, and dug out the slugs. Prying the bullets from the polylaminate was a beast. The 10-millimeter jacketed hollow-point bullets had mushroomed into disks the size of a quarter. Pike guessed their weight at about two hundred grains. Most 10-mil hollow points weighed in between one fifty and one eighty, so these were heavy. Pike rolled the disks in his fingers, and called John Chen.

Chen's phone rang. By the fourth ring Pike expected his voice mail, but the ringing continued. Chen finally answered on the tenth ring. He sounded lethargic.

"Hullo."

"John, Joe Pike."

"Did you find her?"

"Yes. She's safe. She's here with me now."

Chen hissed a soft sigh, like a deflating balloon.

"That's really good news. So good. I'm glad."

"Can you talk?"

"No reason I can't."

"Three men were shot tonight in the Los Feliz hills. A ten-millimeter pistol will be found with the bodies."

Chen made the sigh again, but said nothing.

"Two weeks ago, a U.S. Marshal named Kemp was killed with a ten up in Palmdale. The ten in Los Feliz is the murder weapon."

"Okay."

Pike barely heard his response.

"John?"

"Yeah?"

"The Los Feliz gun will give you Kemp's killer. He works for Hicks. You can tie Kemp's murder with the people who kidnapped Isabel. They're the same."

Chen said, "Hicks. That's something."

"The same ten killed Karbo, so this gives you the button on Karbo's murder. Run the prints from Los Feliz, you'll name the shooter. The marshals want his name. You can give it to them, and Hicks, and all of it."

"I'm sorry, Joe. I can't."

Chen's voice was so sad he seemed to be melting away.

"What's wrong?"

Chen did not respond.

"John? What is it?"

"Harriet and her spies. They followed me to the impound yard. She fired me."

"Because you helped me?"

"I didn't tell them about you. I wouldn't rat you out. Not you or Elvis. Not ever."

"Tell them."

"And feel even worse about myself? Not in this life."

Chen hung up.

Pike started to call him back, but didn't. Isabel came down the stairs. She stopped when she saw him.

"What's wrong?"

Pike tossed his phone on the table.

"I'm good."

"You don't look good. You look pissed off."

She was wearing a white terry cloth robe and fluffy white slippers. Her hair was damp, and slicked behind her ears. Pike stood. He wanted to catch up with Elvis, but not until he was sure Izzy could stay by herself.

"Hungry?"

"I'd rather call Carly. She's gotta be frantic."

"Sure. May I speak with her first?"

Isabel looked surprised, and made a sloppy smile.

"Fine by me. You crushing on my bestie?"

"Ground rules. No one can know where we are until this is over. Don't mention Los Feliz, or what happened. After, tell her whatever you want, but for now, she'll only be scared. Make sense?"

Isabel nodded.

Her phone was on the table with the others. Pike handed it to her.

"Dial, and let me speak first."

Izzy thumbed in the number and gave Pike the phone.

Carly answered on the first ring, screaming.

"IZZZYYYY!!"

"Not Izzy. It's Pike."

"Hey. Why is this you?"

"She's safe. She's with me. I'll put her on."

"Oh, thank God! Thankyouthankyouthankyou. OhmiGod."

"Carly? She'll be off the grid for a couple of days. Don't tell anyone we called."

"Can't I tell Joyce?"

"Who's Joyce?"

Isabel said, "Joyce is her mom."

Carly shouted, "I HEAR YOU!"

Isabel shouted back, gleeful.

"I HEAR YOU, TOOOOO!"

Pike was wishing he hadn't agreed to the call. He offered the phone to Isabel, but held it a moment longer.

"Don't tell her where we are, or what happened, or what we're doing. You can tell her everything later, but not now. Copy?"

"Copy!"

Isabel grabbed the phone.

Pike was pleased. They chattered and giggled, but Isabel kept it simple. She told Carly she was fine, and safe, and promised to tell her everything soon. She didn't want Carly to worry, and Joe was taking good care of her. The call ended quickly, and left Izzy beaming.

"I love that girl. Joyce is like my second mom."

She put down the phone and the beaming stopped. She adjusted her glasses.

"I remembered two more."

"This makes eight."

"A second man was waiting around the corner last night. I told you, remember?"

"I remember."

"He was blond. A real thin face. I only saw him once."

"And the other?"

"In Los Feliz. He was younger than the others, maybe the youngest. Kinda big, and creepy. His voice was weird. Like a whisper, but not on purpose."

Five down out of eight. Hicks had two soldiers left.

"He kept showing me a knife. He would show me the knife, and whisper, but I couldn't understand what he said."

"He the one bruised your arms?"

"Uh-uh, no. Hicks. Hicks kept shaking me."

She suddenly turned and went to the bar. She pointed at the one-sheets.

"Your friend, Peter, is he in movies?"

"He makes movies."

"Peter Alan Nelsen? The director?"

Pike nodded. He wanted to go watch her house with Elvis, but she needed to talk.

She dropped into an oversized leather lounge chair and pulled up her legs.

"I thought so. His name is on the posters. How do you know him?"

"He needed help. Elvis and I helped. After, we got to be friends."

She sprawled back, and let her arms and legs starfish off the chair.

"If I had that money, I'd live in a house like this, here on the beach. I wouldn't live in a tiny house with bad sprinklers."

"I believe you."

She pushed up from the chair and returned to the bar.

"I don't know what to believe."

"You do."

Isabel scowled.

"Excuse me? My mother and father had a life I knew nothing about. I might have relatives. Aunts and uncles and cousins. They told me my grandparents died before I was born. Did they? Are my grandparents still alive?"

"Find out."

"Oh. Sure. Knock knock knock, hi, I'm the witness's daughter."

She veered away from the bar and slalomed between the foosball machines.

"I don't want another family. I don't want to be the witness's daughter. I like being me."

Pike wished Cole were here.

"You haven't changed. You're you."

Isabel made a frustrated *grr*.

"I'm not! They lied, and lies aren't real. Don't you get it? Everything I thought I knew about myself is a lie, so I'm a lie."

Isabel looked younger than her twenty-two years, and now, resentful and frightened, she could have passed for a child. Pike had kept his life simple. Simple was good. Simplicity brought order and peace.

"Did you love them?"

Isabel rolled her eyes.

"What kind of question is that?"

"Were they good to you?"

This time she didn't respond.

Pike lifted the vest. Once the panels were split, they were no longer guaranteed to stop a bullet. He strapped it on anyway.

"I joined the Marines when I was seventeen. That age, a parent has to sign. My mother was scared, so I made my father. I told him I'd kill him if he didn't sign the permission."

Isabel stared, and narrowed her eyes.

"No way. Did you really?"

Pike slipped the Python into its holster, and clipped the holster onto his hip.

"I threatened to beat him to death. I would have."

"You actually threatened to kill your father."

Pike remembered the day well. They were in the kitchen. Pike and his father. His mother was in the yard, hanging clothes. The old man had just gotten home from work. He poured a triple shot of Old Crow over ice. He was raising it to his lips when Pike stopped him.

Pike said, "Yes."

"You can't be serious. I don't believe you."

Pike cocked his head.

"No?"

Isabel doubled down.

"No."

"What do you remember most about your mother? A special thing. In a word."

Isabel didn't hesitate. She didn't have to think.

"Singing. She sang to me. When I got bigger, we sang together. Around the house, on walks, in the car."

She smiled, enjoying the memory, and repeated the word.

"Singing. I remember her singing."

Pike tried to imagine Isabel and her mother singing. He couldn't quite build the image, but singing was a fine memory.

Isabel said, "Now you."

"My mother?"

"In a word."

Pike didn't have to think, either.

"Bruises."

Isabel's smile collapsed. She shifted uneasily.

"I'm sorry."

Pike shrugged. Those things happened years ago.

"Nobody enters the program for fun. Whatever they told you or didn't, they were hiding from bastards like Hicks. Your folks did a good job."

Isabel stared at him quietly. She adjusted her glasses, glanced away, and wet her lips.

"He asked why I hired a bodyguard."

"Hicks?"

"I told him I didn't. He called me a liar. I told him you weren't. He said you had to be my bodyguard. You sure as hell weren't my boyfriend."

She adjusted her glasses again.

Pike said, "You okay staying alone?"

"I live alone. I'll be fine."

"There's food."

"I'll watch TV."

Pike clipped a speedloader to his waist, and zipped his go-bag.

"You're sure?"

Isabel flushed and made a face.

"This is kinda embarrassing. I *am* an adult."

Pike picked up his keys and readied to leave.

"What he said? Hicks? He's an asshole."

Isabel smiled.

"Thank you."

"I'll stay in touch."

"I wish I could see his face when he realizes I'm gone. He'll be really, really mad."

Pike didn't think Hicks would be angry. Hicks would be scared. He had fallen behind, their roles were reversed, and Pike controlled the battle space. Whoever Hicks worked for would be mad. His boss would be livid.

On the far end of the table, Spot's cell phone began barking. Woof-woof-woof, woof-woof-woof. A ringtone.

Isabel said "OhmiGod! Someone's calling!"

The barking stopped. A few seconds later, the other phone buzzed. Boris's phone had been set to vibrate, and now it buzzed so hard the phone crept across the table.

Zzz-zzz-zzz.

Pike and Isabel went to the table and watched the phone. It reminded him of a fly with a damaged wing, unable to fly, carving a desperate circle as it died.

When the phone stopped buzzing, Pike stowed the phones in his go-bag and left.

40.

Hicks

Hicks headed back to the mansion, pissed off and irritated with the cowboys. The old man was a bugfuck psycho, but the time crunch was real. Hicks had sent Ronson and Stanley to search the girl's home. They should have finished while he was with Riley, but neither had called. Hicks dialed Stanley to raise hell. He got Stanley's voice mail.

Hicks immediately called Ronson.

Another recording.

Hicks's irritation flashed into worry. Stanley and Ronson were pros. Hicks had taken five scores with Stanley and eight with Ronson. They would have answered.

Hicks had left a dude named Wallick to stay with the girl. He phoned Wallick next, hoping he'd heard something.

Voice mail.

Hicks angrily slapped the dash.

"Does *everyone* suck?"

If those guys were outside smoking dope again, he was gonna shoot someone.

Six minutes later and totally pissed, Hicks turned uphill toward their house, and saw a helicopter circle the ridge. Its searchlight flashed like a lightsaber, probing the houses below.

Hicks slowed to a stop. He watched the chopper, and felt queasy. Horns blew behind him, pissed-off neighborhood chumps anxious to get home. Hicks pulled to the side, and watched the circling bird. LAPD Air Support. He couldn't tell whether the chopper was over their house or two ridges away.

Hicks wiggled out of his jacket, stripped off his holster, and pushed the gun under his seat. He stuffed his jacket under next to prevent the gun from sliding out, and joined the cars heading home.

Two black-and-whites were pulled to the side around the next curve. They weren't stopping cars, so Hicks and the locals continued. The helicopter disappeared, but appeared again as he wound higher. Each time it reappeared, the helicopter seemed larger.

Brake lights ahead finally flared, and the free pass was over. A police car blocked the street, and the cars ahead lined up to speak with the waiting officers.

Hicks joined the line, and waited his turn.

An occasional car was allowed to proceed, but most were diverted onto a connecting street, or forced to turn around.

Hicks tried Ronson and Stanley again. Nothing. He tried Wallick. Nothing. Hicks was scared.

The last two members of his crew were Stegner and Blanch. Neither man had been at the house when he left. He tried Stegner first.

Answer.

"Yo. S'up?"

"Where are you?"

"Scarfing chicken. I'm at Roscoe's. Want me to—"

Hicks cut him off.

"Have you heard from Ronson or Stanley?"

"No. They looking for me?"

"What about Wallick?"

"Uh-uh. What's up? Is something wrong?"

"Stay away from the house."

"What's—"

"Stay away."

Hicks reached the roadblock, and put away his phone. A K-9 officer readied her dog farther up the street. The dog meant a suspect had been cornered, or was believed to be in the area.

Hicks rolled down his window as the roadblock cop approached. Buff dude in his thirties, tight hair, calm eyes. The whump-whump of the helicopter was loud. The searchlight flashed beyond the ridge, and the helicopter circled away.

Hicks said, "Hey, Officer. What's going on?"

"Someone heard shots, so we're checking it out. Sorry about the roadblock."

"Shots? Holy crap. Where?"

The cop ignored his question.

"I know it's a pain, but we can't let anyone through until we know it's safe. You a resident?"

Hicks knew better than to lie. If he claimed to be a resident, the cop might ask to see proof.

"I'm picking up my girlfriend. On Glendower. Can I get up there?"

The street they were on led to Glendower, but Glendower was beyond the mansion. Hicks had studied the area. He knew every possible route up to and away from the mansion, and could draw a map of the neighborhood from memory.

The officer waited for the helicopter to pass before he answered.

"Not from here you can't. No promises, but you might be able to reach it if you come up over by the Greek."

The Greek Theatre was a popular music venue in a canyon to their east.

Hicks didn't move.

"The shooting. Was it up by her?"

"We're still securing the area."

The cop stepped away, and motioned toward the detour.

"Give her a call. I'm sure she's fine."

Hicks didn't argue or waste more time. He wanted to punch the gas and scream down the hill, but turned as the officer directed and followed the detour. Then he turned uphill again, and followed the map in his head to the end of a cul-de-sac.

Hicks knew of five locations from which he could see the mansion and its immediate neighbors. He had sought out and used these locations to assess the home's suitability. Now, what he saw left him feeling sick.

Hicks climbed out of his car, and stood in the center of the cul-de-sac. The air was chill, but he didn't notice.

The cul-de-sac offered an unobstructed view of the rear of their house. The arched windows and glass doors were bright, and cops moved past the windows. The helicopter circled above, sweeping the pool and the deck and the neighboring homes with the light of ten million suns. A Medical Examiner's van passed on a lower street, on its way to the scene.

Hicks watched the officers moving through the house, and felt as if he were floating. His hands and face felt numb.

He took out his phone, and called Ronson.

Voice mail.

He called Stanley and Wallick.

Voice mail.

If they were alive, they would have answered. If they escaped, they would have called.

Hicks stood in the middle of the street, watching the helicopter.

Whump-whump-whump.

He climbed into his car, locked the doors, and sat with his hands in his lap. His crew had been arrested, or they were dead. Either way, it was over. Done. Maybe the girl got hold of a phone and called the cops. Done.

Maybe she grabbed a pistol. Done. Maybe a neighbor got nosy. Done.

Hicks closed his eyes.

Taking scores safely required information, so Hicks had developed sources in useful positions. He took a breath, loosened his hands, and called a freelance video stringer named Lex Ramos.

"Lex, Jack Tully, how're you doing?"

Tully being one of his seven aliases.

Ramos spent most of his time glued to police and EMS scanners, listening for newsworthy accidents and mayhem he could sell to local news outlets.

"Jack T, mah man, what up?"

Ramos sounded like he'd had a few.

"Got a problem, brother. A personal thing."

"I'll do my best. How can I help?"

"My girlfriend is freaking out. The cops are all over her neighborhood. Choppers, dogs, the works. Streets are blocked, no one can get up there, and they won't tell her what's going on. She's scared, man. Thought she heard gunshots. Can you find out what's goin' on?"

"This is happening now?"

"As we speak. I'm surprised it's not all over your scanners. The police are everywhere."

This was the bait. Being a freelance stringer, Ramos sold footage only if he beat local news teams to a scene.

Ramos said, "What's her location?"

"Los Feliz. North of the boulevard, just west of Vermont. Up in the hills."

"Yeah, okay. That'll be Northeast Station. I'll call you right back."

LAPD split Los Feliz into east-west service areas. Hollywood Station handled the western end. Northeast Station handled the rest. Ramos would call a contact at the Northeast Station.

Hicks quickly called Stegner.

Stegner answered instantly, his voice low.

"What's going on?"

Hicks spoke firmly, trying to hide his fear.

"The house is done. Cops are all over it. Air Support. We're done up here."

Hicks thought he sounded good. Level. Calm.

Stegner wasn't.

"Are you kidding me? What the fuck? What—?"

Hicks shut him down.

"Listen. Are you listening?"

Stegner paused. His voice was so soft when he answered, Hicks barely heard him.

"I'm listening. Where are you?"

"I'm safe. We need to move fast now, so listen. You're gonna have to call Blanch. Tell him everything I'm telling you. Tell him do not come back up here. Do not go back to the house. Okay?"

"What happened?"

"I don't know. Something. I can't reach Ronson, Stanley, or Wallick. I don't know if they're dead, in the can, what. For all I know, the girl is dead. I don't know."

"Why dead? What are you talking about, dead?"

"Listen. Pay attention. Go sit on the girl's house. Watch her house."

"What?"

"Leave now. You gotta get there right away, but be careful. A shitload of cops might drop on her place."

"Watch her house? Are you crazy?"

"Listen. We don't know anything right now. We know nothing."

"We're done, man! This thing is over!"

Stegner was getting loud.

"Calm down."

"Fuck calm."

"Listen to me. Listen."

Hicks waited, but all he heard was heavy breathing and silverware rattling in the background.

"I called a guy. He's gonna find out what happened, and let me know. It shouldn't take long. We just gotta wait."

"Wait my ass. If we wait, all we're waiting for is the cops."

"We don't know what happened."

"The cops happened, man. We're done. It's over."

"Maybe not. If it isn't, we still have a shot."

Stegner sounded whiny.

"How can it not be over?"

"What if she isn't dead? What if, somehow, she escaped? She has nineteen million reasons not to go to the police."

Stegner didn't answer. He was thinking.

Hicks said, "A lot of money is riding on this. If we

lost some guys, heaven forbid, I pray we didn't, but if they're gone, well, our shares are bigger. You want to walk away from money like this? For a couple of hours?"

"Why would she go home?"

"I don't know, Jason. Maybe she won't. Maybe she'll stop by, grab a few things, I don't know. Maybe she needs account numbers or safe-box keys. All I'm saying is, she might. Right now—now—we have to respond as if she's alive. Are you with me?"

Stegner was slow with his answer.

"I guess."

"You know someplace besides her home she'd go?"

"No."

"Me, neither. So watch her house. Keep your eyes open."

"What if the cops have her? Or she's dead?"

"Then it's over and out. We're gone. As soon as I find out, I'll let you know. Okay?"

"I'm not going to sit on her house forever."

"I don't expect you to. If the police show up, get your ass out of there and let me know. If the girl shows up, call. I'm counting on you."

Stegner said, "Mm."

"Call Blanch. Tell him I'll be in touch. I got a job for him, too."

Hicks hung up before Stegner could speak.

Hicks felt better. The first glimmers of a plan were coming together, and the tension faded from his body.

Hicks thought about the girl, and the police across the canyon, and the many different ways the police had come to be there. The odds of her being alive seemed pretty good, and seemed better the more he thought about it. And if she was alive, he had a pretty good idea how to find her.

Hicks was deciding what to tell the cowboy when Ramos called. Three deceased males had been found in a residence. The men had not been identified, and appeared to have died in a gunfight. It was unknown whether additional individuals were involved, but no other persons, living or dead, had been found. Ramos phoned from his car, on his way to the scene.

Hicks hung up with a nervous resolve.

He knew what to tell the cowboy.

Hicks raised his phone again, and called.

Riley answered.

"Yes, Mr. Hicks?"

"We have a problem."

Riley's silence sounded like death.

"Tell me what happened."

"Joe Pike happened. We need to talk."

41.

Riley refused to discuss it on the phone. He told Hicks to meet him outside an all-night café on Hillhurst, not far away. Hicks arrived first, which surprised him, and pulled into a little parking lot next door. He half expected a cowboy to step up and start blasting, so he kept his gun handy, and called Blanch.

"Stegner get you?"

Blanch answered in the creepy hoarse whisper.

"Is it over?"

"So far as I know, she's still alive. She wasn't at the house when the cops arrived."

"Mm."

"Tell Stegner. Tell him to stay on her house."

"Shall I keep him company?"

"No. You'll be with me. First, call the area hospitals. Make up some crap like you heard your sister was shot, and find out if she's been admitted."

"I know what to say."

"I gotta deal with the shitkickers. I'll pick you up when I finish."

"Of course. Where shall I be?"

"Sunset and Fairfax, the southwest corner. There's a big parking lot behind the drugstore."

"I'll be there."

Riley's car pulled up at the curb. Riley saw Hicks, and stared.

Hicks raised a finger, the finger saying hang on. He slipped the pistol into his pocket.

"Now listen, I'm here on Hillhurst to meet Riley—"

Hicks twisted around to see the café's sign, and repeated the name.

"Shouldn't take more than ten minutes. I'll call when I leave. If you don't hear from me, or I don't show up—"

"I understand."

Riley stepped from his car, and approached.

"Gotta go. They're here."

Hicks climbed out to meet him. Two more cowboys appeared, but remained by Riley's car. They were big ol' boys with empty eyes, and stood out among the Hillhurst hipsters like a couple of Brahman bulls.

Riley didn't offer his hand, and neither did Hicks.

Riley said, "We're disappointed."

"I'm disappointed, too. What'd your boss say?"

"I'll tell him when I know how this happened."

Hicks was so angry he wanted to throw fists, but he tried to stay calm.

"Remind the man my advice was to back off, and

approach the girl slowly. But no. We did it his way. Fast and stupid."

Riley's eyes were as flat as two plates.

"What else should I tell him?"

"Tell him I was wrong. She has the money. She's had it all along. I believe we can get it."

"I'm listening."

"The dude who canned Karbo and Bender. Pike."

"The Samaritan."

"According to the police report, he was, yeah. Her customer, they said. Even Karbo and Bender bought it. They were wrong. He wasn't."

"I don't see how this matters."

"I saw him take down Karbo and Bender. The way he hit those guys, he put them down like nothing."

Riley glanced at his men.

"So he's rough. These boys are rough."

"He was at her home this morning. If he was only a bystander, why would he be at her home?"

Riley frowned, but now he seemed curious, so Hicks kept going.

"I made a couple of calls. Pike wasn't just some guy who happened to be there. He's a professional operator."

"An operator. Meaning, what, a commando?"

"A professional soldier, Riley, what they call a private military contractor. The dude is high-end muscle for hire. I think she hired him."

Riley seemed interested for the first time.

"A bodyguard?"

"Yes."

"You're saying she's with him?"

"Riley, listen, I'm talking out my ass, okay? For all I know, she shot my guys, but I think he found her, and busted her out. And I'll tell you something else."

"What?"

"He's after the money. That's why he was at the bank, and why he was at her home. He wants the money."

Riley glanced at his men.

"Do you know where to find him?"

"He lives here. I can find him if I need to, but I think I can find the girl."

Riley glanced at his men again.

"You're down three people. We can help."

"If she's with Pike, I'll take you up on it."

"I'll let my employer know. He'll be upset, but I'll talk to him."

Hicks watched Riley return to his car and the car pull away.

Hicks stood in the parking lot, hand in his pocket, gripping the pistol. He counted to sixty. Young hipster dudes and funky chick poets passed, all staring at their phones. They laughed, and smiled, and even talked to one another, but all of them stared at their phones.

Hicks climbed into his car, and called Blanch.

"On my way. You there?"

"I'm here."

Hicks pulled out of the lot. He felt good. Confident. Hicks was absolutely certain he knew how to find her.

42.

Riley

His employer lived two hours ahead. Riley didn't like disturbing his boss at such a late hour, but the old man was used to it. With business interests stretching across four continents, the old man often took calls at odd hours.

"Pull over up ahead. Anywhere."

The driver, Pitchess Lloyd, guided the big sedan into a gas station and up to the pumps. His other two men, Terrence and Charlie, pulled in behind them. Like Pitch, Terrence and Charlie were security operators in the old man's organization. Pitch swung open his door.

"I'll top her off."

"Grab a candy bar, would you? Whatever they have. I'm starving."

They'd been on their way to dinner when Hicks dropped the bad news.

Pitch said, "You bet. Want a pop?"

"Just the candy. Get something for yourself. Ask the boys."

Pitch hadn't missed any meals. The car swayed when he climbed out.

The old man's phone rang nine times before he answered. The old man had staff to field calls, especially in the middle of the night, but he'd given Riley special access.

His voice sounded phlegmy with sleep.

"Hello? Who is this?"

"Riley. Sorry to wake you, sir."

The old man cleared his throat.

"Let's hear it."

"Ms. Ryan's daughter is gone. Hicks lost her again."

"Meaning what, did he kill her?"

"She isn't dead, so far as we know. She's missing."

"Hang on."

Riley heard shuffling before the old man continued.

"Is Hicks with you?"

"I just left him. He's looking for her."

"How'd he manage to lose her? I thought they had her locked in a house."

"There was a shooting. Hicks was with me when it happened. Three bodies were found, but not the girl. He believes they were his men."

"He doesn't know?"

"He wasn't able to reach the site. What he knows, he learned from a source."

The old man huffed.

"And just like that, she's gone."

"No survivors were found. Only dead males."

The old man was quiet for several seconds.

"I guess she let those boys have it. That would've been something to see, wouldn't it? This little girl cutting them down. That how you see it?"

"An outside player might be involved. The person who interfered with our first attempt."

"Ah."

The *ah* sounded sarcastic and harsh.

"This is how Mr. Hicks explains it?"

"It's possible."

The old man went silent again. Riley didn't know what to say, so he let the silence ride. The old man finally finished thinking and filled the silence himself.

"Twenty-four years, eight months, thirteen days, and some odd hours."

"Sir?"

"That's how long I chased the bitch. Missed her by what, a year?"

"Just about."

DeeAnn Ryan had died eleven months ago. Three weeks later, purely by chance, a drug runner Riley knew from Miami mentioned a rumor he'd heard, that a U.S. Marshal out in the California desert helped hide a witness from the New Way trial. After twenty-four years, eight months, thirteen days, and some odd hours, this was the first real lead the old man had. He told Riley to run with it. They didn't know she was dead. They knew nothing about her until Ted Kemp told them.

The old man said, "Hicks did all right with the marshal. Came through real well, finding that fella and making him talk."

"He did."

"But now, with this girl, I don't know. It's one shot of bad news after another. Makes me wonder what's going on out there."

"He seems to think he can find her."

"Maybe he's thinking about running off with my nineteen million dollars."

"I don't think so, sir. Not Hicks."

The old man laughed.

"He's a thief. Thieves steal for a living. Of course he'd take my money."

"Not with me on deck."

"All right, then. I'm going back to bed. I want you to do something—"

"Yes, sir?"

"If you get any good news, call me. I could use a little good news after all this bad, so call with something good."

"I will, sir. Right away."

"One other thing—"

"Sir?"

"Watch your back. I don't trust him."

The old man hung up.

Pitchess had paid for the gas, and was waiting outside. When Riley put away his phone, Pitch climbed in, and held out a bag of trail mix.

"This is all they had. Sorry."

"It's fine. Thank you."

"Where to?"

"Dinner."

Riley opened the trail mix, and considered the old man's warning. After twenty-four years, eight months, and thirteen days, the old man wouldn't let anyone stop him. If anyone got in his way, someone would pay the price.

43.

Hicks

The rain returned at the edge of the Sunset Strip. Hicks hit Fairfax, and turned into the parking lot. Blanch's car waited on the last row, away from the lights.

Hicks parked in front by the entrance, and made sure Blanch saw him approach. He let himself into the shotgun seat, and pulled the door.

Blanch turned off the radio.

"Am I driving?"

"Yeah. You got more room."

Blanch filled the space behind the wheel like a swollen toad someone shoehorned through the window.

Hicks said, "What's that smell?"

"Chocolate mint chewing gum. Would you like a slice? It's sugar-free."

Hicks thought the sickly-sweet smell was disgusting.

"Nah, I'm good. Let's get going. It isn't far."

Blanch backed from the space, and started away.

"I assume we're going to her home."

They were in Isabel's neighborhood.

"Stegner's on her home. We're going a few blocks past."

Hicks loaded the address in his moving map.

Blanch nodded, and kept nodding, like one nod wasn't enough. His head rose and fell like a dashboard dog.

Hicks did not enjoy being with Blanch. The dude gave off a disturbed vibe, and was off the charts, squirmwise. This was why Hicks brought him on. To make the marshal give up his witness. And he had. Scaring the shit out of people was Blanch's specialty.

Hicks studied Blanch for a moment.

"Can I ask you a question?"

Blanch smiled.

"Of course you may."

Hicks felt awkward bringing it up.

"The girl."

"Ms. Ryan?"

"She didn't hold anything back, right?"

"I assume you're asking about the money."

"Yeah, the money. What I'm asking is, do you think she fooled us?"

Blanch pooched his lips, making a show out of considering the question.

"Why, no, she didn't fool us. She feared me on a very deep level. I can tell, you know. I always can. It's like having a gift."

Creeped. Hicks. Out.

Blanch smiled.

"She told us what she believed to be true. Of this, I am certain."

Hicks gazed out the window. Between the cloying stink and the creepiness factor, Hicks thought he might hurl.

"Yeah, okay, I thought so, too. You mind if I crack the window?"

"Not at all. Please."

Hicks cracked the window. The hit of fresh air was a lifesaver.

Blanch said, "And now, may I ask a question?"

"Sure. What?"

"Whether this money exists or not, you and I agree, the young woman knows nothing about it."

Hicks glanced over, bothered.

"You don't think there's money?"

"Honestly? No, I don't. Nor does it matter. The gentleman believes."

Hicks felt annoyed.

"So what's your question?"

"Well, as of now, Ms. Ryan may be giving our descriptions to the police. Why are we trying to find her?"

Hicks's first impulse was to lie, but he told Blanch the truth.

"To buy our way out of this."

"How interesting."

"I drove a hard bargain before I agreed to this gig. That's why our upside is big."

The old man had agreed to pay a percentage of the find. Forty percent of the total recovered, over and above a flat one hundred thousand dollars paid in advance. None of them expected to recover the original nineteen million, not after twenty-five years, but even if they only recovered ten, Hicks would receive four million dollars to split with his crew.

Blanch peered ahead.

"We're approaching Ms. Ryan's street."

"Keep going. Six or seven blocks ahead. On the left."

Blanch peered up Isabel's street as they passed.

"Poor Stegner. He must be bored."

Blanch turned back to Hicks.

"Apologies. You were saying?"

"Point is, this kid isn't a person to him. She is nineteen million dollars. She is *his* nineteen million dollars, and this is the second time we lost her."

Hicks took a breath, and felt tired.

"You understand what I'm saying?"

Blanch appeared vague.

"I don't believe I do."

"Look. This kid doesn't know squat. But we have to find her, and hand her over to him, and hope it's enough. The dude is dangerous. You see these cowboys? He's got a hundred dudes like them. Two hundred. Who the hell knows?"

Blanch considered this, and slowly nodded.

"You believe he will kill us."

"Yes, Blanch, I believe he will kill us. He wanted Karbo and Bender gone, didn't he? Gone."

Blanch made a dainty smile.

"We are dangerous, too."

"I don't want to spend the rest of my life looking over my shoulder."

Blanch gazed ahead.

"Nor do I. Are we close?"

Hicks checked his phone's moving map.

"Two more."

"On the left."

"Yeah. Coming up. Here—"

They turned up a dark, residential street five blocks east of Isabel. Lined by sidewalks, overhanging jacarandas, and modest, single-family homes, the street was similar to Isabel's in every way.

Hicks said, "Slow now."

He spotted a street number.

"Coming up. On the right."

Blanch touched the brake, soft as a kiss.

They stopped.

A white Volkswagen Beetle sat in the drive. The same Beetle Stegner saw at the Ryan girl's house.

Hicks said, "This is it. Let's go."

They walked up the drive.

44.

Stegner

Stegner bagged the last piece of fried chicken to go, and hustled out to his car. Stegner kept a multi-channel scanner tucked beneath his seat, which was preloaded with the frequencies used by LAPD and the L.A. County Sheriffs. He scooped out the scanner as he drove, and brought up the Hollywood Area Dispatch channel.

The chatter on Hollywood Dispatch was minor and unrelated to Los Feliz. He shifted to Hollywood Tactical, and the scanner crackled to life.

The transmissions were short, disjointed, and often in code, but Stegner monitored LAPD radio traffic the way normal people listened to Top 40 radio. He quickly understood the scene, and knew they were screwed.

The Los Feliz house was a war zone. Hollywood detectives were at the scene. Homicide Special detectives were inbound. EMS and a Medical Examiner were present. Assistance for the Medical Examiner had been requested. A criminalist was inbound. K-9 was at the scene, but not yet deployed. Patrol units were door-knocking for witnesses and searching for blood trails.

Stegner changed channels to Air Support Tactical. A voice directed the bird to light up a slope below a particular house. Air Support was hunting, which meant the cops believed—or had reason to suspect—someone had gotten away.

Stegner lowered the volume. He was angry with himself for agreeing to watch the girl's house. Stegner knew better. Hicks knew better, too. Stegner had known Hicks for twelve years, during which they had taken nine scores. Stegner knew Hicks to be smart, meticulous, and thoroughly professional, but the first rule—the absolute, no exceptions *RULE*—all professionals lived by was this: At the first sign of heat, split. The instant Five-O sniffed, split. Drop everything, abandon the gear, bail. Crooks who broke the rule went to jail. Or died.

Isabel Roland Ryan's little house was less than a mile away, and coming up fast. Stegner knew he should run, he wanted to run, but he decided to take a look.

He passed her street, rounded the block, and cruised down Isabel's street at a stately twenty miles per hour. The sidewalks were deserted. After-dinner strollers and dog owners were avoiding the rain, even though the rain had ended.

Stegner passed her home without slowing. The porch was lit, the windows were dark, and the driveway was empty. He rounded the block again, only this time he approached from the opposite direction. This pass, he clocked the cars along the curbs, checking for silhouette heads and unnatural shapes. The cars appeared empty, but the rule didn't give two shits about appearances. He wanted a closer look.

He pulled over halfway up the next block, tucked his pistol under his shirt, and strolled back to her house along the sidewalk, rechecking the cars. He saw no kids making out, no moms copping a smoke, no SIS spooks watching her house. Stegner had a fearful respect for LAPD's Special Investigations Section. An SIS team got wind he was part of an armored-car crew, and shadowed him for eleven weeks, forcing him to drop out of the crew. The SIS had cost him sixty grand.

When Stegner reached her home, he made sure the neighbors weren't watching, ducked into the shadows, and circled her house. Deserted. He returned to his car, and found a better place to park, a pretty good spot below her house and across the street. The space was small, so his rear end blocked part of a driveway. Screw it. This late on a rainy night, the homeowner wasn't likely to notice, and Stegner didn't plan on spending the night. He settled in, and turned the scanner's volume down to a murmur.

The street was wet. A few minutes later, the surface glistened when headlights appeared. Stegner slumped low, making sure his silhouette did not break the line of the headrest. A compact car swished past. Three minutes later, another car passed. Nobody.

Stegner grew antsy. Sitting outside her house felt like camping at ground zero. He wondered what Hicks and Blanch were doing. Blanch was crazy, so he didn't count. Stegner knew better, yet here he was. He wondered if he was crazy, too.

Stegner tried to decide if the girl could identify him. Unlike Hicks, Stegner believed she was with the police. She'd only seen him once, for maybe ten seconds, when they grabbed her. She probably didn't remember him well enough to work with a sketch artist, but she might be able to describe his car.

Stegner adjusted the mirrors to see if anyone was behind him. He muttered.

"This is bullshit."

The next car approached from the rear. Headlights flashed in the sideview. Stegner remained still as the lights grew brighter. An SUV passed, and kept going.

Stegner took out his pistol, and held it. He imagined a line of police cars racing up to her house. He would be trapped. He wondered if Hicks had lost his mind. Dudes in the can had a term for being stupid. Money-drunk. They got so fixed on taking the score, they stayed when they should've run. Hicks was smart, but he might be money-drunk. Stegner wondered if he was money-drunk, too.

Another car passed. Then two.

Stegner remembered the last piece of chicken. A thigh. He ate it. The damned chicken was even better cold.

The scanner still whispered. Stegner upped the volume. The helicopter was still lighting up the neighborhood, and the cops were still searching.

Stegner wondered if any of their guys had gotten away. Hicks believed they were dead, but Hicks didn't know. Failure to answer a call was not proof of death. One of their guys might have been nabbed. The girl might not be able to describe him, but Ronson or Wallick could name him.

Stegner shifted, and tried to stretch. His back hurt from hunching sideways. Stegner had served time only once, twenty-four months for armed robbery, released after three due to overcrowding. An old con named Marty Plumb, in for life on a third-strike bank robbery, had warned him about lingering at a crime scene. "Only dipshits and slackjaws think they can beat the clock. First sign of trouble, get your ass gone. If you wait, you're only waiting for jail."

Stegner checked the time again.

More headlights approached. Stegner slumped. A Mercedes swished past.

Stegner watched the Mercedes disappear, and decided. This is it, I'm done.

Stegner called Hicks, figuring to let the dude know. Hicks didn't answer.

Voice mail.

Stegner hung up. He kept a basic go-bag in the trunk beneath the spare tire. It contained two thousand dollars and three unmarked keys. The keys opened storage spaces located near three different freeways leading out of the city. Each space held a larger go-bag containing ten thousand dollars, IDs, an alternate license plate, a 9mm pistol, a .223-caliber semiautomatic rifle tricked out to fire full-auto, toiletries, and clothes.

Stegner would not phone Hicks again. He would not

return to his apartment, or say good-bye to his friends, or tell any living person his intentions or whereabouts. He would simply go, and not return until he knew with certainty he had not been implicated in any crimes associated with Isabel Roland Ryan.

Until then, Hicks, the girl, and the fucking cowboys could fuck off.

The stress and the pressure vanished. His back stopped hurting and his shoulders relaxed. Having decided to leave, Stegner felt great. He was gone, baby, gone.

Yippee-ki-yi-ay, motherfuckers!

Stegner started his car. The engine roared to life, just as his driver's-side window shattered. A large black pistol appeared. Stegner saw only the pistol. He did not move. The muzzle floated before him like a great staring eye.

The pistol was watching.

45.

Joe Pike

Cold drops sprinkled his arms and head. Pike barely noticed.

"Grab the wheel, ten and two. Both hands."

The man grabbed the wheel. Short blond hair, lean cheeks, stubble.

"What's going on? Is this a robbery?"

Pike opened the door with his left hand. The Python did not move. Pike hipped the door aside, and covered the man's left hand with his own.

"The right hand stays put. Do not let go with your right. Do you understand?"

"If you want my wallet, take it. You can have it. Take the car."

"I won't ask again."

The man's eyes were big as plates.

"The right stays put. Okay. Sure. Could you please not point the gun at me?"

"Let go your left. Relax your arm. Don't fight."

The man did as instructed.

Pike twisted the hand, and locked the wrist.

"Right hand up. Touch the top of the window, and step from the car."

The man slowly reached toward the top of the window, and a pistol clattered onto the street. Pike ignored it.

As the man stood from the car, Cole stepped from behind the vehicle, scooped up the gun, and shut off the engine and lights.

Pike said, "We good?"

Meaning, were the neighbors watching?

Cole said, "We're good. I got it."

Pike pushed the man against the car, and pulled his hands behind his back. Cole bound his wrists with a plasticuff, then slipped behind the wheel to search the car. Pike frisked the man, found nothing dangerous, and walked the man to his Jeep.

"Are you the police? C'mon, man, I didn't do anything wrong. Am I under arrest?"

Pike opened the rear driver's-side door, pushed the man inside, and climbed in behind him. He pulled the door closed, took out his phone, and snapped the man's picture. The man cringed when the flash went off.

"What are you doing?"

Cole climbed into the shotgun seat, and flashed the man's phone.

"Phone and wallet. Has a scanner in his car. Guess what he's listening to?"

The man said, "So? It's a popular hobby."

Pike checked the photograph for clarity, and texted the picture to Isabel. She called immediately.

Pike said, "What do you think?"

"OhmiGod. It's him. Where are you?"

"He's here. I'm putting you on speaker."

Pike put the call on speaker, and asked her again.

"Do you recognize the individual?"

"He's one of the assholes who kidnapped me. The one around the corner. YOU ASSHOLE!"

Pike said, "Call you later."

Pike hung up. The man glanced from Cole back to Pike, and wet his lips. They were finished with acting.

"You're him. The guy."

"I'm him."

Cole said, "He's him."

The blond man waited for Pike to say something, but Pike said nothing. The blond man filled the silence.

"All right. So call the police."

"No police. This is a private matter."

Pike brought up the picture he'd taken of Boris. Dead in the hall. He let the blond man see.

"What's his name?"

The blond man glanced away, but his gaze returned to the picture.

"Where'd you get this?"

"I took it. What's his name?"

"Ronson. This was you? At the house?"

Pike showed him the picture of Spot.

"Name."

"Stanley. Now listen, you got me, okay? Be cool."

Pike held up the shirtless man's photo. The blond man answered before he asked.

"Wallick. Don't kill me, okay? I don't want to be part of your collection."

Pike lowered his phone.

"Your name."

"Jason Stegner. I'm Stegner. God's honest truth."

Cole said, "DL says your name is Richard Mills."

"It's a fake. C'mon. I'm Stegner. Jason Stegner. I swear."

Cole said, "Why are you here, Mr. Stegner?"

"The girl. We thought she might come back. Something happened, but we didn't know."

Cole said, "She isn't 'the girl.' She's Ms. Roland."

"Sure, whatever you want."

Pike said, "I want Hicks. Where is he?"

"Looking for the girl. For Ms. Roland."

"Looking where?"

"I don't know. Hicks told me to watch her house. I don't know where he is."

Cole said, "When you want to see him, where do you find him?"

"Wherever he says. I call him or he calls me. Like that. We don't hang out."

"You work for Hicks?"

"Yeah."

"Who does Hicks work for?"

"I don't know. Some guy. A drug dealer. Hicks calls him the cowboy."

"You don't know his name?"

"Hicks didn't tell us. He's like that. The less you know, the less you can tell."

"Like now."

"I would tell you. Believe me."

"The cowboy. Is he here in L.A.?"

"Hicks talks to a cat named Riley. Riley's here with some other guys. They work for him. Riley calls, Hicks jumps."

Pike thought for a moment.

"You're going to call him."

"The cowboy?"

Cole sighed.

"Hicks, stupid. Keep up."

"I just called. He didn't answer. I got the voice mail."

Cole said, "You're going to call."

Stegner's phone rang, cutting him off. The ring sounded like the Road Runner from the old Chuck Jones cartoons. Beep-beep, beep-beep.

Cole glanced at the screen, showed it to Pike, then showed the incoming number to Stegner.

"It's Hicks. This is him."

The phone rang again. Beep-beep, beep-beep.

Pike said, "Kill it."

The beeping stopped.

"Why's he calling?"

"Returning my call? I don't know."

Pike thought for a moment. He took Stegner's phone, and touched the screen. The phone asked for a password.

Pike said, "Password."

Stegner told him. Pike opened the phone, and set it

aside. He showed Stegner the picture of Spot. A refresher.

"We're going to call. Tell him you couldn't answer because a man walked by. A man with a dog. You couldn't move."

Stegner nodded.

"Okay."

"Give us away, it'll be your picture I show the next man."

Stegner's jaw flexed. He wet his lips.

"What do you want me to say?"

"Say you need to see him, whatever you need to say so we end up face-to-face."

"Okay."

"What's the number?"

Pike entered the number. The speakerphone rang loudly in the quiet confines of the Jeep. Hicks answered on the third ring. His voice was high and excited.

"What the hell, why didn't you answer? I need you."

Stegner started to tell him about the man and the dog, but Hicks cut him off.

"I don't care. You know Sandy's Fish Shack, on PCH out in Malibu?"

Pike and Cole traded a look. Malibu. Stegner shrugged at Pike, looking for direction. Pike mouthed the word, no.

Stegner said, "No. Never heard of it."

"Goddamnit, look it up. Out by Tuna Canyon. Get your ass out there. Now."

Pike mouthed, why?

Stegner said, "Why?"

"Because I told you to, Stegner. Blanch and I are heading there now. I found her, man. She's in Malibu."

Pike whispered into Stegner's ear.

"Tell him to pick you up."

Stegner said, "I don't know Malibu. What if I can't find it? Swing by. Pick me up."

"It's on PCH, Stegner, you'll find it. The cowboys are coming. We'll hook up at Sandy's and get her. I know where she is."

Then he added.

"She's with Pike."

The line went dead. Hicks was gone.

Pike handed Stegner's phone to Cole, and took a roll of duct tape from the cargo bay.

Stegner saw the tape, and tried to wiggle away.

"Hey, man. I tried. You saw. I did what you wanted."

Pike stepped out of the Jeep.

"Lie down."

"Don't do this. I tried. You saw me try."

"Lie down. Give me your feet."

Stegner started crying.

"Don't kill me, man. C'mon."

Cole said, "If he was going to kill you, you'd be dead. Just do it."

Stegner curled on his side in the fetal position. Pike checked his wrists, then wrapped his ankles with tape.

Stegner still blubbered.

"Stop that, man. Please. What are you doing?"

"I'm not killing you. Is that okay?"

"Uh-huh."

Pike climbed behind the wheel. They headed for Malibu. He called Isabel Roland, and prayed she would answer.

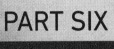

PART SIX

MALIBU

46.

Riley

They were having dinner at a storefront restaurant in Koreatown, just off Olympic Boulevard. The K-town restaurant, located in a faded brick building with exhaust-stained awnings, looked shabby from the street, but online food groupies and L.A.'s best restaurant critics had raved about the place. Now, halfway through a meal of three-way duck, eel with knife-cut noodles, pork *bossam*, and bone broth with organ meats, Riley agreed with the five-star reviews. His guys didn't share his appraisal. Terrence and Charlie eyed their food like it was watching them, and poor Pitch had stayed with the cars. Said he'd grab a hamburger later.

Riley didn't expect to hear from Hicks so quickly, so the call surprised him. He was polishing off the duck when his phone rang, and he saw Hicks's number. He immediately left the table.

"Pay up."

He answered as he headed for the door.

"Hang on. I can't hear."

Riley stepped out into a weepy drizzle. Pitch scrambled out of the car to get Riley's door, but Riley got it himself. He slid into the passenger seat, and wiped his face.

"I'm here. What's up?"

"She's in Malibu. She's with that guy, the bodyguard. Pike. I'm rolling out there now."

"Waitaminute. Where?"

"A beach house. A fucking movie director owns it. No shit. I got the address."

Riley hesitated. A Malibu beach house owned by a movie director sounded like bullshit.

"Are you certain she's there?"

"I got the information from a friend of hers. A chick Stegner saw with Pike at the girl's house. They all know each other, Riley. You see? Now they're shacked up in Malibu."

Terrence and Charlie came out of the restaurant, and stood in the rain, watching him. Riley motioned them to their car.

"Pike is with her now?"

"I have to assume he is, don't you think?"

"How many men do you have left?"

"Me. Blanch. Stegner's on his way."

They wouldn't be enough.

"Her friend might be useful."

"I brought her. You offered to help, Mr. Riley. Did you mean it?"

"Happy to help, Mr. Hicks. Where should we meet?"

Hicks named a place called Sandy's Fish Shack, and

gave the address. Sandy's would be closed, so they would meet in the parking lot. From there, they would check the girl's location, and do what they needed to do.

Riley checked the time.

"We're in K-town. How long to reach you?"

"Doesn't matter. Pike took out three of my guys tonight. Two of those boys were good. I'll wait."

Riley hung up and passed the address to Terrence and Charlie. Pitch loaded it into his driving app, and rolled for the freeway.

Riley thought he should feel excited, but he didn't. He felt a kind of distant resignation, and wondered if the chase would finally end.

He checked the time. It was late back home.

His employer answered right away. Sleep had been elusive.

"Yes, who's speaking?"

"Me, sir. Riley. Sorry if I woke you again."

"I couldn't sleep. What happened now?"

"Good news this time, I hope. Hicks says he's found her."

"Well, damn. So soon."

"We're driving out there now. I'll let you know what we find."

The old man hesitated, and Riley knew he was thinking the same running thoughts that had kept him awake.

"Step easy. He might be up to something."

"He sounded believable. I think we might have her."

"Step easy anyway. All right?"

"Of course."

"Hang on."

The old man cleared his throat, and sounded as if he was choking. He coughed up something phlegmy, and then he was fine.

"These damn allergies. Worse every year. You have allergies?"

"Sometimes. In the spring."

"I'm a snot machine. And this stuff they sell? Nothing works. Puts me in a damn black mood."

"Sounds awful."

"It is. Now listen, been thinking about this, and I want to say something. I never should have hired someone out there, no matter his reputation. You tried to tell me, but I didn't listen. I was wrong. I apologize."

Riley was touched.

"No need, sir. Please."

"Okay, well, I do. Now one more thing."

"Yes?"

The old man's voice turned hard.

"Clean this mess up."

"Yes, sir."

"I'm tired of this bullshit. Girl or no, clean it."

"I hear you."

"Hicks and his boys, whoever else knows. They gotta go."

"No witnesses."

"Tonight."

"Yes, sir."

"If you get the girl, bring her here. If you don't, no

matter. I hunted her goddamned mother for twenty-five years. I'll damned well hunt her."

"We'll find her."

"You're damned right we will. Call me when it's done."

"Have a good night, sir."

The old man hung up.

Pitchess looked over. Riley started to say something, but thought better of it. They were on the freeway, moving west. Before them, a river of red taillights stretched to the sea. Riley imagined they were glowing red lemmings, marching toward madness. He thought they were beautiful.

47.

Joe Pike

Pike put the call on speaker. Cole held the phone as Pike drove, weaving through traffic like an open-field runner. Pike fired a growl at Stegner.

"Don't speak."

Cole jabbed Stegner's head.

"He means it."

Isabel answered with a cheery greeting.

"Don't be late for dinner, honey. It's getting—"

Pike cut her off.

"Isabel. They're coming. I want you to leave the house."

She didn't respond.

"Did you hear me?"

"Where should I go?"

Her voice was small, like a whimper.

"Elvis and I are coming. We're on the way. When I hang up, I'll call Detective Braun. The police will come."

"How did they find me?"

Cole shook his head. Don't mention Carly.

"Leave the house now. It'll be cold, so grab some robes. A couple of beach towels. Something warm."

"Where am I going?"

"The beach. It's dark. Walk to the water. When you're facing the water, turn right."

"Turn right. Okay."

"Turn right, and walk. Count houses. At the fifth house, you'll see a lifeguard station."

"Will someone be there?"

"No. Not at night, but you'll see it. I'll come for you at the lifeguard station. Wait for me. Don't leave. Stay at the lifeguard station. Okay?"

"Okay."

"Leave now. Grab the robes and go. Take your phone. I'll pick you up at the lifeguard station."

"When?"

"As soon as I can. Go. Leave now. I'm coming."

"I love you."

The line went dead. She was gone.

Pike said, "Braun. The number's in recent calls."

"LAPD doesn't serve Malibu. Malibu contracts with the Sheriffs."

"Braun can coordinate."

Cole found Braun's number and dialed. Braun's phone rang once before his voice mail answered.

"Braun, it's Pike. Isabel is in danger. This is an emergency, Braun. Call me."

Cole lowered Pike's phone, and dug out his own.

"I'll call the marshals. Maybe we'll have better luck."

Pryor Gregg answered on the first ring.

"That you, Cole?"

"Want your bug back?"

"What do you want?"

"Pike's here. You're on speaker. We know where she is, and we know where Kemp's killers will be. You interested?"

Gregg shouted for Steinaway.

"Damn right I'm interested."

Cole filled him in and told him about the fish shack.

"Coordinate with Braun. Don't charge in with the cavalry. We don't want to scare them off."

"Don't tell me how to do my job."

"I think I just did."

Cole lowered his phone.

Pike adjusted the rearview to see Stegner.

"Sit up."

Stegner squirmed into an upright position, leaning forward because his hands were behind his back.

"What?"

"Hicks said the cowboys are coming. How many?"

"Four, maybe. If Riley comes, four."

Cole twisted around to see Stegner.

"Muscle?"

"All I've ever seen them do is stand around."

"So you've seen them."

"Once. When they came in. Hicks and I picked them up. Brought so much stuff, we needed two cars. I drove the second."

Pike glanced at the mirror.

"What kind of stuff?"

Stegner made a smirk, hidden in the shadows.

"Long duffels. Hard-sided cases. Heavy as hell."

Cole glanced at Pike.

"Muscle."

Cole looked back at Stegner.

"What do they look like?"

"Shitkickers. That's why we call them cowboys. Got the boots, got the big buckles. They're big, too. Real big boys. Jumbo."

Pike didn't care how big they were.

"From Texas?"

"No idea."

"You met their plane. Where'd it come from?"

"Dude. We picked them up at Van Nuys Airport. They flew in on a private jet. We drove right up to the plane. It was totally cool."

Cole glanced at Pike, and cocked his head.

"Someone has money."

Stegner enjoyed talking about it, and kept going.

"No shit, right? I asked how much a plane like that cost, and the shitkicker, he said it cost eight million bucks. Eight million!"

Pike glanced in the mirror again.

"They didn't say who sent them."

"Not to me. Riley called him 'my employer.' 'My employer' this, 'my employer' that. I started calling Hicks 'my employer,' but he made me stop."

Pike's phone rang, cutting him off. Braun.

"A U.S. Marshal just called. Is Cole there?"

"I'm here."

"What's going on?"

Pike filled him in, and described the plan. Braun wanted to have the sheriffs flood Malibu with cars, but Pike cautioned against the high profile.

"If they see cars, they'll leave. We don't want them to leave. We want to catch them."

"Keeping this woman safe is what we want, Pike. Let's scare the bastards away. We'll catch them later."

"We need them to find who sent them. We don't know who's after her, Braun. The man who sent them hunted her mother for twenty-five years. Now he's hunting Isabel. You think he's gonna quit?"

"Okay. Tell you what. I'll have the sheriffs post a couple cars close by. Not too close, but close if we need them. You driving your Jeep?"

"Yes."

"I'll let'm know. I'll set it up with Lost Hills Station, and coordinate with the marshals. I'll find DeLako and get out there."

"Call when you're close."

Cole lowered the phone.

None of them spoke. The Jeep fell quiet. The wipers arced their metronome beat. They crossed the 405 into West L.A., but still had a long way to go.

Stegner finally spoke, a quiet voice in the backseat darkness.

"Please don't kill me."

Pike didn't answer. Isabel should have left the house by then. She should have reached the lifeguard stand. She should be safe. Pike told himself these things, but found no solace. All the shoulds in the world meant nothing. Isabel would not be safe until he reached her.

48.

Hicks

Sandy's Fish Shack sat off the inland side of PCH, sharing a potholed parking lot with a surf shop and a dive shop. Sandy's dished out fried fish sandwiches and fried fish tacos from a little white takeout stand. Fishing nets on its sides and surfboards guarding the service window gave the place a dated cowabunga retro vibe. When Hicks rolled up, the businesses were closed and the parking lot was empty. A security lamp burned on the far side of the dive shop, but it didn't do much. Hicks crunched across the parking lot and parked by the fish shack.

"He should be here. Where is he?"

Stegner.

Blanch said, "Traffic?"

"Traffic sucks for everyone. We're here. We drove the same distance."

Hicks dug out his phone, found Stegner's number, and called.

Voice mail.

"Would you answer your damn phone? We're here. Where are you?"

Hicks checked his GPS. He had googled the address for Peter Alan Nelsen's beach house, and loaded it into his map. Nelsen's was close, which was why Hicks chose the fish shack as their rendezvous point. He expanded the image, and guesstimated a point-to-point distance. If her girlfriend was right, Isabel was less than four hundred feet away.

Hicks pushed open his door, climbed out, and studied the line of homes farther ahead. They were clusters of light in the darkness, slashed by occasional passing headlights. The GPS pinpointed her exact location, but Hicks couldn't tell them apart.

He pocketed his phone, and leaned into the car for his gun.

"I'm gonna take a look. Scope out the place. See how to do this."

"I'm sure they'll be here soon."

"Great. They can wait for me to get back."

He gave Blanch the keys.

"In case. Otherwise, hang out."

Hicks tucked the pistol under his rain jacket and hustled across the parking lot. He ducked through a gap between passing cars, and followed the map. Beachfront homes formed a solid wall along the highway, but an occasional path to the beach appeared between them, mandated by the state so people other than millionaires could enjoy the sand. Hicks was freezing. He zipped the rain jacket, pulled on the hood, and walked faster, trying to get warm. The dot marking Nelsen's house moved steadily closer, and soon he was almost on top of it. He slowed, and finally saw it, three houses away. A big concrete block set behind tall hedges. Hicks slowed even more, and no longer felt cold. He rested his hand on his pistol, thinking about Pike. He didn't want to face Pike alone, but if the dude didn't see it coming, if Hicks had a shot, he would take it. Finish this thing. End it.

Hicks strolled past, and casually glanced through the gate. The damn house had no windows. It was a bunker with a metal door, ugly as hell, and side gates too tall to climb. Hicks saw no cameras, but places like this had cameras out the ass. The little motor court was well lit, but held no cars. The lack of cars bothered him.

Hicks continued past the next house, then turned around and walked back to one of the trails that led down between two houses to the beach. Hidden from passing cars, the beach was much darker. He let his eyes adjust, and took off his shoes and socks. The beach was empty. The sand was wet, and cold, and difficult to walk on. Most of the homes were dark, but the lit homes were open to the world. People who lived on the beach wanted to see the beach, so the backs of their homes were glass. Like they were fish in a fishbowl. Everyone walking past saw them, their possessions, and their business. Hicks shook his head. A res-burg crew he once worked with had feasted off fools like these.

Hicks approached Nelsen's home carefully. Like every other home on the beach, the back of Nelsen's bunker was glass. The lights inside were on, filling the interior with a bright glow. A well-lit deck jutted from the house to the sand. He saw no one outside or inside the house.

Hicks moved closer.

The bottom floor looked to be a long room. He saw couches and chairs, a bar, what looked like a pool table, but no people. Bedrooms were above. Sheer drapes had been drawn across the glass, but from down on the beach, he couldn't see if anyone was in bed. No cars, nobody kicked back, watching TV. Hicks grew worried. The friend might have given him old information. Pike and the girl might be gone.

He crept closer, risking the light cast by the house. A person inside might see him, but if she was here, this was how they would reach her.

At the edge of the deck, Hicks froze, and crouched low to the sand. His pulse hammered. The sliding glass doors stretched across the width of the house were open. Not much. Maybe six inches. Hicks craned his head, looking up and down the beach, and along the side of the house. He saw no one. Nothing moved in the house. He started to text Blanch, but stopped. Screw it. He was here. He wanted to know.

Hicks drew his pistol, and moved to the opening. He listened, but the house was silent. No music from upstairs. No voices. The full length of the big room was visible. He saw food in the kitchen, a small bag on a large table, and what looked like towels draped on a couch. He touched the door wider, and stepped inside.

The house remained quiet. He crept to the stairs, and listened again. He half expected to hear Pike and the girl going at it, but didn't. The thought made him grin. Shoot the bastard right off her.

Hicks moved well in the house, and knew how to move quietly. He'd hot-prowled plenty of homes during his res-burg days, sneaking through bedrooms while residents snored. He checked upstairs, and was down again in less than a minute. Someone had spent time in the big master bedroom. Most likely a woman. He found long hair in the sink.

Hicks did not linger. He was the man in the fishbowl now, and wanted to leave. They were gone, but likely close, probably out grabbing dinner. He wanted to surprise them.

49.

Riley

Riley peered ahead, squinting.

"Is that it?"

Pitch leaned over the wheel, hesitant.

"Looks like. Yeah, that's it. The fish."

Riley was irritated with how long it had taken to reach Malibu. He'd thought, Malibu, okay, it was right up the beach from L.A., but it felt like they were driving to San Francisco.

Pitch eased the sedan off the highway onto a pockmarked turnout that damn near beat them to death. Terrence and Charlie bumped along behind.

Pitch said, "There he is. Car. Behind the fish place."

Riley looked around at the crappy little buildings and wide-open parking lot. He wondered if Hicks was crazy.

"Is the boy nuts, having us meet right beside a highway?"

"He's local. Maybe he knows something."

Riley saw a man standing by the car, but he didn't see Hicks.

"Who's this?"

"I've seen him. The weird one."

"Supposed to be three. I see one."

"Way the hell out here, maybe they got lost."

Riley stepped out of the car. He didn't like the location and he didn't like standing in the open. The thought crossed his mind they were being set up. He felt tight as a bowstring.

"Where's Hicks?"

The man smiled dumbly, and offered his hand. He was a big boy, but not big like Pitch or Terrence. He looked swollen and soft, with wide sloping shoulders and a round puffy face.

"Hello, Mr. Riley. My name is Blanch. It's a pleasure to meet you."

He spoke softly, his voice whispery and hoarse.

Riley ignored his hand.

"Where's Hicks? Hicks and the other man were supposed to be here."

Blanch slowly lowered his hand.

"Well, we didn't know when you'd arrive, so Mr. Hicks went to check the location. He should be back soon. It's close."

"How close?"

The man slowly pointed up the highway.

"There."

Pitchess said, "Supposed to be a third. He go with Hicks?"

"That would be Stegner. He hasn't arrived. I'm sure he'll be along shortly."

Riley glanced at Terrence and Charlie, and Pitchess. Terrence shook his head and spit at a rock.

Riley wanted to kill them right here. Wait for Hicks to return, and drop them right here in the light of the Pacific Coast Highway. But this would leave the third, Stegner. Riley didn't want to tell his employer one got away.

Charlie frowned.

"What's that?"

Riley turned.

"What?"

"Hear it?"

Pitch said, "Yeah."

He pointed at Hicks's car.

Riley heard a thump. Then another. The car thumped again.

Riley stepped past Blanch to the car.

Thump.

Something in the trunk thumped.

Riley looked at Blanch.

"Open it."

"All righty."

The boy made his idiot's smile and opened the trunk.

A young woman lay curled on her side. She was bound with duct tape and cord, and tape covered her mouth. She managed to lift her feet, and brought them down hard.

Thump.

The idiot said, "This is Carly Knox, Isabel's friend. Isn't she pretty?"

Riley walked away, shaking his head. No wonder crazies like Manson and the Night Stalker popped up out here. These people were defective.

50.

Hicks

Hicks saw their cars as he hustled back to the fish shack. Two big sedans, parked behind Blanch. The cowboys stood by the cars, looking as large as grazing cattle. Hicks didn't see Stegner, and felt a stab of concern. Stegner should have arrived. He put in a call as he crossed the parking lot. Voice mail.

"Call me, Jason. I need you."

He pocketed his phone as he reached the others.

Riley looked tense.

"Who'd you call?"

"My guy. Stegner. I don't know where he is."

Riley looked at Blanch.

"Impressive associates. Where is she?"

"Gone. She'll be back. They're close."

Riley grabbed his arm so quickly Hicks was caught off guard. He broke Riley's grip, and pushed the larger man back.

"The fuck's wrong with you?"

Two of the cowboys hovered near Blanch. The third drifted behind Hicks.

Hicks grabbed his pistol but didn't draw. He edged backward, eyes flicking from man to man, but mostly on Riley.

"Wanna go? Go! Do it! You fuck!"

Riley didn't move. He didn't look frightened.

"You told me she was here."

"She's here. She just—"

Hicks searched for an explanation.

"—stepped out for a few minutes."

"Her bodyguard?"

"Him, I don't know. He's probably with her."

The moment of violence passed. Hicks let go of his gun and patted the air, trying to calm Riley's nerves.

"Relax. You'll have her in five minutes. Ten minutes, tops."

"Except for the part how you don't know where she is, or when she'll be back, or even *if* she's coming back. With her bodyguard. A man who killed three of your men."

"I got it covered."

"So do I."

Riley glanced at his bulls.

"Saddle up."

The cowboy named Charlie went to a sedan and popped the trunk. The other cowboys crowded around as Charlie handed out bullet-resistant vests and crop-stocked Benelli shotguns. Watching them strap on the vests, Hicks thought they looked like West Texas linemen suiting up for a championship game.

Riley turned, and Hicks knew the man was making a decision.

Riley said, "So? Where is she?"

Hicks shoved past the herd of cowboys to his car. Blanch stood by the trunk with his hands in his pockets, watching the cowboys.

Hicks said, "Gimme her phone."

Blanch held up a phone.

"The cool thing about nabbing her friend is we nabbed the friend's phone. It was a hoot reading their texts. You should see this stuff. All these chicks do is text each other."

Riley squared off behind him as Hicks tapped the phone.

"Stop wasting time. If you don't know where she is, take us to the house. We'll find her."

"Relax, Riley, and learn something. Read enough of their texts, and you can sound just like them. Carly, for instance. Especially when you send it from Carly's phone."

Hicks finished typing.

"Get in your car, Riley. We don't have to find her. She'll come to me."

Hicks sent the text, and went to get Isabel.

51.

Isabel

The roiling, rushing crash of breaking waves thundered across the sand. Isabel huddled beneath the lifeguard stand, waiting for Joe. She had bundled herself in three of the thick terry robes, but they were already damp. She was cold. Isabel held her phone underneath the robes to keep it dry.

The lifeguard stand was an elevated wooden shack the size of a closet. It sat on posts four feet above the sand, allowing the lifeguards a better view of the surf. Now, at night, it sat shuttered and empty. Isabel sat between the posts, watching the mouth of an access path that emerged between two homes. Joe hadn't mentioned the path, but here it was. The beach was so dark the path was swallowed in shadows.

Her phone vibrated with an incoming text.

A wave of relief hit her so hard she almost gasped.

Izzy assumed the text was from Joe, who had finally arrived, but when she checked her phone she saw a text from Carly.

Iz! Hey, gurl, I'm here! Where are you?

Isabel read the text twice, and felt totally confused. She typed a response.

> Where here? I don't understand.

A few seconds later, Carly responded.

> The Bu! At PAN's. I had to see it. And you!
> But nobody's here. 🙁

PAN was shorthand for Peter Alan Nelsen, which Izzy had used when they texted earlier.

Isabel felt a rush of panic. Her heart raced so fast she trembled.

> You're here? NOW???

> Duh! At the door!
> Which nobody answers! 🙁

> GO! GET AWAY FROM
> THE HOUSE! RUN!

> This isn't funny. I drove all
> the way out here.

> PLEASE go! Those men are coming.
> They know I was there.
> They'll hurt you!

For real?

YES!!! RUN!

You're scaring me.

RUN! Get away!

Now I'm really scared.
Where are you?

Go, baby! Get in your car,
drive away! PLEASE!

I'm scared! Are you close?
I'll come to you.

I'm waiting for Joe.

I'll wait with you.
I'll pick you up. PLEASE!

Carly would get herself killed if she didn't leave.

Okay. Drive to the access path. It's
five houses away. There's a sign.
Wait in the car. I'll jump in.

xoxo

Isabel pushed to her feet and stumbled toward the path. The wet sand gave, and sucked at her feet, but once she reached the path, she moved quickly between the houses.

She popped out of the path at the edge of the PCH shoulder, looking for Carly's Volkswagen. Peter's house wasn't far. This time of night, with almost no traffic, Carly should have been waiting.

Isabel stepped to the edge of the highway. She looked toward Peter's, then turned, and looked behind her. Carly's white Beetle was nowhere, and neither was Carly.

Isabel grew afraid. The highway seemed deserted. No cars approached, and she saw no other people. Joe had said he was close, but Joe hadn't arrived. Isabel backed away from the shoulder. She wished she had never left the lifeguard stand. Joe told her to wait, and that's where she should have stayed.

Isabel ran back along the path, but suddenly stopped. A shadow moved ahead. A man, coming toward her.

The man said, "Gotcha."

Isabel turned, and slammed face-first into a second man.

The man threw his arms around her. Isabel screamed.

52.

Joe Pike

They rolled past Tuna Canyon on an empty black ribbon. PCH was deserted. As if people sensed something worse than rain was approaching. The wipers shhchoonked, shhchoonked, brushing aside a sprinkle.

Cole murmured in the Jeep's quiet darkness.

"Close now. Quarter mile. Ahead on the right."

Pike saw a dim light, and called Isabel.

"We're close. You okay?"

"I'm freezing."

"I'll see you soon."

Pike hung up and called Braun.

"Quarter-mile east. You?"

"I'm a mile behind you."

"The marshals?"

"Inbound."

Cole said, "What about the sheriffs?"

"Two two-man cars. I hope this isn't bullshit. DeLako gets cranky when I pull her away from her boyfriend."

DeLako spoke in the background.

"Eat me."

Pike slowed as the fish shack rolled into view. A single car sat beside the building, but Pike saw no one in or around it.

"We've got a car here. One vehicle."

"Is it them?"

Stegner leaned forward to see.

"That's Blanch."

Cole said, "I don't see anyone."

"The car, not Blanch. That's his car."

Pike relayed the info to Braun.

"Stegner says it belongs to one of Hicks's people. Looks empty."

"Wait for us."

"Isabel's just ahead."

"I'm right behind you. Wait."

Pike didn't want to wait.

"I'll drive by and keep rolling."

"Just wait. The marshals are right behind us."

Pike drifted onto the shoulder and into the parking lot. Cole drew his pistol and rolled down his window. Pike slowed, and crept past the car.

Cole said, "Stop."

Cole climbed out, and peeked into the car.

"Empty."

"Let's roll."

Cole came back to the Jeep, but stopped as he was about to get in, and turned back to the car.

"I heard something."

Pike shut off the Jeep.

Cole took a step back toward the car, then looked back at Pike.

"I heard it again. Something's in the trunk."

Pike climbed out, and joined Cole at the trunk.

Thump.

They both heard it.

Thump.

Then something went mmm-mmm-mmm.

Braun and DeLako and the sheriffs' cars arrived as Pike popped the trunk. Carly Knox looked up at them. She was bound with duct tape and cord, and duct tape covered her mouth. The instant she saw them, she frantically tried to speak.

Pike lifted her out, and cut off her binds.

DeLako said, "Holy shit, who's this?"

"Carly Knox. Isabel's friend."

Carly clawed the tape from her mouth.

"They tricked her. They didn't find her at Peter's, so they used my phone to trick her. They pretended to be me so she'd tell them where she was, and she did. I heard them. She thought it was *me*!"

"How long ago?"

"Five or six minutes. I don't know—they just left!"

Pike ran to his Jeep.

"She was at the lifeguard stand, just west of here."

Braun stopped him and opened the backseat door.

"Hang on. Stegner has to go with these guys."

Braun waved two of the sheriffs closer.

"Ms. Knox can stay with us. The marshals are al-most here. You should wait."

Pike dragged Stegner out, dropped him, and climbed behind the wheel.

"I'm not waiting."

Cole piled in, and Pike hit the gas. Two sheriffs scram-bled to their car, but Pike did not slow.

53.

Pike braked hard when he reached Peter's gate, and crept past the motor court.

"I make two sedans. They're here, Braun."

"How many?"

"Can't see in from the front. ETA on the marshals?"

"Anytime. I'm calling in more sheriffs."

"Call you back."

Pike dialed Isabel. Her phone rang six long times before voice mail answered. Pike climbed out, and motioned for the sheriffs. They gathered between their cars.

Pike pointed out the access path.

"We'll check the house from the beach. You guys post here, but stay back. If anyone tries to leave, stay back and follow."

The older dep nodded.

"We got it."

Pike and Cole ran down the path to the sand, passed the lifeguard stand, and jogged toward the house.

Peter Alan Nelsen's beachfront home glowed like a

lamp. They slowed as they neared, and crawled to the deck. Hicks and Isabel stood by the bar, Hicks gripping her arm. Blanch stood near Hicks, smiling. A tall, trim man in a western suit stood facing Hicks. The man wore a polymer vest over his jacket, and they seemed to be arguing. Pike made the man in the suit for Riley. Three bruisers the size of trucks also wore vests. The vests went well with their shotguns.

Cole nudged him.

"The glass door is open."

Pike called Braun.

"Isabel is in the house. Six males. Four with vests, three shotguns. Two deps are out front. Cole and I are in the rear."

"Copy that. DeLako's coming."

"Vest."

"She's good."

Pike recited a four-digit number.

"Say back."

Braun repeated the number.

"Tell DeLako. It's the entry code to the front door."

"I understand. Stand by. The marshals are here."

Gregg's voice came on the line.

"Cole?"

"Pike."

"We have four cars here and Air Support on station. I have a SOG team in the air. ETA twenty. What do you want to do?"

"Set up and wait. Avoid a hostage situation. Let them leave. Take them down on the way out."

"Sounds good."

Cole nudged Pike again.

"Something's up."

Pike murmured into the phone.

"Wait one."

Cole shifted, staring at something in the house.

"Not good. Not good not good."

Riley took Isabel's arm. He pulled her from Hicks. Hicks shouted, and waved his hand. Isabel stood between them.

Cole drew his pistol.

"Dude on the left. Watch the spread."

"I see it."

Back to Gregg.

"Something's wrong. They're arguing."

The cowboy to Riley's left circled toward Blanch. Blanch noticed, and turned to keep him in view. The remaining two cowboys drifted right, and Hicks started shouting.

Cole drew his legs under him, ready to go.

Pike's heart slammed into a slow heavy roll.

Braun came on the line.

"Pike? It's Braun. What's wrong? What are they doing?"

"Arguing. They're gonna pop."

The rough men arrayed themselves like chess pieces. Tension spiked. Pike saw it in the cant of their heads and the way they moved. They were three heartbeats from killing one another, and Isabel was trapped in their hell.

Braun said, "Pike, damnit. Hang on. Let us get set up. We're setting up now."

Pike slipped the Python from its holster. Cole looked over and nodded.

"What are you doing, Pike? Pike?"

Pike put away his phone.

The cowboy at the bar raised his shotgun.

A pistol went off.

Pike stood and ran to the light.

Cole ran with him.

54.

Hicks

Hicks pulled Isabel across the sand, Blanch huffing and stumbling behind them. She fell, but Hicks jerked her to her feet. She tried to twist away, but not as strongly as before. The chase had worn her down.

"I don't have any money. I don't know anything about the stupid money. You're all obsessed, and I don't know what you're talking about."

"Blame your mother. She left you holding the bag."

"She did not! She didn't take his money. I wish she had!"

"Me, too. I was in for forty percent."

"Well, I'm *sorry*! But she didn't, and I DON'T HAVE IT! I'd give it to you if I had it. I CAN'T!"

Hicks, who usually didn't give a shit one way or the other, felt bad for her.

"Doesn't matter. He thinks you do."

"Tell him!"

"I did. People believe what they want to believe."

"*Please* let me go."

"Wouldn't do any good."

"My boyfriend's coming. He's coming right now."

Hicks knew this to be true, and wanted to be gone before Pike arrived.

Hicks reached the deck. Riley and his shitkicker goons were grouped by the bar, talking. Hicks had hoped to see Stegner, but Stegner was a no-show. Prick. Hicks tugged Blanch close.

"Keep your eyes open."

Blanch studied the men, his puffy face floating in the night like a large balloon.

"Oh, yes."

Hicks dragged Isabel across the deck and into the house. All four cowboys turned, making Hicks think of a herd of cattle.

Riley stepped forward.

"So this is Ms. Ryan."

"My name is Roland."

Hicks didn't stop. He wanted to get her into a car and away from the scene. He towed her toward the door.

"C'mon, Riley. Let's go. Pike's coming. God knows who else. We gotta split."

Riley touched the girl's arm as Hicks towed her past, stopping them.

"Let him come. We'll handle it."

The cowboys drifted apart, standing there with their shotguns and vests as if they'd done something.

Hicks couldn't believe these people.

"Here she is, Riley. We got her. You want to lose her again? Let's go."

Riley took Isabel's arm, and pulled her to him.

"I have her, but we won't lose her."

Two cowboys stepped from behind Riley. The third cowboy drifted the other way, moving toward Blanch. Hicks glanced at Blanch, and saw him smile. Hicks stared at Riley.

"Are you serious?"

"I'm serious."

"I found her. Here she is."

"We'll take her from here. My employer prefers it."

One cowboy moved to the end of the bar. They had spread like the fingers of an open hand, encircling Hicks and clearing their field of fire. Hicks glanced at Blanch again, and made his own smile. They were going to do it. It was going down, and Hicks decided, then and there, to kill Riley first.

"Your crazy fuck employer can kiss my ass. I didn't fail. She doesn't know."

"She'll know for us."

Hicks glanced at Blanch. A big-ass cowboy sidled up beside him, and Blanch grinned like a loon.

Hicks smirked at Riley.

"You dumb shitkicker, there is no money. There never was. It's all that old man's fantasy."

"Tell me about it."

Riley shrugged.

"I know there's no money. But it doesn't matter. He wants Ms. Ryan, so he'll have her. And he wants you gone."

The big cowboy at the end of the bar brought up his

shotgun. Hicks knew they would try. He was expecting it, and caught that first flick of motion as the barrel came up. Hicks grabbed fast and drew, swung his pistol to Riley, and saw the bright yellow flash as Riley shot him.

Hicks slammed backward into the bar and fell forward to a knee.

He heard Blanch, making a weird Blanch sound as he stabbed the man next to him.

Unh-unh-unh.

The girl shouted a name.

"Joe!"

Hicks saw two men rush in from the deck, then he toppled and fell, and everything went dark.

55.

Joe Pike

They entered the house as Hicks fell. Pike broke left, and Cole broke right. Riley and his cowboys were at the far end of the long room, with their backs turned, but Blanch probably saved them. Knives appeared in each hand, and he spun at the nearest cowboy. He moved faster than big puffy boys should move, and stabbed the cowboy four times fast. Then the cowboy at the bar saw Pike, and Cole shot him.

Riley pulled Isabel close like a shield. The stabbed cowboy pushed Blanch away, scrambled behind a couch, and popped up with his shotgun. He shot Blanch in the face, fired twice at Pike, and ducked out of sight.

Pike moved up the left side of the room, and took cover behind a pinball machine. He fired a shot into the couch, moved forward, and fired again.

Riley fired twice, but Isabel struggled and threw him off balance.

The third cowboy peeked from behind the anthracite table, cranked off four 12-gauge loads as fast as he could pull the trigger, and ducked. Pike beaded up. When the cowboy peeked out, Pike shot him.

Cole moved up the right side, trying to reach the bar.

Riley lifted Isabel off her feet, and moved for cover behind the fireplace. He fired at Cole and fell back.

Riley shouted, "Hit the bar. The bar!"

The stabbed cowboy popped up, fired twice, and vanished. Pike shot at him, but missed. Cole hit the floor, and scrambled behind the bar.

Pike dumped his empties, fed the Python a speed-loader, and took cover behind the jukebox.

Somewhere out front, a siren whooped twice, and the sound of a helicopter was close.

Pike said, "Stop this."

The cut cowboy popped up, fired again, and disappeared.

Pike said, "Stop. Let her go."

Riley fired.

Isabel pushed into him hard, then wrapped her arms around his gun arm, and bit. Riley flung her off, she fell, and Pike shot him.

Riley's head snapped sideways. He dropped like a bag of wet laundry.

The big cowboy popped up behind the couch, fired at Cole, and missed Isabel's head by an inch.

Pike ran forward, firing into the couch. He emptied his gun as he reached Isabel. Pike dove on top of her, and Cole took over, pounding more bullets into the couch.

The cut cowboy popped up six feet away, fired, and ducked.

Pike was out of ammo. He pushed Isabel behind him.

"Back up. Scoot back. Get behind the bar."

DeLako and a sheriff stepped out from behind the stairs. DeLako beaded up, and shouted across her weapon.

"How many?

Pike answered.

"One. The couch. He's wearing a vest."

Two more sheriffs and three marshals entered behind her, and spread to the sides.

DeLako said, "C'mon, man. Be smart."

The bloody cowboy popped up once more. The big Benelli boomed.

DeLako fired three fast times, and the cowboy dropped. Her last two shots weren't needed. Her first shot killed him.

DeLako did not move. She was locked out, breathing hard, and ready to shoot.

"Pike?"

"I'm good."

Cole called from behind the bar.

"Me, too, thanks for asking."

DeLako said, "Who else? Who else is alive?"

Pike looked at Isabel. He touched her hair.

"Isabel. Isabel is alive."

Pike touched her hair again.

"You good?"

Her eyes were red. She tried to speak, but only managed to nod. Words wouldn't come.

DeLako lowered her weapon, and looked at the carnage.

"What a mess."

More deps piled in behind her and moved through the room, securing weapons and checking for wounded. Gregg and Braun pushed through the crowd. Braun went to DeLako. He threw his arms around her, and hugged her, and they stood like that for a while.

Pike looked over at Cole. Cole pushed to his feet and offered a hand. Pike took it, and stood.

Pike walked the room, going from Riley to each of his men. Dead. Maybe their identities or something in their possessions would point to their employer. He looked down at Blanch. His open eyes stared at the ceiling. His smile was gone.

Pike walked over to Hicks. Blood had sprayed from his nose and mouth, and joined the blood leaking from his chest to form a growing pool. Center mass shot, a little high and to the left, an inch below his collarbone. Heart shot. The bullet likely nicked the aorta.

Pike thought, who sent you?

A bubble appeared at the side of his mouth. A second bubble joined the first.

Pike squatted and touched his shoulder.

"Hicks."

Hicks made a crackling hiss.

Pike called out.

"Medics. He's alive."

Across the room, Braun shouted.

"Got a live one. Get EMS in here."

Pike leaned close.

"Who sent you?"

His left eye flickered. He crackled again, and a new bubble appeared.

"Wake up."

Pike dug his thumb into a pressure point. Pike dug deep, and pressed hard on a nerve bundle under his jaw.

Hicks's left eye opened. Not far.

Pike leaned closer.

"What's his name?"

Hicks's mouth worked, but nothing came out.

Pike heard the paramedics, up front in the entry. They were coming.

Pike took off his glasses, and looked into Hicks's eye. The eye looked back.

Pike said, "He killed you. Tell me who killed you."

Hicks's mouth worked.

Pike bent down, and put his ear to the bloody lips.

"Tell me."

Pike stood when the paramedics arrived, and stepped out of their way.

Braun and Gregg were watching him.

Braun said, "It sounded like he said something. What did he say?"

Isabel was watching. She wanted to know.

The paramedics looked up from the body.

"He's gone. Dead."

Braun asked again.

"What did he say?"

Pike put on his sunglasses.

"He said good-bye."

Pike sat with Isabel until Braun let them leave.

PART SEVEN

PERMISSION

56.

Elvis Cole

Four days after the events in Malibu, Cole watched Pryor Gregg enter his office. The hat came first, and kept coming, and finally the marshal followed. Cole marveled at the size of the brim. Gregg's Stetson went on forever.

Gregg stood there, a thousand feet tall, and took off his hat.

"Thanks for seeing me."

"Come for your bug?"

"Nope. Taking off. Wanted to see you before I left."

Cole nodded at the director's chairs.

"Have a seat."

Gregg eyed the Pinocchio clock as he sat.

"The eyes just go back and forth?"

"Sometimes they blink."

Gregg said, "Ha. I bet they do."

"Find out who Riley worked for?"

"Not yet, but we will. Boy had no record. The others, mostly petty stuff. Bar fights and such."

"They worked for somebody."

"We'll figure it out."

"Let me know when you do."

"Anyway, I came by to thank you."

Gregg leaned forward and offered his hand.

"The Marshals Service thanks you."

Cole took his hand. The hand swallowed his.

Cole said, "You don't have to thank me. Nothing to thank me for."

"A marshal was murdered. You helped bring his killers to justice. We take these things seriously."

Cole smiled. Modest.

"You're thanking the wrong person. I was just along for the ride."

"I tried to reach Mr. Pike. He isn't easy to catch."

"Not Pike."

Gregg looked surprised.

"No?"

"A friend of Joe's. He put it together and connected the dots. Joe will tell you."

"Who's the friend?"

"A criminalist. John Chen. He ID'd Hicks and pointed us in the right direction. Matched the guns to the shooters and the shooters to the murder. Without Chen, we'd still be riding in circles."

Gregg mulled over this new information.

"Where can I find Mr. Chen?"

"FSD. The Forensic Science Division. Call them. I'm sure they'd love to hear from you."

Gregg stood. He unfolded himself from the seat, and there he was, up on the ceiling.

"Think I'll do that. And if you talk to Mr. Pike, please tell him I'd like to thank him in person."

"You bet, Inspector. Will do."

They shook hands again, and Cole walked Gregg to the door. After Gregg left, Cole returned to his desk. He picked up his phone, and called Joe Pike.

Cole said, "I told him."

57.

John Chen

John Chen was flat on his back on the floor of his apartment when his phone rang. This was the sixth time the phone had rung in the past forty minutes. John covered his head with his pillow and tried to ignore it.

Chen—defeated, deflated, and mired in lethargy—barely moved. He had so little energy, opening his eyes was an insurmountable effort. Crawling to the bathroom was beyond him. His shame was so great, his humiliation so complete, he'd pulled the shades, locked the door, and turned off the lights. Darkness was too good for him.

Ring.

Chen groaned.

Ring.

What the FUCK? *SIX* TIMES? *SIX* TIMES THIS PHONE?

Ring.

John slowly lifted the phone and checked the caller ID.

Harriet.

Chen covered his face.

Ring.

He knew she'd call. He had to sign the termination papers.

Ring.

Chen answered.

"Hullo."

He hoped the sound of his miserable, heartbroken voice made her feel terrible.

"Johnnn! All is forgiven!"

John looked at the phone to make sure this was Harriet. She sounded bright, cheery, and bubbling with goodwill.

"That was just a nasty spat we had. I hope you won't hold it against me."

John looked at the phone again. Could this really be Harriet?

John said, "What spat?"

"I've been under so much stress, well, I overreacted. I know you won't hold it against me, but I just feel terrible."

This wasn't Harriet.

"You do?"

"I'd like you to come in tomorrow, John. Dress nicely. We'll have guests."

"You want me back at work?"

"Of *course*, silly!"

Maybe she was drunk. She sounded drunk.

Harriet said, "Wear a nice suit. Your court suit. I want you to look nice for the pictures. I'm going to have my hair done."

Harriet giggled. Harriet. Actually. Giggled.

Chen sat up, totally suspicious. Harriet might be taping the call. She probably wanted to trick him into saying something she could use against him.

"Harriet, are you taping this call?"

"What? No, absolutely not! Why would I tape us?"

"I have an expectation of privacy. I do not agree to being taped. I do *not* grant permission."

"I'm not taping us, John. I only want to make sure you're here, and I want to make sure you look nice."

"Why should I look nice?"

"The award."

Chen's eyes narrowed.

"What award?"

"The Marshals are giving you an award. For all the fine work you've done. The United States Marshals! It's federal. We'll have our picture in the trade journals."

John said, "We?"

"Be here by ten. It'll be nice."

"A promotion would be nicer."

"Don't push it, John."

"No me, no trade journals."

Harriet didn't say anything. She was silent for so long, Chen grew worried he had overplayed his hand.

Then she said, "Come early. We'll talk about it."

Chen hung up. He had no idea what she was talking about.

Chen shouted, "*YES!*"

John Chen, soon-to-be owner of a shiny black Tesla, jumped to his feet and danced around his apartment. Naked.

58.

Isabel

Nine days after the events in Malibu, Isabel sat with Carly and her mom in their kitchen. Carly's mom was named Joyce. When Izzy and Carly were small, they called each other's mothers Ms. Knox and Ms. Roland. Later, when they turned twelve or thirteen, Carly began calling Izzy's mom Debra Sue (or, sometimes, Debbie), and Izzy called Carly's mom Joyce. Joyce was still making peace with all these names.

"I just don't see Deb as a DeeAnn. I don't care what they say, DeeAnn doesn't fit her. And your dad? He's an Ed. Always was, always will be."

They were drinking chamomile tea with honey and milk.

Carly said, "Mom. Izzy's going to sell the house."

Joyce sat back.

"Are you getting married?"

Isabel tried not to laugh. Carly rolled her eyes.

"Jesus, Mom. Really?"

"I'm kidding."

Joyce reached across the table, and took Izzy's hand.

"You okay with selling?"

"I think so. I'm not really sure."

"Money?"

"For sure, but ever since—"

Izzy gripped Joyce's hand.

"I don't know. Ever since those people, they were in it, they were watching me—"

She faded away, and ended up shaking her head.

"I feel sad all the time. And weird."

Joyce rubbed her hand.

"You can stay here. You're always welcome here. You know that, don't you?"

Carly said, "I told her."

Joyce smiled, and rubbed her hand again.

"People get born, grow up, and move on. Mom and Dad die, the old place gets sold. That was your mom and dad's house, but if you're worried they wouldn't like it, stop being silly. They wouldn't mind. That house served its purpose. They made a home for you in it. Now you're grown, they're gone, and you should do whatever in hell you want. Your mother—my friend— would be the first to tell you."

Izzy gripped the older woman's hand with both of hers.

"I love you, Joyce."

"I know, sweetie. I love you, too."

Joyce sat back, and grew thoughtful. She patted Izzy's hand, then let go and sighed.

"I miss your mom. I miss your dad, too, but—"

Izzy smiled.

"I know. You were besties. Like us."

She glanced at Carly, and Carly beamed.

"Yes, we were. Since you girls were two."

Joyce fell silent. Izzy thought she might be thinking of those days. Then Joyce pushed back from the table and left the room.

"I'll be back. Have more tea."

As soon as her mother left, Carly leaned closer.

"Have you seen him again?"

Carly was totally crushing on Joe.

"Just twice."

"You should do him. I would *so* totally do him."

"You're gross."

Carly clutched her arm, being dramatic.

"I would beg him. I would say, breed me!"

"You are so far beyond gross. You're disgusting."

"Tell me you haven't thought about it."

"It's not like that. He's—"

"Male?"

"—kinda weird."

"I hate you."

"He's a really nice man. Kinda distant? I don't know how to say it. He's nice."

Joyce came back, and plopped into her chair. She brought back an envelope. It was white, thick with whatever was inside, and sealed with tape. Joyce set the envelope in front of Isabel.

Izzy's name and address were written on the envelope in her mother's hand.

"Mom?"

"This is yours. Five weeks before she died, she asked me to keep it for you."

Isabel looked at the envelope, but did not touch it.

"What is it?"

"Considering what we now know, I'd guess it's the truth. I'm breaking a promise by giving it to you, but what with all this drama, well, you should have it."

"What did you promise?"

"She asked me to hold it until you were twenty-five. I don't know why. She just did. But, hell, you're almost twenty-three, and look what just happened."

Joyce pushed the envelope closer.

"Here."

Isabel picked up the envelope, and turned it over. She pinched the corner, and started to open it.

Joyce touched her hand.

"Baby. This is between you and your mother. She wrote it for you. Take it home. Don't read it with us. Read it with her."

Isabel fingered the edge of the envelope.

She smiled at Joyce, and Joyce patted her hand.

59.

Joe Pike

Eleven days after the events in Malibu, Pike sat with Isabel on the edge of her porch. The azure sky was cloudless. The recent rains were so deep in yesterday they seemed like someone else's memory.

Isabel said, "I don't know what to do."

Pike paged through the letter as he answered.

"What does Carly think?"

"I haven't told her."

"Have you told anyone besides me?"

"I'm too scared. I'm just so—I don't know—*mad*! I feel so *betrayed*."

Isabel's mother had left a four-page, handwritten letter. The pages were small—inexpensive stationery her mother bought at the local drugstore. Pale blue, unlined, with a delicate border of daisies. Pike had read the letter twice.

"You sound like your mother."

"I sound like me. I'm really upset."

Pike read a passage aloud.

I don't know why I did what I did. I guess I was mad.

Isabel hit him with a frustrated glance as Pike continued.

We were scared. Here we were trying to do the right thing, and just like that our lives changed.

Pike lowered the pages.

"She didn't know what else to do."

Isabel spread her hands, exasperated.

"You don't take their money is what you do! You tell your daughter. You don't write a letter she might never see, and keep secrets that almost got her killed."

Pike decided a nod was the best response. He nodded.

DeeAnn had finally revealed the truth.

Dearest Izzy, my sweet baby, At this late date, I must share a difficult truth. I was not always named Debra Sue. Once upon a time, my name was DeeAnn Alison Ryan. Daddy's name was Nick.

DeeAnn described her former life simply, and cut herself no slack in the telling. She had been sickened to learn of the harm being caused by her bosses, and proud to help the FBI, but she and her husband slammed face-first into a grim reality.

Daddy and I didn't know if we could get new jobs, or what kind of jobs we'd get, or where, or even if we'd be shot dead in bed. I wanted to get back at them. Not the FBI, but my bosses. I wanted to punish them. I wanted something for everything we were losing. So I took their money.

DeeAnn skimmed eighteen million, six hundred forty-two thousand dollars from New Way Healthful Choices. She had done so in plain view of the FBI and her criminal bosses, and altered her books to hide the skim. Ed was horrified, but unable to stop her. They filled their attic and four garbage cans with cash, and rented a storage space. Later, after she and Ed had relocated, when she was two months pregnant with Isabel, they rented a trailer, drove back to Texas, and hauled the eighteen-six to Los Angeles. By the time Isabel entered nursery school, DeeAnn had figured out how to set up anonymous, numbered accounts in agreeable countries. The banks, account numbers, identification numbers, and codes required to access the funds were listed on the letter's last page. Pike found himself admiring DeeAnn. Not bad for a bookkeeper who hadn't gone to college.

Isabel waved her hands.

"This is *so* unfair. If I'd known I had the money, I would have given it to them. None of this had to happen."

Meaning, she would have given it to Hicks and Riley.

Pike shook his head.

"They would have killed you."

"Even if I gave it back?"

"For knowing. For being a threat." Isabel closed her eyes.

"What should I do?"

I'm sorry I took it. We talked about giving it to the FBI, but I was too scared. We even talked about burning it. But it was in the accounts, and I guess we got used to it. We didn't spend it.

Pike said, "Call Braun. Tell him. You won't get in trouble."

Isabel stared at the street.

"I guess I should."

"Give it to charity. Build a school. Find a cause."

Isabel frowned, wondering if he was kidding.

"Fix your sprinklers. Buy a beach house. Use it however you like."

"Joe! You're being silly."

Pike wasn't being silly. He was quoting her mother.

The money is yours now, baby. Use it however you like. Keep it or don't, whatever you do is fine by Daddy and me. We love you, baby girl. I love you so much. Mommy did the best she could.

Pike tried to imagine DeeAnn in her early twenties, back before the FBI and the trial. A DeeAnn who looked so much like her daughter they could have been twins. DeeAnn had guts. Pike liked gutsy women.

"Wish I had known her."

Izzy sighed again and adjusted her glasses.

"Right now I'm wishing I didn't. I'm scared."

Pike considered her.

"You won't get in trouble if you turn it in."

"Not about the money. Those men. Whoever sent them still thinks I have it. Nothing's changed. I'm a target."

Pike thought for a moment, deciding what to say.

"Not anymore. It ended with Riley."

Isabel looked surprised.

"But didn't he work for someone?"

Pike shook his head. A small shake. Barely a lie.

"Nobody's left, Iz. No one is after you. You're safe."

Isabel gave a great, relieved sigh, and pressed her hands together in thanks.

"Finally! *Finally!*"

Pike enjoyed the silence that followed. He thought DeeAnn would enjoy it, too. Then Isabel asked again.

"What do you think I should do with this money? Really."

Pike tried to imagine what the younger DeeAnn would have told her future daughter.

"Do what makes you happy. If you're happy, I'm happy."

He patted her leg, and stood to leave.

"Rest easy. I'm around if you need me."

"Call soon?"

"Soon."

Pike stepped off the porch when she stopped him.

"Joe?"

Pike turned back, and found Isabel smiling.

She said, "I wish you had known her, too."

Pike wanted to say something more, but turned and walked to his Jeep.

60.

Sixteen days after Malibu, a dry desert breeze blew from the hills in Nuevo León, sweeping north across the sand toward Laredo. The twin-engine Cessna flew south from Texas, and never climbed more than a hundred feet above the ground. The pilot landed on a dirt strip forty-two miles south of the border. He rolled to a stop, but did not shut down the engines.

"I'll be back at fourteen hundred. Don't be late."

Fourteen hundred was two hours past noon.

"Fourteen hundred."

"I won't wait."

"I understand."

Pike stepped off the wing, shouldered his ruck, and powered up his GPS. The rancho was four-point-two miles away on a heading of three-five-four degrees.

Pike set off at a trot. A quarter mile farther, he picked up the pace. Running was nothing. Pike could cover forty miles in a day.

James Robert Kinnaman, now seventy-eight, an

American, made his first fortune running cocaine from Colombia. The cartel people loved him, and allowed him to branch into heroin, which was transported in container ships from the Middle East to Culiacán, then trucked north to El Paso. These were his glory years, during which Kinnaman amassed a personal fortune somewhere between sixty and eighty million dollars. Also during this time, the FBI and DEA linked Kinnaman and persons employed by him with sixty-two murders. This explained why he lived in Mexico, in an area where cartel cronies made sure the local authorities left him alone.

Pike reached the rancho in twenty-three minutes.

The hacienda was nice. A large, sprawling adobe set in a pool of green. A man with Kinnaman's wealth could afford irrigation.

Pike sat among the creosote and studied the area with binoculars. A man to the left of the house changed an irrigation spigot. A man closer to the house carried a rake on his shoulder. A third man trimmed bushes, and two younger guys were washing three pickup trucks. Workers. Maintenance people. The help.

The DEA believed Kinnaman, who had flooded eastern Mexico with counterfeit pharmaceuticals, also supplied fakes to New Way Healthful Choices. They believed Kinnaman had been an investor, whose funding allowed Darnel and Fundt to expand. This explained why so much of their weekly cash flow had been unaccounted for, and why Kinnaman almost certainly was behind their murders. To ensure their silence.

The old man had a nasty reputation for murdering former associates. And former wives.

Pike slowly circled the hacienda, looking for a way to approach. Forty-four minutes later, the kids washed the last truck, climbed into a beat-to-death pickup of their own, and left. The field people still worked.

Pike drew his pistol and let himself in through the front door. It wasn't locked.

This great big hacienda, the place was empty.

Pike set his ruck by the door, and walked from room to room, the pistol dangling along his leg. Kinnaman was in the kitchen when Pike found him. The man jumped so hard, he grabbed the counter to keep from falling.

"Who the hell are you?"

"Joe Pike."

"How'd you get in?"

"Your door wasn't locked."

The old man pooched his lips.

"Want some coffee?"

"I killed Riley Cox."

Kinnaman squinted.

"What is this?"

"Terrence Semple. Pitchess Lloyd. Charlie Reyes."

The cowboys.

"You get out of here. I don't know what you're talking about."

"Nathan Hicks. The man you sent to find DeeAnn Ryan."

Kinnaman wet his lips.

"You'd best leave."

"Got more names. Want to hear them?"

"I want my money is what I want. That bitch stole my money. I want it."

Pike raised his gun and shot Kinnaman in the chest. A little high, a little to the left, a bit down from the collarbone. Heart shot.

Pike walked over, and looked at the body.

"You can't have it."

Pike shot Kinnaman again. Head shot.

He took a small picture of Isabel Roland from his pocket, and propped it on the counter above the body. It was Isabel's graduation picture, the one where she looked like her mother.

"It's her money now. She's keeping it."

Pike turned from the body, and let himself out. He shouldered the ruck and began the four-mile jog, but after a bit he decided to walk. Pike had more than enough time to reach the Cessna. He enjoyed the desert. The air was clean. The rugged scenery was beautiful. The silence felt right.